STUCK
with the
BILLIONAIRE

TO THOSE OF YOU WHO NEED A LAUGH
AS MUCH AS I DID
WHEN I STARTED WRITING THIS BOOK.
I hope it makes you smile.

ONE

Tessa

"Did you hear the news?"

I finish swallowing a chip, the salty taste pairing nicely with my margarita, and lean toward my friend Bree. Since I met her almost a year ago, I've come to know she's either going to give me an update on serious world events or juicy gossip—with her, I can never tell which.

I glance around our table at my other friends Madison and Erin. Together, they make up a timeline of my life—Madison was my college roommate, and I met Erin at a yoga class during my fitness phase a few years ago.

On girls' nights like tonight, my worlds collide, blending together as well as a strawberry banana smoothie.

"Manhattan's most beloved playboy just crashed his car into a mailbox again." Bree wiggles her eyebrows as she passes me her phone.

I scroll through images of a Ferrari and note the single smashed headlight. I keep studying the article headlines until it all becomes blurry—thanks to the late hour and the number of shots I've had, courtesy of the bartender and my friends.

But hey, I only turn twenty-eight once, so bottoms up.

I stop at an image of said famous playboy. His dark blond hair is tousled, curling at the tops of his ears, but most of his face is covered by the platinum blonde on his arm. Even though Bree complains about this and how she wishes she could see his pouty lips—her words—I can't share in her sentiment.

I actively try not to pay too much attention to him. Unlike my friend, I'm not into celebrity gossip, a topic that Carter Fields tends to dominate. The world knows more of him as an arrogant playboy than as the next CEO of the reputable Fields Company.

"Isn't this his third wreck in a month?" I ask, handing Bree her phone back.

"You should ask him. You're the one who knows him," Madison says, hooking her thumb toward me.

"Shut up!" Drops of margarita fly out of Bree's mouth. She throws her hand over it to try to cover the waterfall, but she's too late.

Erin and I hand her a few napkins while I glare at Madison, who innocently crunches on a chip, her long, red hair falling in waves over her shoulders like a mermaid. It was the first thing I noticed about her when we moved into our stuffy dorm freshman year, and I've always been insanely jealous of it.

When she unpacked dozens of hair products and makeup, I didn't think we'd get along. I was more into theater and doing myself up only when necessary. Even then, I was at the mercy of makeup artists. I pegged Madison as pretentious, but she turned out to be one of the best and most down-to-earth people I know.

The only time I've ever wanted to strangle her before tonight was when she set me up on a double date with her neighbor a few years back. To her credit, she wasn't aware he was into a kinky mix of BDSM and cosplay.

"What?" Madison shrugs. "You don't usually tell people you know him, but *we* are not regular people. It's way past time to put out there." She points around the table, her forest-green eyes unapologetic. In fact, they're sparkling with amusement. She is so enjoying putting me in the hot seat, but I'll get her back for this.

Although, in truth, my connection to Carter Fields was bound to slip out, I guess.

I lean my elbow on the table and rest my throbbing head in the palm of my hand, bracing myself for Bree's inquisition.

Her eyes are as wide as those of the cartoons my brother Graham and I watched as kids. She sputters, "You know Carter Fields? *The* Carter Fields—billionaire, philanthropist, hot as hell? You, Tessa Rollins from Queens, know him and have been holding out on me?"

"*Hot as hell* isn't a noun like billionaire and philanthropist." I smile around my shot glass, then toss it back and bask in the burning stream of tequila sliding down my throat.

Bree leans over the table, nearly knocking over our margarita glasses as she points her manicured finger at me. "Don't go all English teacher on me. I need answers."

"When have I ever done that?" I shrug, exaggerating my innocence. Grammar rules are like my second language, which comes in handy when proofing resumes and personal statements for work, but it's not so fun when I'm hanging out with my friends.

Madison throws her head back, and her high-pitched laugh is loud enough to be heard above the buzzing of the crowded restaurant and bar. "You learned a lot from your single semester as an English major." She snorts.

"As did you." I blink sarcastically in Madison's direction, recalling we were both English majors before I switched to behavioral science, and Madison eventually quit to attend cosmetology school. I steel myself and face Bree again as I say, "I don't know Carter. My brother does."

"I find it hard to believe that he knows Carter and you don't. You and Graham are closer than any siblings I know. You have to know the same people." Bree stares at me like I'm a stranger to her, clearly in shock that I have anything to do with someone of Carter's caliber.

I'm not the type to know trending facts about celebrities, let alone have connections with any of them. On the other hand, Bree's favorite pastime is reading their bios and taking ridiculous online quizzes. At midnight last night, she texted me the results of which *Friends* character she's most like—unsurprisingly, it's Rachel.

She and I somehow fit, though.

Bree's the first friend I made when I started my new counseling position at the career center. She'd asked for my name and invited me out for drinks in the same breath, declaring we'd be friends in her bubbly tone that matches her personality.

She was right. Bree has become one of my closest friends, and Erin, Madison, and I didn't hesitate to bring her into our girl gang.

"Well? Don't hold out on us." Bree waggles her finger at me, and the multi-colored tiles on the wall behind her start to make me dizzy. "I have actual live access to a billionaire hottie, and I need to know everything. Are his dimples as deep and sexy in person as they are in pictures? Does he actually hate the taste of champagne? And does he wear boxer briefs or boxers? That last one is important." She stops to take a deep breath while I blink at her, adjusting to the whiplash of questions she threw at me as fast as balls fly out of a baseball machine.

Erin giggles next to me.

"Don't laugh." I toss a napkin at her, but she only giggles harder. I then turn to Bree and say, "I've really never met the guy. Graham and I are close, yes, but I have my own life and he has his, which includes Carter."

Bree twists her lips in doubt.

"I'm serious! Mads, back me up." I gently smack her arm. "Carter and Graham have been best friends since college, and every time we're supposed to get together for an introduction, Graham gets an emergency call from a patient, or Carter's too drunk or occupied. Usually, *both* of those things happen."

"Occupied with female company?" Erin lifts her brow, turning her phone screen to us. "Seriously, check out the models he dates. They don't even look real."

Bree snatches the phone from her and cringes. "Ugh. No one should look this perfect." She drops the phone on the table with a loud thud, drawing attention to us from surrounding patrons.

"Another round, ladies?" one of the bartenders asks, appearing at the end of our table out of nowhere. He clasps his hands behind his back and faces me. "Anything else for the birthday girl?"

"Yes!" Bree pounds the table with her fist, her cheeks rosy.

I tilt my head, a lazy smile playing on my lips as I say, "The birthday girl has had plenty."

"Oh? And I thought you were going to get wild tonight." He winks, and his smirk is flirtatious. His black hair is buzzed on the sides, and his tattooed arms are sculpted. He's definitely hot and likely knows how to please a woman, but that won't be me.

Not tonight.

I give him an apologetic frown—or at least I think I do. My cheeks have been numb for the last ten minutes. But I have enough wits about me to remember the long day ahead of me tomorrow. "This is the end of the line for me." I tilt my head to the other side, and the ends of my blonde hair barely graze my shoulder, tickling me. A feminine giggle escapes me like this is the funniest thing that's happened all night.

"What is so funny?" Erin asks, glancing around the table.

"Can I actually get a glass of water, please?" I manage, staring up at the bartender. "At this point, I think a bucket would be best."

"Let me know if you change your mind." He winks again, backing away.

Bree covers her mouth, squeezing her eyes closed. When he turns around, she drops her hands and bursts into laughter, along with Madison and Erin.

"Oh my God." Madison's mouth hangs open. "Please, please, *please*, Tessa, you have got to go home with him. You two have been dancing around each other for weeks, and I can't take the sexual tension."

I almost choke on my own spit. "You're kidding, right? I've seen him exactly two times and don't even know his name."

"It's Harvey," Erin offers, her syllables clear and enunciated—she's way more sober than the rest of us.

We all turn to stare at her at once.

"What?" She shrugs. "I like talking to people—sue me."

"That's not helpful." I shake my head.

"It's your birthday!" Bree scoots the basket of chips to the side and grabs my hands. "Do it for us single girls everywhere. Trace those tattoos with your tongue, and let him take you on a dirty ride you'll never forget."

I throw my head back. "You're insane."

"Insanely horny." Bree snorts and waves down at herself. "This is what happens when you vow to stay single forever: the dreaded dry spells between eligible one-night stands. I mean, I'm to the point where even my tight-ass jeans rubbing against my privates is turning me on."

We erupt into laughter, drawing even more attention to our table than we have all night.

"I'll cheers to that." Madison clinks her glass to Bree's, and they finish off their drinks.

"Now, if you'd like to give me Carter Fields's number, I'd reconsider my vow." Bree holds her hands up in a begging manner.

"I don't have it." I wipe the runaway mascara from the corner of my eye. "Like I said, I don't know the guy, and I'm glad for it."

"Oh, please! You're telling me you wouldn't climb this hunk of a man like a mountain, risking your life for pleasure?" She points at her phone again, and on the screen, an image of Carter in a suit pops up.

"Is that your screensaver or something? You pulled it up awfully fast." My eyes widen.

"Maybe." She shrugs.

I've laughed a lot tonight, and so hard I've had to clutch my stomach on multiple occasions. This is exactly what I wanted for my birthday—a fun night out with my girlfriends.

The celebration won't stop here, either.

Tomorrow, I'm driving up to our family cabin to meet my parents and Graham for a week-long celebration. It used to be an annual thing until a couple years ago.

It'll also be a week away from the chaos of the city and a nice vacation from work. It's been too long since I've done either of those things, and I'm more giddy about it than a kid is when going to Disney World.

"So?" Erin nudges me and tilts her head in the direction of the bar, where Harvey nods at us. "Are you going for it?"

"No," I answer immediately and thank the server for the water she hands me. "I need to pack tonight."

"You haven't gotten laid in *ages*," Bree exaggerates, her words slightly slurred. "And I totally get it, but this is your birthday. You should not end it by *packing*." She grimaces, saying the word like I suggested I bathe in mud when I get home.

"I've hooked up plenty of times," I say in my defense.

"This year?" She narrows her gaze at me skeptically.

"*Anyway*." I place both palms on the table and stand. "My new neighbors will surely keep me awake for most of the night, and I have an early morning. I need to go."

"At least someone's getting laid." Madison nudges Erin, who nods in agreement.

"You took the next week off, Tess. What do you need to get up early for?" Bree spreads her arms. *Always so theatrical.*

"I'm meeting my family at our cabin in Connecticut. I told

you this a million times," I say, my cheeks flushed and sore from tonight. "And I'm going to be so hungover, I'll need all the sleep I can manage. My mother cannot see me like this—all grumpy and disoriented." I wave over my appearance. I haven't checked a mirror in over an hour, but I'm positive my mascara is smeared from tears of laughter.

It's what always happens when the girls and I get together, which we try to do at least once a week, even when we're not celebrating anything specific. We all live in or close to the city, are unmarried, and love margaritas, so dinners are a must.

"Since it's late, and some of us *do* have to work tomorrow"—Madison places her hand over her chest—"I'm going to head out too."

"No way. It's only..." Bree pulls on Madison's arm, holding her in place as she checks the time on her phone. "Oh my God, it's midnight. I need to go too, ladies."

I snort. "When was the last time you went to sleep before midnight?"

"You need to pack, bitch." Bree sticks her tongue out at me as she stands and rounds her chair to pull her leather jacket on, then tosses her hair over her shoulder.

The rest of us follow her lead, and on my way out, I glance back at the bar, where Harvey grips the edge, a gleam in his eyes.

Even though there's promise in them—and it *is* my birthday—it's not enough to make me walk over there and ask him to call me after his shift. There's no immediate spark, which has been in line with the guys I've dated lately.

There's nothing about Harvey that tells me it would be different with him.

My mind made up, I step out onto the sidewalk, where I

wave goodbye to the girls and hail a cab. Once I rattle off my address to the driver, I lay my head back, and my mind drifts to the guys I've gone out with in the last year.

As the city lights blur against the dark sky overhead, a sinking feeling settles in my chest, and I dread my dating future. I fear I'm doomed to boring hookups until I take my last breath. What else can I do, though?

Since my official breakup with my one serious boyfriend, Wyatt, I've only gone out with a handful of guys I either met at the gym or at my coffee shop. I've committed myself to dating safe guys, ones I don't feel an instant connection with. I did the love-at-first-sight thing with Wyatt, and it didn't end well, solidifying for me that the whole idea is for fairy tales.

Although it bores me to tears, playing it safe is my only option. The only way I'll keep my heart from getting broken.

Again.

TWO

Carter

I moan, dreaming of last night.

Ginger tells me to go faster, purring in my ear as she slides her hand over my crotch. She fingers my belt buckle, and I press on the gas, riding my Ferrari into the night. We're laughing—a lot—until my vision blurs, and a shadowy figure walks onto the road in front of us. His dark eyes droop in the corners as they stare at me, and his sandy-blond hair matches mine.

What's my father doing here?

My brakes screech to a halt of their own accord, and the headlights illuminate his frown.

My eyes snap open.

"Fuck me," I croak as a stab of pain slices through my forehead.

I try to stretch my arms above my head, but my knuckles hit the leg of the glass coffee table I'm lying under.

As I blink, my dad's face fills my vision again, except this time, it's on my ringing phone screen. With careful movements, I reach my hand out from underneath the coffee table and grab my phone, wincing from my headache. I'm more disoriented than I was the week I flew to Italy, back to New York, and then to Tokyo. It took me almost a month to get my body back in the correct time zone.

This moment may be worse.

"What the hell happened last night?" My dad's voice is far too loud for eight in the morning, even if I didn't have this insane hangover. "You could've gotten yourself killed!"

"It's so sweet how much you care about me," I coo as I squirm in my spot on the rug, the fibers tickling the back of my neck. "But I'm fine. Thank you for calling. I'm surprised you're not at breakfast with Mom yet."

He sighs, and from the sound of it, I know my response isn't enough to deter him. "It's the fourth time this week you've been seen with that… that… *Ginger.* It's the third time this month you've damaged your very *expensive* car. The media are already speculating, saying you're having a nervous breakdown and should consider therapy. Or rehab." He sighs again—*God, his fucking sighs.*

He has one for every occasion and level of disappointment he wants to express. One for when I'm late to a meeting, even if I'm only tardy because I'm helping a kid find his mom.

For when I make too many jokes during our lunches.

For when I forgot the Rolex he gave me for my birthday in the bathroom of a club after getting handsy with a bar bunny.

I grunt, mentally calculating which category this sigh

falls into when he interrupts me, "Son, are you having a breakdown? Is there something I need to know?"

Through gritted teeth, I say, "No, Father. For the millionth time, no. Besides, I figured it'd be a good thing to be seen with the same woman multiple times in a row for a change. Isn't that what you want? For me to settle down?" I fight a grin. My sarcasm is thicker than a cowboy's southern accent.

He huffs. "Don't fuck around, Carter."

I almost bite my tongue to avoid the comeback I'd like to give him. "Why did you really call, Dad?"

"Because of your behavior," he bites out. "We're too close to the board's decision to screw up now. You want to be CEO of the company, yes? If you've changed your mind, please spare me the devastation and tell me now."

I press the heel of my palm into my closed eye, exasperated we're having the same conversation we keep repeating lately. It gets worse the closer and closer we get to the good ole board making decisions for *our* family's company like they're the Volturi.

I can almost feel bile rising in my throat—I should not know that name, but I made the poor choice of spending the night with a sexy woman I met at a fundraiser, who turned out to be a *Twilight* fanatic.

"I'm waiting," Dad says, and I imagine him tapping his foot like he does during our meetings when he's not impressed by what he's hearing.

I want to tell my father that this position is what I've worked for all my life. That he and the board will have to pry it out of my cold, dead fucking hands, but I opt for the less dramatic response, lest he attributes my snark to a meltdown.

"Yes, Dad. I want to be CEO. Last night, I was letting

off steam, and things got out of hand. That's all. I wasn't even drunk behind the wheel."

"So, you hit a mailbox *sober*? Somehow that's worse."

I clench my jaw, but deep down, I'm more disappointed in myself than he is. Ginger and I were reckless last night. It was fun, but definitely not the smartest choice I've made.

Now, although I haven't seen anything yet, I'm positive the world is speculating—as they always do. But this time, their ringleader is my father.

Great.

There are murmurs on his end before he says to me, "It's simply not natural to continue being so careless and irresponsible at your age. You're forty and—"

I mockingly gasp and correct him. "I'm thirty-five."

"You should have a respectable wife by now. A modest, genuine woman on your arm. Maybe even some children. Who will continue our line? Our legacy? We have a family fortune and reputation to uphold. What will become of our empire, Carter? And for the love of God, don't say Ginger will have any part of it." He finally takes a breath, which turns into a cough, and I picture his face reddening as he continues glowering at his phone.

Ah, the family fortune.

He never can resist bringing it up. As if I could actually forget.

If I'm not careful and don't cut this conversation off here, I'll get another lecture about how my great-great-grandfather started it all—during the Great Depression, no less. Even though his wages were cut, he was one of the lucky bastards who didn't lose his job entirely.

He laid the foundation for what is now Fields Company

like he did when he built railroads: one steel track at a time. He had an idea, saved every dime he could, and scoped out properties using his father's ancient compass and a worn-out map. I'm inclined to believe he couldn't even read the map and landed on a piece of prime real estate by accident and a little luck, but I don't voice this thought.

It would be disrespectful, given how hard the man worked and what he built. After all, I wouldn't be who I am if not for my great-great-grandfather.

People thought he was crazy. All they saw was a barely educated blue-collar man sick with delusion.

But thanks to his so-called *pipedream*, my family and I are at the top of the list of Manhattan's elite real estate developers, having recently expanded our business overseas. I'm giddy like a schoolgirl to get moving on those projects. They're providing a different kind of challenge, which I thrive on, and the meetings in Europe are a pleasant change of pace too.

The beaches.

The ladies.

The—

"Are you listening to me?" Dad's deep and raspy voice rings out.

I jolt where I still lie on the floor and bump my head on the glass of the coffee table. "Christ," I grumble, cringing as my head falls back onto the rug with a soft thud.

"What the hell are you doing?"

"Dad, I got it. It won't happen again."

"I wish I could believe you." I can't see him, but I'm certain he's giving me his disapproving frown. The same one that haunted my subconscious while I slept.

"Is there anything else?" I ask, staring at the sun rays

casting across my ceiling from the window behind the couch.

"We think it's a good idea for you to lie low until the charity dinner in a couple weeks. You won't be in the office, but you can take a few business calls as needed. Just nothing that requires you to be in public. And for the love of God, no Ginger. Or any other girls, for that matter. You cannot give the media any more gossip to make them money."

I carefully maneuver myself around the dangerous table and struggle to sit up as the crick in my neck screams at me. "Two weeks?"

Can I go that long without being in the office? I use it almost as much as this penthouse.

"I've already spoken to your assistant and told her to reschedule your meetings and that you'd be—"

"Wait. Hold on. You already talked to Yara about all this? What did you tell her exactly?" I dig my fingers into the side of my head and massage my temple, trying not to lose it with my father.

He's retiring soon.

He's *retiring*.

I repeat this sentence in my head a few times as he continues, but it doesn't make me feel any better right now.

"Why the hell does that matter? I told her what she needed to do. That's all you need to know," he says, his tone matter-of-fact, leaving no room for rebuttal.

Except it doesn't sit well with me. I'm imagining he told Yara, my sweet, long-time assistant, that I'm incapable of handling myself and that I'm actually the yahoo the media is making me out to be as of late.

I remember a time when they portrayed me as the adorable ten-year-old who got a helicopter for his birthday. An actual helicopter that a man named Felix flew when my father asked him to take us to Martha's Vineyard, where my father showed me our new beach house.

Those days are long gone, though, and in their place are stupid headlines that make my father and the board think I'm incompetent to do the job I've essentially been doing for ten years.

Except, as CEO instead of my current position as president, I won't have my overbearing father meddling in my affairs.

"Carter, don't get bent out of shape because I spoke to your assistant. She works for the company, which I'm still in charge of."

I press the phone screen to mute my mic and let out a shaky groan full of anger.

A few more weeks.

Only a few more weeks until he steps aside.

I can do this.

I click to unmute the mic and say, "Fine. I'll hang out at our place in the Poconos. I think I'd even love it." I can already imagine the peace and quiet in the mountains. I could play some golf, sneak Ginger up there, or maybe call my *friend* Erica—

"No, you can't go there. The house is being renovated, remember? Your mother thought it necessary to update the kitchen."

"Didn't she do that last year?"

"She did. Then last week, she saw her friend Cynthia's kitchen with a different colored marble, and *we simply had to have it.*" He uses a high-pitched voice when he imitates Mom, the mockery in his tone the equivalent of an eye-roll.

I flinch. My dad loves my mom, but their relationship is very… strained, according to their therapist. I can think of many other words, but I'll take the one from the professional.

"Martha's Vineyard, then," I suggest.

"Ah, they're still fixing the flood damage." There's shuffling on his end again, then heavy breathing as if he's rising from a chair and it takes more energy than necessary.

I believe it does for him, since he's seventy and unhealthier than a homeless dog.

He and I are similar in many ways, especially when it comes to business, but our physical health is not one of them. While he calls walking into the office exercise and lives on a diet of whiskey and cigars, I maintain balanced meals—indulging on baked goods on occasion—and exercise with Miles, my personal trainer and friend, four times a week. Whenever I've asked Dad to join us, he's cackled louder than he would if I were to wear a chicken suit to work.

"You can stay with your cousin Daisy and—"

I scoff. "You're joking, right?"

"Daisy and her family are perfectly delightful," he says evenly, but I know he doesn't mean it. Even he himself has called Daisy and her husband boring. I believe the exact words he's used were *trite* and *dull* and that he'd rather sink into a mud puddle wearing his Armani suit than spend five minutes with them.

I clench my fist in my lap. "I'd rather sleep in a tent in the woods than listen to her husband's nasally tale of the minnow fish. I'll find somewhere else."

"You're right." He quietly chuckles, then grows serious again. "Two weeks. Don't stay at your penthouse or Ginger's. I mean it, Carter. Find somewhere no one can track you down, and give this mess time to breathe. I can't have the board thinking you're too irresponsible to run a company, even though you don't seem to know how to drive a car in one lane."

"Love you too, Dad."

Once the line goes quiet, I toss my phone to the side, and it thuds against the marble floor. Over my shoulder, the fireplace roars. Half-filled glasses litter the coffee table. A broken plate rests on the couch, its pieces laid out like a puzzle.

I put my hands on the edge of the couch and coffee table to hoist myself up. Scanning the kitchen counter, I find a few open bottles of whiskey and vodka, one tossed on its side. *A wild night, indeed.*

How did I even end up on the floor of my penthouse—alone?

I scratch the back of my head and freeze when images from last night flash through my mind.

Ginger.

Her friend Skye was here too at one point.

There was a lot of sex.

I peer over my shoulder, glancing upstairs in the direction of my bedroom. *Am* I alone?

Gripping the back of my throbbing neck, I tiptoe across my five-thousand-dollar rug that my interior designer claimed is *so me*, then grimace when my feet hit the cold marble floor. I climb up the stairs, and sure enough, Ginger and Skye are asleep on my king-size bed. They're buried under the sheets and cuddled in the middle, seemingly content.

As if they don't even miss me.

Suddenly, a sting of… *something* hits my chest. What the fuck is that? Regret? Guilt?

Loneliness?

It can't be.

It's my father. His nonsense about marriage got to me—it's the only explanation.

After all, I'm Carter Fields. I don't have serious feelings of love and longing for commitment. Case in point, the scene in front of me—two naked women lying on my bed—is the extent of my capability.

On top of that, I'm happy with this lifestyle.

"Why stare when you can join us?" Ginger rasps, stretching her arm above her head. As she does so, the sheet falls, exposing a pink nipple.

I move toward the edge of the bed and tip her chin up as Skye stirs on the other side. "Good morning, beautiful."

Ginger moans like she did when I was between her thighs last night, arousing me all over again.

I steel myself, suppressing the urge to crawl back into bed—the same urge that brought them here to begin with. Crossing the open area toward the bathroom, I call over my shoulder, "I'm sorry, but I need to get dressed and head out."

As I move to close the bathroom door, I catch a glimpse of Ginger's pout as she throws the covers off and swings her legs over the edge of the bed. The door clicks behind me, and silence consumes me as I grip the edge of the bathroom counter.

This is the only place in the house—and in my life—I seem to get any peace and quiet. The only thing missing in here is a minibar, which I've debated adding on several occasions, but I always talk myself out of it. It would be too weird to bathroom drink, and although I'm many things, I'm not *that* guy.

I take a deep breath like I'm inhaling the silence.

From the sounds of it, though, I'll be getting plenty of

time to myself over the next two weeks. So, instead of reveling in it now, I push off the marble counter to get ready.

A few minutes later, I hear the faint ding of the elevator when the girls leave. I should feel bad for not walking them out, but it's not the way we do things. On the contrary, we have an understanding—one that doesn't involve flowers and romance—and it works.

It's how I've always done these types of things, even before Ginger.

It's what I know.

Humming under my breath, I hurry through a shower as best my brutal hangover will allow. I have to reach out to the wall to steady myself on more than one occasion, dizzy and out of breath like I am after my workouts with Miles.

Once I step out and onto safe ground, I'm a little more balanced and sober. I wrap a towel around my waist, and when I open the door to my bedroom, a thick cloud of steam behind me, Whitney is in my room, pulling the sheets from the bed.

I chuckle when I see her rubber gloves—she went full-on, elbow-length gloves today. She must've seen the girls leave earlier and wanted an extra barrier while cleaning.

"Good morning." I lean on the doorframe as warm water droplets run down my bare chest.

She quirks her eyebrow at me like she's been doing for years. "Good morning, Mr. Fields. Another wild night, I noticed?"

"Of course. I have to uphold my prestigious title of Manhattan's Most Notorious Billionaire somehow."

"Playboy. I believe it's Most Notorious *Playboy*, Mr. Fields." She glares, but the kind woman can't contain her smile. Whitney's too entertained by my antics to be outraged, although the hint of disapproval in the twitch of her lips is always present in the recent months.

"Same difference, am I right?" I smirk.

She shakes her head as she finishes getting the sheets off the bed and ready to wash. After she brushes past me—eyebrow still quirked—and out of the room, I get dressed, my head throbbing with every lift of a finger.

Because of my current state, I had to forego shaving in the shower for fear I'd slash my chin open. That makes three days in a row, and I'm long overdue for a haircut. Instead of bothering to tame any of it now, I throw a hoodie over my white T-shirt and cover my head with a Harvard ball cap—my favorite incognito look, although it doesn't usually fool the media.

No, to get by them, I'd need plastic surgery to change my entire face.

With as good as my disguise will get, I grab a small bag and toss in as many comfortable clothing items I can find, a welcomed contrast to my tailored suits.

As much as I love my job and am looking forward to finally taking over, this break is coming at the perfect time. If I didn't know any better, I'd say my subconscious had this planned all along, mailbox incident and everything.

Packed duffel in hand, I head downstairs, where Whitney has picked up the glasses from the coffee table and is now after the broken plate. I drop the bag by the stairs and wave to her. "Let me get it."

"No, no—"

"You're going to cut yourself. Let me," I insist. "Besides, I'm assuming this is the culprit for the gash on my thumb, and we have unfinished business here," I joke, holding my hand up to show her the battle scar.

She sighs, much like my father did earlier, and the wrinkles around her eyes grow in numbers when she gives me a half-pitiful smile. "I'll get you a Band-Aid, but you're going to need stitches."

I place my hand on her forearm. "I'm fine. I think the bleeding stopped somewhere around my tenth shot. Alcohol is known to coagulate blood, no?"

"Quite the opposite."

"Meh." I shrug.

She tsks under her breath, then offers, "Coffee?"

"I'll take a small cup to sober the rest of the way up." I walk toward the couch, where the offending dish lies. "I'm going to grab more on my way to a friend's."

"Mr. Fields, your father told you to lie low." She puts her hands on her hips.

I'm not surprised she already knows my father's plan. He tells her everything in order to keep me accountable, as if I'm still ten years old.

"Ah, always looking out for me." I wink, then pick up the broken pieces of the plate and walk them toward the trash. I toss them with a clink, then turn to face her, leaning over the kitchen island. "This is an actual friend. You remember Graham from college, right?"

"Oh, yes, Graham is wonderful." Her expression lights up as she sets two ibuprofen pills and a cup of black coffee in front of me. I notice a single ice cube almost completely melted in the dark liquid, and I appreciate how thoughtful Whitney is. The woman thinks of everything. "Now he's a good friend to have on speed dial."

"Whoa, whoa. I think it's the other way around for us." I hold up the coffee, thanking her, and take a sip. "Also, you never light up like this for me. I'm hurt."

She grabs my ear and tugs, reminding me of the way my mother would do the same when I was a boy. Whitney tugs harder, though. "You, Mr. Fields, are the reason I have so many wrinkles at fifty."

"I'll take that as a compliment."

She clicks her tongue, her face animated, and continues cleaning the kitchen.

I take a few more gulps of my coffee, my head practically healed now, and back away. "See you after my exile is up." I wiggle my eyebrows at her as I sling the bag over my shoulder and step onto the elevator.

On my way down, I dial Graham's number. After five rings, I'm about to give up, but he finally answers as I arrive on the bottom floor.

I steel myself for the press, whom I can see through the glass doors outside as I cross the lobby. Nodding to our security guard, I say to Graham, "Remember Trixie from college? I'm calling in my favor."

On the other end, he groans. "Oh, God…"

"Don't sound so scared."

"Well, with you, I never know if you only need me to remind you of your last date's name or if you need a kidney. But bringing up Trixie means something even more serious than either of those."

"Shut the fuck up." I chuckle as I slide my sunglasses into place, scooting them up the bridge of my nose with my free hand and bracing myself for the media frenzy. All it'll take is one person to recognize me—and they will—but hopefully I'll have made it at least halfway past them before they do. Sighing, I say to Graham, "I need a place to stay. Somewhere secluded to hide from prying eyes—aka outside the state of New York—and if memory serves, you have a cabin somewhere in Vermont?"

"Connecticut," he corrects. "You can definitely stay there. Whatever you need, man."

"You're a fucking lifesaver." My shoulders sag, relief flooding my body. "Otherwise, I would've had to call up Cousin Daisy."

"The one with the husband who can't stop talking about four-eyed fish and estuaries as spawning grounds?" His distaste mirrors my own.

"That's the one. So, really, you're doing me a couple favors." I chuckle again. "Send me the address, and I'll be on my way." I stop short of the door, turning my back to it as I wait for his response.

"Oh, today? Shit. Wait—" He mumbles to someone in the background, and I use it as an opportunity.

I nod to Shepley as he opens the door for me, and I make it three feet outside the building when the first flash goes off. A commotion follows as more cameras go off, and people spout questions as if they're paid for each question they ask me per second. Trevor, my head of security, appears at my side out of thin air. I was surprised by his stealth at first, but I've gotten used to it by now, three years later.

And I'm even thankful for it.

He leads me to my car of the day, the Maserati. Once I'm inside, Trevor closes the door behind me, and a few seconds later, I'm taking off through the streets of Manhattan. Graham's voice sounds again through the Bluetooth on my radio, echoing through the speakers. "You good?"

I shift in my seat, exhaling. "Always am. The key is to keep my head down, even though I'm not the one doing anything wrong."

Silence answers me.

"You still there?" I take a right and continue down a narrow path a few yards before I come to a stop at a red light. I glance at the screen, thinking Graham was called away. As a physician, he's hard to get ahold of during the day to begin with, but it's even harder to maintain a conversation for longer than a few minutes at a time.

"Carter, I'm going to need to go here in a second. My next appointment is almost ready for me." There's shuffling on his end, then, "Listen, I'll send you the address for the cabin, but we'll all be up there this week to celebrate my little sister's birthday. You remember me talking about Tessa, right?"

"Of course." I nod. How could I forget? Although I've never met her, I practically know her given how much Graham's talked about her over the years. "Will she be pissed if I crash?"

"No, she's cool. Besides, I can't keep you two from meeting forever."

I furrow my brows. "What do you mean?"

"She'll be fine," he continues, distracted like he's already checked out. "Besides, I owe you, right?"

I smirk. If I could see his face, I'm sure my best friend would be winking.

We end the call, and I pull over when my phone dings. Contrary to what the world might think, I'm not a reckless driver.

Once I'm safely parked out of the way of traffic, I grab my phone to check the address Graham sent and use my thumb and forefinger to pinch the screen, zooming in on the map. I've never seen so much green surrounding a location.

For a split second, I regret agreeing to this, but still, I tap *Go*.

Staring out the windshield, my car still in park, I squint at the bright sun like I'm seeing it for the first time. I may be doing this for my father, but the truth is, I haven't taken a real break or vacation since college—since before I was old enough to work at Fields Company. The trips I take around the world involve extensive research and business meetings. Although I squeeze in some *extracurriculars*, I don't get many full days to myself.

I glance back down at the red dot indicating my destination, and I work my jaw back and forth as I contemplate turning around toward JFK Airport, instead.

The sandy beaches of Fiji or Greece would be a much better alternative to an old cabin with my college buddy's family.

Graham may be the best friend I have, but his cabin isn't exactly my idea of fun for my first real vacation in years.

As if he can hear me, I receive a text from my father.

Boss man: You better not be getting on a plane to Fiji or some shit. Reporters still exist out of the country, you know.

I can practically hear his sarcasm dripping from each letter, and it makes me scoff.

My phone vibrates again with another text.

Boss man: Hide, Carter. I mean it.

I put the car in drive and ease out of my spot. *Cabin it is, then.*

I roll my window down as I zip through the streets of New York. The cool wind filters into my car, rustling the bill of my hat like it does the leaves on the sidewalk. Ah, the secrets this city would tell, from its most elite to its deepest member of the underground.

Annika Covington, the Upper East Side's most beloved socialite—one the media dubbed as America's girl next door—enjoys threesomes and a bottle of vodka more than she does family dinners and her volunteer work.

Marcus Grant, tech genius and philanthropist, would rather spend the night with a twenty-something hooker than his wife and children.

Then, there's me.

I should be ashamed to be grouped with them. Our lives aren't wholesome like my father constantly advises. Beyond that, I should be upset right now instead of smiling from ear to ear. After all, I'm on my way to hide at an old cabin to avoid further embarrassing myself and my family, but as I cruise through the city, I can't find it in me to feel the gravity of the situation.

I am who I am, just as Annika and Marcus are.

Just as a yacht floats on water. As a glass of whiskey burns. As a party needs a host.

I let my arm hang off the side as I come to another stop. A red Mercedes pulls up next to me, and I catch the young brunette driver's attention. I wink at her, and she smiles, dipping her head. I bet she's blushing.

When the light turns green, I raise the volume on my radio and continue cruising toward my hideaway. As the buildings blur on either side of me, I silently praise my life, and despite what my father begged me for this morning, I hope it never changes.

THREE

Tessa

*Is Manhattan's Most Eligible Bachelor Finally Settling Down?
Spotted (Again): Carter Fields with Supermodel Ginger Myers.
Fields's Ferrari vs. a Mailbox. Who won?*

Scoffing, I lean against the wall of the café, my attention glued to my phone while the morning bustle gets going. I keep scrolling the numerous articles, scanning headlines that range from humorous to truly ridiculous. How is Graham friends with this joke?

He's been friends with Carter since college—for fifteen years—and I've never met him. For some unholy reason, Graham thinks inviting Carter to the cabin for my birthday celebration would be the best time to introduce us.

It's supposed to be family only, as it's been in the past.

"Tessa?"

I lift my head at the sound of my name coming from behind the counter and find the barista holding up a drink—my salvation.

As expected, the noisy couple next door kept me awake until long after two in the morning. Their constant moans and pants sounded like they had five people in the room for a giant orgy.

I wanted to barf.

My mouth waters as I push my thick-framed glasses up higher on my nose and make my way to the front for my much-needed drink. I woke up long before my alarm—a treacherous habit—and had two cups of coffee in my apartment to nurse my hangover.

But they weren't enough to soothe me awake from my eighth sleepless night in a row, nor were they infused with the uniquely rich and bold flavor of an espresso shot like this.

I reach the counter as the barista calls my name a second time and slides my coffee forward. My latte in hand, I skirt around the newly formed line and pull my phone back out.

The image at the top is much like the others: clean-cut billionaire Carter Fields in an expensive, well-tailored suit from some designer I'm too inferior to know, a matching shiny watch, and a blindingly gorgeous woman on his arm like an accessory.

Is Fields Done Playing the Field?

"Oh my God," I mumble to myself.

Rolling my eyes, I take a tiny sip of the coffee to test its temperature, but I'm so distracted by my phone that my sip is more of a gulp.

Too hot.

The liquid burns the roof of my mouth, and I jolt, bumping right into another person.

I glance over with an apology on the tip of my tongue, but the woman I ran into doesn't even spare me the opportunity.

Instead, she tosses a scathing glare my way, her plump red lips pouting like I spilled my coffee on her, even though I didn't.

Scoffing, I smooth my sweater down with my free hand and inspect for any damage, finding only a single brown spot over my chest. Relieved, I grab a napkin on the way out the door as the café continues filling up.

Stepping outside, I dab at the setting stain like it's enough to rid myself of it. The next thing I know, I hit a hard chest, causing my glasses to fall to the tip of my nose. The lid flies off my cup, and my morning caffeine boost spills down the front of me.

"Ah!" I jump back, holding my arms out. If I was in anything other than my thick turtleneck sweater, that shit would've left a brutal mark on my skin.

"I'm so sorry." Two large hands grip my elbows, steadying me. "Are you okay?"

Disoriented, I blink as he glances between me, over his shoulder, and then back at me, his teeth raking over his bottom lip. He shrugs in a sheepish manner similar to Graham when he's hiding something.

When I see the awful woman who bumped into me walking away behind him, her curvy hips in a skintight skirt, I can't help my scowl.

I've had enough of this morning.

It's my first day of being twenty-eight, and it sucks balls. I'm running on zero sleep, the coffee I spent more than an e-book's worth on just spilled down to my belly button, and my brother's annoying friend is crashing my family vacation.

On top of it all, this jerk was too busy checking out a woman instead of being more careful.

He holds his hands out. "Please. Let me buy you another coffee—"

"Don't bother." I wave him off and rush back inside, only to find the line is now three times as long as it was when I first arrived. *Great.*

"Hey, I'm really sorry." A gentle hand touches my arm, and when I turn, it's the guy from outside. He's wearing his hat low, and his eyes are still hidden behind Ray-Ban Aviators, even though we're inside now where the sun's not blinding us. "I should've been watching where I was going, but—"

"But a nice ass caught your attention, instead, right?" I blurt, adjusting my glasses and jutting my chin up.

His arm falls as we take a step up in line. "That's not what happened."

"Oh?" I cross my arms, unsure of why I'm even entertaining this conversation other than there's nothing else to do until I get my new cup of coffee. I'm not leaving here without it.

"A woman needed directions, so I gave her some. I was being a friendly New Yorker. You know, battling the stereotypes that we're prickly and rude."

I relax my stance a fraction, furrowing my brows.

"That's all. I just wanted to make sure she knew where she was going. She has a job interview and was nervous." He shrugs as if he did what any Good Samaritan would do.

And it's true. I don't know of many guys in the city other than Graham and my father who would help a stranger.

Maybe that's why the woman was rude. She was nervous

and flustered because of a job interview. Of all people, I understand that very well. Many of my clients come to me in a big bundle of nerves right before their interview.

Which definitely makes me feel like I stepped in a pile of dog shit.

"Oh. I'm sorry…" My voice trails off as he starts to remove his sunglasses, but just when I'm about to glimpse the color of his eyes, he pushes them back into place again.

Odd.

I run my gaze over him, traveling from the top to the bottom of this stranger, trying to get a sense of him. His beard appears too scruffy for someone wearing a Harvard ball cap. His confident posture, on the other hand, is something I'd expect from a prestigious Ivy League grad—Graham's one of them, after all.

Even though half this guy's face is covered, there's something familiar about him. About his square jaw. His lean but sculpted frame. His touch on my elbow before should've felt foreign, but instead, it was something more than friendly.

I spot movement over his shoulder through the glass windows and notice a man outside with a large camera hung around his neck. He's peering inside the coffee shop like he's looking for someone.

Before I can think more of it, he walks away, shaking his head.

Can this morning get any weirder?

I blink the Harvard guy back into focus, gathering my thoughts. "Do I know you?"

He steps back, glancing around, then dips the hat lower over his forehead. "I don't think so."

"I feel like…" I shrug off any thoughts other than getting

my hands on another cup of coffee and offer him a small smile. "Never mind."

He places his hand on my arm again, his touch confusingly warm and comforting. "Let me buy you another coffee. Maybe another sweater too?"

I shake my head. "Not necessary. I have extra clothes in my car."

"As all unsuspecting citizens should." He cracks a smile. Even though it's not enough to erase the worry from between his brows, it's a charming grin, nonetheless, one complete with perfectly straight white teeth and dimples.

Fucking dimples.

"I'll take you up on the coffee, though," I manage, tearing my attention away from the cute lines in his cheeks.

"After you." He spreads his arm to the side for me to continue forward in line.

My hand trembles as I gesture it over myself and say, "This is my fault too. To tell you the truth, I wasn't watching where I was going, either. And I shouldn't have assumed you were being a sleazy pervert checking out that woman."

He hangs his head, chuckling as he stuffs his hands into his jeans pockets.

"That's so not me." I wave my hands in front of my face like I'm denouncing the devil. "I don't know what came over me."

"Sounds like you know too many sleazy pervs," he teases, and I wish I could see his eyes. Would there be a twinkle in them? An amused look in them as we fall into this easy banter?

"They're everywhere, actually," I say, letting a soft laugh escape. "And right before I ran into you, I ran into a woman because I was on my phone. So stupid."

"It's a dangerous thing these days." He leans in to let a patron by, and the hint of his woodsy scent makes my mouth water more than the smell of coffee. We're now standing side by side, my shoulder to his bicep, and warmth radiates from him like heat from the fireplace at the cabin, drawing me in. "I swear, we act like we can't live without our phones, but people did just fine without them a hundred years ago."

I nod, my lips curling in the corners. "The sad part is, I wasn't even reading anything important."

His hat covers the top of his forehead, casting a shadow over his expression, but I imagine if I could see all of him, I'd see his brow lifted, his interest piqued. Why does he seem so familiar? My instinct that I know him fades even more as we talk, and that nagging itch is replaced by a tingling sensation. I'm overcome by it as though I've never seen a good-looking man before—half of one, anyway.

"Forget what I said. I love wasting time on my phone. Do tell what nonsense you were reading." He nudges me with his shoulder.

I laugh as we step forward, getting closer to the counter, my brown-stained shirt almost forgotten. I use my thumb to unlock my phone and turn the screen toward him. "I was reading dumb gossip."

"Oh?" His body tenses.

"I don't normally bother, but I had to check out the latest news on Manhattan's most beloved man-child." Rolling my eyes, I scroll down. "I mean, Carter Fields is almost forty years old and doesn't know the difference between the gas pedal and the brake. This guy has crashed his car way too often than is socially acceptable."

"There's a social standard for that sort of thing?"

I shrug. "I don't know, but three in a month is too many."

His perfect posture falters as he shifts on his feet. "I'm…" He clears his throat. "I mean, I heard Carter's only thirty-five."

"And I'm twenty-eight and a day," I tease, exaggerating my exact age.

"Besides, I hear this *man-child*, as you so eloquently put it"—he swipes the corners of his twitching lips—"does a lot of charity work. Very generous."

I make a noncommittal sound.

"Tell me, what types of men do you prefer, then?"

There's a trace of humor in his voice, but I almost don't notice it. Instead, I'm distracted by his full lips, the bottom one slightly bigger than the top. It gives him a unique charm.

I tuck my hair behind both ears as he stands firmly in place, his head tilted as he waits for my answer like it's important.

He's a very intriguing stranger, for sure, and I'm thrilled by the mystery of him. I'm even tempted to ask him to hang out here until I can unravel it.

I clear my throat, stepping forward in line. "Well—"

"What can I get you?" a high-pitched voice behind the counter interrupts.

I turn to my left, unnerved by the butterflies in my stomach. Surprisingly engrossed in this conversation, I didn't realize we were so close to the front.

Once we finish with our order—a new caffè latte for me and an Americano for him—he stands with me on the waiting side of the café and leans down. From this close, his cologne invades my senses, and it's easier for me to hear him when he says, "So? Tell me your idea of the perfect man. Your boyfriend, perhaps?"

I inhale a sharp breath like he asked what color my panties are. "No, no boyfriend. No perfect man, either, but if I meet him, I'll be sure to let you know."

"You'll give me your number, then? So you can let me know?" His hoarse voice is in my ear, sending shivers down my spine.

"I walked right into that one, didn't I?" I manage a small smile through the turmoil in my head and chest.

"Literally." He rocks backward on his heels, his wide grin victorious.

"Tessa?" the barista calls, setting a new latte on the counter.

"Tessa?" the mystery man repeats, and his previous smirk falls slack.

Guess he didn't hear me give my name to the barista when we ordered. It was loud, and the noise in here has only grown since we first stepped in line.

I want to ask him what his name is. I gave mine for both of our orders.

I want to give him my phone number too, but… I shouldn't.

"Um…" I grab our coffees, and once I hand him one, I lift mine to clink against his. "Thank you for the coffee, but I have to go."

"Right." He drops all humor and stills, facing me. It makes me feel like he's studying me, but I don't wait to find out. It wouldn't do me any good, anyway.

Waving over my shoulder, I weave through the line and dart out the door, my heart thundering. Once my feet hit the sidewalk and I suck in the fresh midmorning air, I run my hand through my short hair, bogged down like it's already late in the evening.

Who was I in there? So easily chatting with a good-looking guy while my stomach did backflips?

An immediate connection is what that was.

It's the one thing I've been actively trying to avoid for almost a year, but I can't deny how exhilarating it was.

Shit.

My phone vibrates in my hand, snapping me out of my trance.

Graham.

I take a sip of my coffee, pushing away thoughts of the Harvard guy's mouth so close to my ear. It's not normal to have such an extreme reaction to someone I don't know and will never see again. With a deep breath, I settle my nerves and ease the nagging knot in my stomach that can only be described as butterflies—unwanted as they are.

"You have some explaining to do, big brother." Holding the phone to my ear, I pick up the pace toward my car, but not before glancing behind me. I don't see the Harvard guy, though, and I'm more miffed than I should be.

The smart part of my brain says *good riddance.*

But the other part of me wonders why he didn't try harder for my number.

"Carter needs my help. I couldn't say no," Graham says, his voice soothing. He's used this tone on me all my life when he's needed a favor, whether it was to lie for him when he missed curfew or to be his designated driver on the rare occasion he goes out drinking. I've never been able to refuse him, and he knows it too.

I scoff. "And you thought a simple text to let me know he's going to be joining us would be enough for me not to lose it?"

"I was going to call after you had a chance to do your research and calm down."

"What do you mean?"

"I know you've already researched every exaggerated snippet of Carter's life in the media."

"I didn't realize I was so predictable." I turn the corner and walk between the lines of cars on the sides of the road until I reach mine.

"No, I just know you too well."

I carefully set my coffee in the cupholder and shut the car door behind me. "Well, I did do my research to see what your old friend has been up to since college, but I can't say it calmed me down."

Graham's voice drops when he says, "I know what people say about him, but he's not the immature asshole they make him out to be. Give him a chance."

I sigh. "He must be important enough for you to let him crash *my birthday*."

"I know, and I'll make it up to you. I didn't want you two to meet this way, either." He mumbles something, but he continues before I can ask for clarification. "I wouldn't do this if Carter didn't need me. We've had each other's backs since college, and he's saved my ass a few times. He never lets me forget one time in particular." He chuckles. "I swear, if I would've known what Trixie was up to—"

"Dr. Rollins, your ten o'clock is ready," another voice sounds from his end.

Graham addresses me again. "I need to go, sis."

"Wait, who's Trixie? And when is Carter supposed to—"
The line goes silent.

I chew my lip, holding in the rest of my sentence like a

sneeze, and toss my phone to the passenger seat. That's the life of a physician—drop everything when it comes to a patient. I'm used to it from both Graham and our father. Before he retired, anyway.

His office is always bustling, and Graham and Dr. Blythe—his partner—run around it like the people on Wall Street, rushing from one patient to the next.

So, I let it slide each time Graham abruptly hangs up on me. What else can I do?

Checking my mirrors, I pull onto the road that will take me out of New York and up past Hartford, Connecticut, the same road I used to take a few times a year. As always, I turn the volume on the pop station higher and let my mind drift as the tall buildings transform into trees.

My family and I go up to our cabin for holidays and birthdays, but I missed Labor Day. Graham's birthday was in June, but we didn't meet at the cabin since his schedule was too loaded. I've been too busy with work as well.

While I was in graduate school, though, I went up there to study or simply get away from real life, especially after my breakups with Wyatt.

He and I dated on and off for a year until I realized *off* was the better option for my sanity, and I filed that period of my life away under a "bad decisions" folder in my brain.

While we were together, Wyatt drove me crazy, but our chemistry was palpable. It was my first time getting sucked into an otherworldly feeling. One of passion and heat that made me constantly feel drunk in his presence.

That feeling was our downfall, though.

Merging onto the interstate, I laugh at myself. It's been a year since I last spoke to Wyatt, yet it feels longer. So much has happened since then. I'm another year older, with a real job and my own apartment in Brooklyn.

I've traded mind-blowing sex and an unhealthy relationship for the occasional *safe* man.

I pass signs for New Haven, and the closer I get to the cabin, the more my heart swells.

As shadows of trees dance across the hood of my car and windshield, happy nostalgia replaces the dread that usually comes with thinking of Wyatt. When I stop at the same gas station we always came to when I was a kid, I'm consumed by wistful memories. Dad would fill the car up, and Mom would get me juice and plain Lay's chips. She knew how much I hated the different flavors back then—a habit I grew out of as I got older.

I put my car in park next to one of the pumps, fill my tank up, and grab BBQ chips from inside. Once I'm on the road again, the city of Hartford in my rearview mirror, I admire the river, the trees covered in light reds and fading greens, and the air filled with early signs of fall.

I'm cautious as I drive down the winding road, careful of the steep drop-off where there should be a shoulder, until the cabin comes into view. I inch down the gravel driveway, and my breath hitches as I roll to a stop.

My family's quaint wooden cabin stands before me, two grand oak trees towering over it on either side like they're keeping it and my memories safe.

Leaving my bags, I get out and walk up to the porch where I run my fingers over the deep red window shutters. The white rocking chairs by the door are chipped and faded, but they're sturdy. In the past, Mom and Dad would sit out here in the mornings, sipping coffee and enjoying the sunrise while Graham and I would sleep. When we'd wake, we'd beg them to come inside for French toast, Mom's breakfast specialty.

Daniel and his wife, Marie, are the closest neighbors half a mile up the road. They're also good family friends. My parents probably called to let them know we'd be arriving today. They always grab these chairs from the shed out back and make sure the heat is turned on for us.

Once I'm seated in a chair, I open and close my eyes, enjoying the breeze on my cheeks like a soft caress.

Late September might be my favorite time of year. Even though the mornings and evenings are chilly, it's still warm during the day. Unlike midsummer, this is the perfect season since it's not so hot to melt ice cream.

Not everyone agrees, though. In the city, it seems early fall is colder for people who aren't native to the area, like some of my clients. I work with people from all around the world, and each fall, those from the South especially, come to me covered in enough thick winter gear to brave Mount Everest. It always makes me smile.

I'll miss my clients this week, but this will be a much-needed break to recuperate and bond with my family.

Smiling, I continue rocking, enjoying the peace this place offers, unlike the city. Birds flap their wings in the distance. The sun filters through the leaves on the trees. The air is fresh and hopeful as the new season settles upon us.

Silence.

Until a passing truck jolts me from my spot.

Exhaling with contentment, I return to the car for my bags, checking my phone on the way.

There's no word from Graham or my parents, but that's

not unusual. They said they'll be here this evening, and they will be.

I hum as I grab my bags and mentally list the things I want to do before everyone else gets here. Who knows when the playboy will show.

As I make my way inside, I glance back at the mailbox at the end of the driveway. I have half a mind to tape off a protective perimeter around it before he arrives.

Snorting, I open the door, drop the bags at my feet, and take a deep breath. I inhale years of history and traditions, which I plan to keep intact as much as I can, starting with this week.

I close the door behind me and check the pictures along the walls and across the mantle above the fireplace as the memories continue to assault me.

Wyatt hated this cabin. One of his reasons was the family pictures. He'd say he felt like my parents were watching us the entire time he and I would visit.

On top of that, he and Graham never got along. Their arguments were so childish, fighting over the last bag of chips or who would sleep on the couch since we only have three bedrooms. Wyatt knew he'd sneak into my room after Mom and Dad went to bed, but he just liked pushing Graham's buttons.

I had to play referee between them so often it made me dizzy.

Thank God I don't have to do that now. Beyond benefiting my own mental health, breaking up with Wyatt has helped Graham and me get to a much better place in our relationship.

All is as it should be now.

After an hour of welcomed silence, I'm halfway finished

with my freshly brewed cup of decaf coffee and three chapters into the newest Nora Roberts romance when there's a knock on the door.

From my spot on the window seat, I peek through the blinds, but the man's back is to me. In the driveway, a Maserati is parked behind my Subaru, making me snicker. Only a spoiled billionaire would drive an expensive sports car through winding roads and down a gravel driveway without flinching.

I open the door, expecting the clean-cut pretty boy whose images are plastered all over the internet, but his black hoodie, the scruff along his jaw, and his unruly hair curling over his ears surprise me.

"I didn't know when you…" My voice trails off when I notice the Harvard ball cap and aviators.

"Hey, Tessa." He flashes his dimples, but instead of causing a jolt of welcomed electricity like they did this morning, they send me into a panic.

All air leaves my lungs, and my knees buckle.

"Oh my God." I slam the door in his face and lock it. How the hell did the coffee shop guy find me all the way up here?

Did he… follow me?

"Oh my God," I mutter again, my heart racing.

"Tessa?" His voice is muffled by the barrier between us and also the blood rushing to my ears.

With trembling hands, I grab my phone from the couch and dial Sheriff Thompson. "It's Tessa. I need your help at the cabin." There's more knocking on the door, and suddenly, I can't breathe. "Please hurry."

FOUR

Carter

I t didn't click until the barista called her name. It's why she seemed so familiar.

Graham's little sister, Tessa. She's the only woman Graham's ever made—and kept—a serious commitment to. They have the same blue eyes and distinct features, but her cheekbones are more defined. And pink. I thought about her pink blush during the entire drive to the cabin.

Tessa Rollins.

She was a young teen when I first met Graham, and she never visited him on campus since she couldn't drive yet. I only ever saw a picture of her when she was fourteen, with braces and long hair. After college, Graham and I stayed in touch, especially since we both live in New York City, but he never introduced me to Tessa.

She's definitely a woman now.

Short, wavy-styled blonde hair. Bright smile. Witty and smart.

Graham would kick my ass if he knew I tried to get her number, but to my defense, I didn't recognize her. Not with those sexy glasses and womanly curves. Although, even if I would've, I don't think I would've stopped myself.

Her lips were pink and full, and I couldn't help staring at them as she spoke, even though she was insulting me without knowing it was me.

I mean, a *man-child*? What the fuck?

It's possibly the worst dig I've received in a long time, mostly because it came from those sultry lips of hers.

She wasn't wrong about everything, though. I was definitely checking out the woman outside the café, but I couldn't admit it to Tessa. Although I didn't even know who she was, I didn't want her first impression of me to be that I'm a *sleazy pervert*.

I tap the steering wheel as I drive around the curve, and the GPS spouts directions toward Graham's family cabin.

I'm still stunned she didn't recognize me after all the pictures she was scrolling through, although I will admit, I'm not looking like myself today. Not with my beard and messy hair under my hat. On top of that, my sunglasses covered half my face, so I don't hold it against her.

I wouldn't have had to keep the sunglasses on if I weren't being followed. Cameramen and reporters have no fucking boundaries when it comes to chasing a story, even if there's no story to speak of.

The dry tone of the GPS sounds, directing me to turn right, and I find myself leaning into every winding curve until a little wooden cabin comes into view.

Once I'm parked in the driveway behind a Subaru, I smooth my hair back and put my ball cap on. Straightening the bill, I step out of my car, and the gravel crunches beneath my feet as I study my surroundings.

There are a lot of trees.

The rows of them seem to extend for miles. It's so quiet here, I can almost hear the leaves break from the branches and fall. I inhale deeply and cough like I'm allergic to nature and its freshness.

This is the kind of place I imagine writers would enjoy. They could sit on the porch as the sun rose and set, contemplating all of life's wonders, none of which I have the answers to.

Unless I'm asked for a sarcastic response—now that, I'm good at.

My shoulders relax. Paparazzi won't find me here, and I can hide out in peace. It'll be a change of pace for me. I'm not exactly known to thrive in quiet, secluded settings, but there's a first time for everything, right?

Still, the thought of being trapped here for days without clubs, models, or my office makes my skin crawl. As I walk up to the porch, the main thought that keeps me moving is that Tessa might make things interesting.

My heart races as I knock on the door and face the rocking chairs. They've certainly seen better days. Soft thuds cross the floor inside and grow louder before the door swings open.

I spread my arms in a grand gesture. "Hey, Tessa."

Her mouth falls open, and her expression transforms from relaxed, maybe even a little dazed, to pure terror. "Oh my God," she says and slams the door shut.

There's another click and a slide from where she bolts the door, locking me outside.

What the hell? She seemed so much friendlier this morning. Toward the end of our run-in, anyway. Our conversation was effortless, and—wait… is there a bear behind me?

I stiffen, ready to bolt and scream louder than Whitney claims I did as a kid.

Slowly, I spin in place and check the small front yard, but nothing's there.

"Tessa?" I knock on the door again, but there's no answer. Pacing the porch, I call Graham, who answers on the first ring for once.

"I was about to call you. Make it up to the cabin okay?"

"I'm outside, but Tessa slammed the door in my face. You didn't tell her about Carmen in college, did you? About the curse that crazy psychic cast on me?"

He snorts. "No. Why?"

"Trying to think of reasons I already could've scared off your perfect little sister."

"Maybe you're just not as charming as you think."

I scoff. "That's definitely not it."

"I'm heading back to the office from lunch. I'll call her."

"Good, because I feel like I'm being hunted by a bear." I spin in place again, scratching the back of my head.

"Nah. Bears don't go after spoiled billionaires. Your money makes them sick."

"Fuck off." I hang up, laughing, but I still check over my shoulder for any eight-foot grizzly monsters.

I wait a few minutes, but she still doesn't appear. I knock on the door again, which echoes in the silence, until sirens sound in the distance. Turning around, I find a cop car with flashing lights racing toward us, leaving a cloud of dust in its wake.

It stops in the driveway right when Tessa emerges from the cabin. "Sheriff Thompson, hi!" She brushes past me toward a tall and lanky man stepping out of the police car.

The sheriff? What the hell is going on?

As they talk, the man looks over Tessa's shoulder at me, his expression wary.

Instinctively, I pull my hat farther down over my face.

The sheriff stalks toward me, and beside him, Tessa skips to keep up with his long strides. "Is this the intruder?" He clears his throat, pointing at me. "The stalker?"

My eyes bulge out of my head. "The *what*? You called the sheriff on *me*?" I pin Tessa with my glare.

She shakes her head and waves her hands as she steps between the sheriff and me. "This is all a misunderstanding. It's silly, really. This is my brother's best friend. He's staying here for the next couple weeks. But I didn't recognize him."

He nods as I scoff. "So, you called the sheriff?" I ask again, placing my hands on my hips.

She doesn't look at me as she apologizes to him, promising to bring homemade brownies to him and his wife this week for his troubles.

Blood boiling, I take the steps onto the porch and stand by the door, keeping my head low as I wait. Once he's convinced I'm not an unhinged predator, the sheriff waves goodbye and gets into his car. I remain fuming as he spins his tires, flinging rocks in every direction, and backs out of the driveway.

When it's just the two of us again, Tessa slinks toward the porch, her head dipped as she stops in front of me. Worrying her bottom lip between her teeth, she finally looks up.

"I'm supposed to be here to hide, not have the police come to my doorstep and cause a scene." I seethe, pacing beside her.

She flings the door open, tossing over her shoulder, "Relax. There's not a single person around for at least half a mile. You're safe."

She acts like she didn't almost get me fucking arrested.

Wouldn't that have been something? Dozens of headlines flash through my mind with images of me in handcuffs, all of which only fuel my rage.

I follow her inside, my mind reeling as sarcasm drips from every word. "Apparently, you're not safe, though. You have a stalker."

"What was I supposed to think?" She whirls around, stopping me in my tracks less than a foot from her. "I meet a random guy in a coffee shop, and a few hours later, he's on my doorstep over a hundred miles away from said coffee shop. How else should I have handled the situation? Please enlighten me!"

I yank the sunglasses off and remove my hat. Running my hand through my mess of short curls, I snap back, "You seriously didn't recognize me? You were checking me out all morning on your phone."

"Half your face was covered, and you look like you haven't gotten a haircut in a year." She crosses her arms, and her voice is unsteady when she says, "Also—I was *not* checking you out."

"No, you're right. You were judging me. What was it you called me? A *man-child*? Much better." I bump her shoulder with mine as I brush past her, my entire body tense and irate.

She could've cost me everything—my reputation, job, and entire damn future—all because she didn't take a second to think.

She squares her shoulders and juts her chin up at me. "I stand by my statement."

We lock eyes for a beat, the door shut behind us, closing us inside. The added tension makes the room feel a lot smaller, and I'm about ready to explode with this much pressure built in my head of all the what-ifs and potential outcomes of her little stunt.

I squint at her, refusing to back down. "You have no idea the damage you could've caused."

"Yeah, right. Like your deep pockets wouldn't have been enough to save you." She stares pointedly at me.

"This isn't a fucking joke, Tessa. This is my life." I inch toward her, chest heaving.

She extends her reddening neck forward, morphing her expression into one of mock sympathy as she brings her hands to her chest. "Oh, I'm sorry. I forgot everything is about poor little Carter." Scowling, she stands upright and changes her voice back to the stern tone she held moments ago when she says, "God forbid I think about my own safety."

We stare at each other, coming to a standstill as the air around us shifts.

What the hell am I supposed to say now? Or do? Offer my apologies?

Fuck that. I didn't do anything but ask Graham for help.

Now, his uptight sister is giving me hell with her infuriatingly smart mouth.

I lick my lips as she breaks our staring contest and steps around me with a huff. She rushes toward a room on the other side of the fireplace, leaving behind a cloud of flowery scent.

I inhale a deep whiff—I can't help myself—and curl my fists at my sides.

Breathing in through my nose and out of my mouth, I

turn from side to side, taking in the pictures scattered around the room. There are so many pictures, both old and more recent, of the Rollins family hiking, next to a Christmas tree, and in front of this very cabin.

I march to the far corner and run my hand over the Afghan folded neatly over the back of a maroon recliner. The couch next to it and in front of the small fireplace looks worn. The edges are starting to fray like dead ends of hair, which according to many of the socialites I know is "beauty suicide."

I stand next to the couch and place my hands on the back, pushing up and down to see how much give it has, then take a seat. It might not look like much, but it's comfortable as hell, as is the rest of this cabin.

It's what home décor magazines might call cozy.

And then, there's Tessa.

My gaze falls to the hall where she disappeared. She hasn't made a sound since, either.

I throw my head back and stare at the wooden fan hanging from the ceiling as a low laugh escapes me. I'm fucking delirious—it's the only explanation. This whole morning has been a whirlwind.

I drag both hands down my face as Tessa finally emerges, but she doesn't stop to make small talk or even ask me what food I'm allergic to as part of some evil plan of hers. She must've been cooking up some way to torture me, right?

Instead, she bolts toward the kitchen, taking small but hurried steps along the way, and the pads of her sock-covered feet slide across the hardwood every couple of steps.

I follow her every move, studying her as I would a business associate to determine a strategy to gain the upper hand. She doesn't meet my gaze, though, as she reaches into a cabinet for a glass and fills it with water. With a full glass in hand, she starts back toward her room.

"This is how we're going to play it for the next week? Seems a bit immature. But wait, that can't be right. You're the grown-up between the two of us, no?" I lean forward, resting my elbows on my knees, my lips twitching.

She stiffens and spins on her tiptoes like a ballerina until she faces me. "I'm going to my room to read quietly while we wait for your babysitter. Because unlike you, I can take care of myself without needing someone to slap my wrist and handle my problems for me."

I run my fingers over my knuckles, glaring back at her as I steady my voice. She knows how to hold her own, that's for sure.

And I respect that.

Even though I'm the one she's lashing out on.

"So, while you chew on what I'm sure will be a witty and intelligent comeback, I'll be in my room reading the swoony heroes of Nora Roberts's creation."

"Ah, might they be the perfect men you referred to this morning? The ones who don't exist?" I ask, my voice low and laced with so much amusement I can hardly contain myself. I run my knuckle across my bottom lip, suppressing a grin, and her gaze falls there, following my movement.

Her eyes flash back up to meet mine. "I don't need to explain myself to you."

"No, but you're still telling me *plenty*." I wink.

Roughly exhaling, she whirls around so hard, she almost spills her drink. The slam of her door makes me jump in my spot, and I finally let my laugh loose.

I've been here for less than an hour, and already, Tessa's most certainly making my visit interesting.

FIVE

Arrogant asshole.

I let my head fall back against the wall with a thud for what feels like the hundredth time in the last thirty minutes, during which I've read exactly one sentence of the book now resting in my lap.

All I can think about is Carter. I finally got a look at his hazel eyes, and they're nothing like the pictures online. They're the color of a magnificent sunset, smoldering and intense.

They knocked the freaking wind out of me. It's a miracle I kept myself relatively composed out there long enough to string a sentence together.

And it pissed me off to have such a reaction to him. His stupid grin was smug and knowing, like he's got me all figured out.

He's under my skin.

I knew this week would be a train wreck, and if the past few hours in his presence are any indication of what to expect from the rest of it, we're headed right for a fiery crash sooner rather than later.

My parents better be on a damn flight already.

They've been on a couple's trip to Hawaii over the last week—their third trip this year. It's what they enjoy most during their retirement, other than their time spent with Graham and me. And it makes me happy too. Not only are they generally more relaxed than I've ever seen them, but they always have amazing pictures to show us, allowing me to live vicariously through them.

I don't know when it happened, but my parents are more fun than me.

I check my phone for any update on their whereabouts, but I find nothing from them or Graham. Where are they? My foot bounces on the bed, and I close my book, giving up on making any progress on what happens next. I click through my contacts until I get to my mom's and give her a call.

After the third ring, her voice booms through my speaker. "Hi, honey! Or should I say, birthday girl."

I smile, comforted for the first time today. I hear my dad whispering in the background, but other than that, I don't hear much else. No airport intercom announcing passengers' last chance to board. No chatter or urgency in their voices like they can't talk right now because they're going through security.

Nothing.

"Where are you guys?" I ask, pacing next to my bed, one hand on my hip.

"Ask her," my dad hisses. "She'll be fine."

"Okay, okay," Mom assures him.

"What's going on?" I take a seat—I think it's best to be sitting down for whatever's coming.

"Sorry, sweetie, but here's the thing. Anthony and Sheila are moving to Costa Rica next month, remember?" She doesn't wait for my response before she says, "I don't know why they insist on giving up their place in the city. Their apartment overlooks Central Park, and there's a waitlist three times the length of an American Medical Association manual. But it's always been their dream to open a little tiki bar on the beach, and it'll make them happy. It'll also give your father and me an excuse for a tropical beach vacation." She giggles, and I can hear my father again in the background.

I run my fingers through my hair, practicing the patience I've learned in my adult life with deep breaths and enough pause to consider what she's saying.

But I come up empty.

"I remember you telling me of your friends' decision, Mom, but why are you telling me all this now?" I hug one knee to my chest, resting the heel of my foot on the edge and sinking into the mattress.

"Of course," she says. "The thing is, Anthony and Sheila asked us to stay another night. I know it's a lot to ask, honey, but we won't see them much between now and the time they move. They have so much packing to do. It would just be one more night, and then, we will fly right over to Connecticut to celebrate your birthday."

"Oh."

"But we don't have to. I know this week is important. You say the word, and we'll get on the next flight out." She takes an audible deep breath like she's holding it in anticipation of my answer.

It reminds me of all the times when I was a kid, and I'd ask her if I could stay at a friend's house over the weekend—just one more night, five more minutes, or one more movie. Except now our roles are reversed. What kind of alternate reality is this?

I drop my leg, and my foot hits the floor with a soft pat. "It's fine, Mom," I say as I run my palm down my thigh over my cotton leggings. "I'll see you tomorrow, then?"

"Yes! We will be there by your time tomorrow evening." Her voice reaches a higher pitch than before, and I again imagine myself as the mother in this scenario where the teenage daughter is jumping up and down, clapping with enthusiasm that she gets to spend more time with her friends.

Once we say our goodbyes and end the call, I sigh, but I can't help my smile. Graham and I thought retirement would be hard on them. We figured they'd run back to work after only a month, but it's been almost a year. It's like they're in their early twenties again.

They've found their strides, picking up new hobbies and traveling. My mother discovered pottery and has even taken up reading for fun. My father has a newfound appreciation for nature and its inhabitants, so instead of studying human charts, he's studying birds and animals in the forest.

Some days, it's like Graham and I are getting to know our parents all over again. The new versions of them, anyway.

I laugh under my breath as I stand and make my way to the door. With my hand on the knob, I pause, remembering… *Carter.*

He hasn't made a sound since I closed myself in here,

and remembering his presence in the living room makes me seethe.

I wish I didn't need that glass of water earlier, just so I wouldn't have had to see his stupidly gorgeous face. What has he been doing out there?

Or is he even still here?

Did I get lucky and scare him off?

Then, I could have the cabin to myself to read and relax in. I could make brownies in peace and sing at the top of my lungs. No one but the squirrels and birds would hear me.

For a brief moment, I grin at the mental image, but then, the happy bubble pops with a needle—Carter being the needle.

I lean my ear to the door and hear the low buzzing of the TV and rustling like he's searching his duffel bag.

Exhaling, I let my hand fall away from the door, and I resume my position on my bed, back melting into a wall of pillows against the metal headboard and swoony book in hand.

Not five minutes later, the repeated drilling of a woodpecker into a tree outside my window grows louder and louder as I stare at the same word in my book, my eye twitching.

Slamming the paperback shut, I grunt and jump off the bed, then march toward the door. I yank it open and storm around the fireplace, my steps heavy with purpose and determination not to let this day be ruined by my parents' absence, Carter's annoying smirk, and Graham's delayed arrival—which he has yet to call about.

When my gaze lands on Carter, though, I stop in my tracks, my aggravation caught in my throat. He sits on the couch, his legs sprawled open in front of him. A laptop is propped between them, and he types away on the keyboard, the light from the screen illuminating his face.

I push my glasses higher on my nose and tug on the hem of my sweater, suddenly squirmy.

This image in front of me is so different than the ones on the internet. The photos I found this morning show a party boy—a strong and powerful one, but a party boy, nonetheless.

Sharp suits and A-list friends ranging from Manhattan socialites to Hollywood superstars. Online, Carter's the guy everyone wants to befriend, or sleep with.

But here, he's sitting on a slightly worn couch in a hoodie and jeans, his eyes blue from his computer screen and concentration etched into his expression where his dimples should be. He's still sitting with impeccable posture, exuding the power I assumed he would from the pictures, but he's less intimidating.

He even seems… normal.

"Are you going to stare at me all evening, or do you care to join me?" He glances up, and his eyes resume their natural hazel color.

"I'm not staring. I…" I hold my head up. "My room's not so quiet, so I'm going to read right here on the window seat, if you don't mind."

"Not at all. Besides, this is your place." He watches me, his expression and body language relaxed like he has the upper hand in some twisted game.

But I'm not playing.

"That's right." I nod and make my way to the holy grail of reading nooks, feeling his gaze on me the entire five steps, but I don't dare turn toward him again. My attention averted,

I nestle onto the red cushion of the window seat, adjusting the pillow behind me and curling my knees up to my chest.

"On that note, I hope you don't mind that I helped myself." He holds up a glass with dark liquid in it—whiskey. "I would've asked, but your door was closed. Seemed like you wanted to be left alone."

"I did, and I do."

"Message received." He focuses on his computer again and takes a sip of his drink, one I'd love to have myself, but I refrain.

I'll need to drive to the store soon for groceries, and if I'm not careful, I'll get carried away with the alcohol. I don't want to drive drunk and hit a mailbox or anything.

I snort under my breath as I flip the book open to the page I left off of.

In my periphery, I catch Carter's head snap toward me, but he doesn't say anything. After a few minutes of silence, though, he smirks at his phone, automatically drawing my attention to where he sits on the couch.

His laptop is forgotten, and instead, he strokes his bottom lip with his thumb and forefinger as he reads whatever's on his phone. I can only assume he's talking to a woman.

Supermodel Ginger Myers, perhaps.

Who else would put a dopey smile like that on a guy's face?

I twist my lips in disgust and turn back to my book, but his voice ringing through the silence stops me. "Something bothering you?"

"I'd have to care, which I don't, in order to be bothered, which I'm not." I throw my legs over the edge of the seat and stand, finally admitting defeat. I will not be solving the mystery of this book anytime today.

"What's your problem with me? Other than the fact you thought I was a stalker earlier today." He sets his phone aside and stands between the door and me, his chest wider than I realized, and a silly thought enters my mind—how long would it take me to run the tip of my finger from one side to the other?

I snap my attention up to him.

"You were a lot more pleasant at the coffee shop this morning. You know, before you knew who I was." He folds his arms across his magnificent chest.

"Maybe that's the problem. I learned who you are." I sidestep him as a low chuckle rumbles out of him, and I head toward the kitchen counter to grab my purse. "I'm going to the store."

"All right, but I have a question." He holds his finger up. "Nothing major, but where will I be sleeping?"

I nod toward where he was just sitting. "The couch, of course."

Now it's my turn to be smug, and I enjoy it more than a margarita during girls' night out.

Maybe I'll play his little game, after all.

SIX

Carter

Tessa moves farther into the living room and pats the couch. As she points to the folded blanket and pillow on one end, she says, "There are only three bedrooms—mine, Graham's, and my parents'—so you can sleep here."

I blink at her, then the couch, then back at her. "I'm sorry, I don't think I understand."

"I'm sorry too." She juts her hip out in challenge, obviously enjoying this. "I'm sorry this isn't The Ritz and I can't meet your expensive and luxurious needs. Instead, I have a couch, and I'm sure it's better than the floor you probably woke up on."

I start to offer my retort, but I'm taken aback. "How did you know?"

She laughs under her breath, which makes her thick-framed glasses fall lower on her nose. She uses her slender finger to push them back into place, and my jaw drops as if she licked her damn finger. "You're a typical party boy."

"Lucky guess." I tilt my head, focusing on our situation instead of how her lips might pucker if she sucked on her finger. My voice is much harsher than I intend when I try to save face and say, "Also, don't lecture me about wealth and luxury, okay? From where I'm standing, you're doing just fine." I wave around the room, then stop on the mahogany china cabinet by the breakfast table. It's filled with fine china plates that even my extravagant mother would approve of.

Tessa purses her lips, squaring her shoulders again—her defensive stance. "I'll have you know, my parents grew up in Queens with little to their name while they put themselves through school. Before they retired, my father was a doctor, and my mother was a therapist. They splurged on this place to provide somewhere for Graham and me to make memories. The china was my grandmother's, which she passed on to us. They all worked for this and weren't handed a cent, unlike *others*." She stares pointedly at me.

My usually perfect posture crumbles. "Shit, I didn't—"

"You don't have to be here. In fact, I'd prefer you weren't. But Graham said you need our help. Take it or leave it." She points to the couch, then disappears into a bedroom, closing the door behind her.

I assume she'll go to the store later, then.

"Fuck." I rub my hands down my face, then stare at the couch. "Guess you and I should get better acquainted," I mumble to it.

Sighing, I tilt my neck from side to side, working the tension out of my shoulders. I've never had a woman be so infuriating. This day has held too much excitement—after a long drive, no less.

I spin in place, taking in the cabin again. The cobblestone fireplace, the fabric sofa, and the red-and-green plaid blanket draped over it. The pillows have owls on them, and their eyes follow me as I turn toward the windows. The curtains are held in place to the sides by brass hooks, and the blinds are pulled up, allowing more natural light inside than I've ever seen. There are so many windows lining this place, it's like I'm standing out in the open.

I'm exposed, in more ways than one.

I walk to the mantle and pick up a framed picture of a young Graham and Tessa. They stand in front of the cabin, knee-deep in snow. Their cheeks are red, which is probably because of the cold, but I'd like to think it's because of how much they laughed that day.

Even though I feel like shit—the whiskey's done nothing to take the edge off—this picture makes me smile.

I've always known Graham to be close with Tessa, but it's nice *seeing* them together like they are in the pictures. It's obvious how strong the bond is between them, as it appears to be between them and their parents as well.

I might be stubborn and believe in my judgement, but I'm man enough to admit when I owe someone an apology. After all, I'm disappointed in myself more than I'm frustrated with Tessa.

I make my way around the fireplace, taking in more family pictures as I drag my feet to Tessa's door and raise my knuckles to knock.

Her cheeks are flushed when she answers. "What?"

"I'm sorry."

She tilts her head, frowning with doubt.

"I am. I was a dick for implying you're spoiled or something. You're not. I'm just…"

She turns her ear toward me and watches me expectantly.

"Look, you called the sheriff on me, okay? I think we're even." I turn on my heel and head back to my *bedroom*.

"That's your apology?" She chases after me and yanks on my arm to face her.

I open my mouth to respond but stop when I notice the blush spreading down her neck. My gaze travels over her simple leggings and the loose sweater that falls right below her ass. I like this better than the one she had on earlier—the one that was drenched in coffee after we ran into each other. Unlike her turtleneck, this top scoops across her chest, barely hanging off one shoulder.

It gives me a hint of the swell of her breasts, but it doesn't show cleavage. It's modest to an average person, but to me, it's sexy in a different kind of way.

She's unlike the women I usually meet at galas and high-end bars in the city. In particular, she's nothing like Ginger.

All of a sudden, my dad's words about a respectable young woman ring in my head as I study her eyes. They're fuming, but underneath, there's a layer of kindness and warmth.

And for some unknown reason, part of me hopes she shows me that layer over the next week.

"You're the marrying type," I blurt, grimacing. "I mean…"

She scoffs. "As if there'd ever be a scenario where I'd marry *you*."

Instantly, I relax and lean forward with a wink. "I meant in the general sense, but it's good to know where your head is at."

She crosses her arms over her chest, pushing her breasts up higher like they're begging me to check them out. "Don't flatter yourself."

"Why would I need to when you're doing it for me?" I step toward her and rest my arm on her doorframe, breathing her in while I fight my urge to take another long look at the top curves of her tits.

"You are so arrogant." She seethes, her nostrils flaring as she gives me a once-over.

I raise my eyebrows. "See something you like?"

With a huff, she puts her hand on my chest and shoves me backward, then slams the door in my face. From what I can tell, that will be a regular occurrence this week.

Chuckling to myself, I walk back to the living room—my *glamorous* sleeping quarters for the next several nights—and am about to sit on the couch when her door flies back open.

Tessa's chest heaves as she stands in front of the fireplace and demands, "Why did you say it like that?"

"I'm sorry?" I squint at her.

"You said I'm the marrying type like you're offended by such a thing as marriage and commitment and love," she says, her breaths releasing in flustered pants.

I grin. "Not offended, but I tend to be allergic to your kind. In fact, I'm surprised I haven't broken out in hives already."

Her hands drop to her sides as she brushes past me.

"It was a joke." I follow her into the kitchen, and my shoulders sag as I witness the downfall of my comedic genius.

Tessa is really testing me and making me question all the things I used to pride myself on.

"So, you *don't* find me and my lack of a boob job

repulsive?" She places her hands on her hips, jutting one out and standing her ground.

"Who said anything about a boob job?" As if I was just waiting for an excuse to finally look again, my gaze immediately falls to her chest, but her loose sweater leaves too much to my imagination.

She wraps her arms around her breasts, covering herself as her eyes bulge out of her head like I invited her to have a threesome. "Don't check me out."

"It's your fault. When boobs are involved, I have to investigate."

"You're such a child." She throws her hands up. "Last night, I was surprised how a grown man could crash his car into a freaking mailbox, but after knowing you for five minutes, I totally get it."

I step toward her, now matching her heated stance. "It's not my fault I never learned how to drive while receiving a blow job."

Her jaw drops, and her hands fly to her chest.

I lick my lips as we stare at each other. "Aren't you missing your pearls?"

"What're you talking about?" She drops her hands to her waist to grip her sweater and pulls it tighter around her.

"I always thought such a strong, disgusted reaction to sex, oral or otherwise, required pearls to clutch," I quip.

Her blush is a darker crimson than before, covering her neck and both cheeks. Her blue eyes, traced with a touch of eyeliner and a soft coat of mascara, pop with surprise.

They're magnificent.

After a short pause, she moves toward me, and with every step, she visibly steels herself, replacing her shock with fire. Her breath is hot on my cheek when she says, "I'm not repulsed by it. On the contrary, I enjoy sex. It's cheap fucks I don't care for, unlike you."

She doesn't wait for me to answer. Instead, she crosses the living room, hips swaying to their own angry tune. The back of her sweater lifts an inch with each step, teasing me with a full view of her ass.

Tessa's something else—quick-witted, passionate, and sexy as hell. The woman draws attention without even trying.

Even when she's spewing insults.

Her lips look sweet and skillful. Her hips and ass were made to grab.

It's all I'm thinking about while she closes herself in her room for what seems like hours. The store is obviously low on her to-do list for the day, right under drawing up a list of ways to torture me this week, I'm sure.

Why the hell does even the thought of that excite me?

I squirm in my seat on the couch, idly changing channels on the TV. The screen blurs as I'm consumed with thoughts of Tessa and her lips close to my skin.

Her words low and seductive.

Her breasts pressed against my arm when she leaned up to whisper in my ear.

There was desire there. An intense heat between us, urging me to silence her with a kiss so deep and punishing, she'd be so turned on she'd forget she was mad.

Or, she'd just use her rage to *punish* me back—I'd be fine with either option.

I exhale, roughly running my hands through my hair.

Fuck me.

I need to get a grip.

Blinking the TV above the fireplace in and out of focus, I try to wrap my head around my current situation.

I can't just apologize again—it would seem futile at this point. Besides, the last time didn't go so well. It only led to another argument, which led to more heat between us, and that's why I'm now squirming in my seat with an agonizing stiffy.

How screwed up am I?

"Didn't take long for you to get comfortable," Tessa mutters, walking back into the living room and jostling me from my seat.

How long have I been staring at the TV?

"Excuse me, but I'd appreciate it if you knocked when you came into my bedroom." I wave my arms around at my unpacked duffel on the floor and the clothes littering the place like red solo cups after a frat party.

Not my best look, but I'm just getting comfortable.

"You've been here for five minutes, and you've already made a mess." She steps over my pile of clothes toward the door. "Do I seriously have to remind you there's no maid? You're going to have to pick up after yourself."

"Ah, man, and here I thought this *was* The Ritz," I mock.

She takes a deep breath through her nose and releases it out of her mouth. "And I thought I'd get to spend my birthday week with my family, not some spoiled billionaire who doesn't know how to even do his own laundry."

My face immediately falls as I clear my throat to respond, but what can I say? That I didn't think twice about the mess until she walked in here and pointed it out?

I guess I do rely on other people too much for that sort of thing.

"I'm going to the store to get groceries and ingredients for brownies to take to Sheriff Thompson and his wife. Need anything?" she asks.

"Nope, no luxury items for me." I give her a tight-lipped smile, standing from the couch when a thought occurs to me. "I've never met someone who's so close to the sheriff and his wife. How do you know them?"

She hesitates, searching my face for something, although I'm not sure what. Does she think this is a trick?

Her voice is lighter when she finally answers, "Trina and my mom play Bridge together when we stay here. They have two kids around my age too. Graham and I used to play with them every summer."

"That's really… nice." I nod, bobbing my head slowly, and something passes between us as we stare at each other.

Is she letting my genuine compliment sink in? Because I am capable of such a thing. I might be rough around the edges, but my parents taught me manners.

"Okay, well, I'll be back in a minute." Each word rushes out of her, and she bolts before I can say anything else.

Blowing out a frustrated breath, I sit back down and grab my phone, only to find several new emails and texts. Skimming through, most of them are questions regarding my sabbatical. To the first couple people, I said I got an early start and gave up work for Lent. After all, why not have a little fun with it? A sentiment they did not appreciate, given the circumstances, so I kept to the script I was given from then on.

As I toss my phone to the side and rest my head back to stare at the ceiling, I suddenly feel guilty for all the *fun* I've been having lately.

The flash of regret I felt this morning is glaring and blinding me.

It seems the closer I get to this promotion, the more intent I am on self-destructing.

What the hell does that even mean?

The sound of the TV is muffled as I wrack my brain to answer that question for myself, but after thirty minutes, guilt still consumes. On top of that, I'm disappointed that Tessa only sees me as the screwup the rest of the world believes I am.

I've never been ashamed of my lifestyle before, but now, I have the overwhelming desire to change Tessa's mind.

SEVEN

Tessa

That irritating man.

The obnoxious, confusing, aggravating *man-child*.

I pace the aisles, making three loops around the store without buying anything as I alternate between pulling my hair and fanning myself.

What the hell was that back at the cabin?

Before I left, Carter looked at me like he was a Rottweiler and I was wearing Lady Gaga's unique dress of meats.

It's why I rushed out of there as quickly as possible.

Instant connection with him this morning or not, and even if he wasn't Graham's best friend, Carter is the exact opposite of the kind of guy I'm looking for. He's trouble with a capital T, and I want *safe*.

I vowed not to let myself get wrapped up in stupid things

like chemistry and heated attraction again. It's been working fine too, and Carter Fields will be no different.

"Focus," I mutter to myself as I open the grocery list on my phone.

I stroll through the aisles and grab ingredients to make my famous homemade brownies. Well, they're not famous in the same vein as Carter, but around these parts, my baked goods are well known.

I grab enough flour, eggs, sugar, cocoa, butter, and chocolate chips to make three separate batches—one for the sheriff, another for our neighbors up the road, and the third to keep at the cabin for us to munch on during the week. I like to bake but refrain from doing so at home since I started living alone and no longer have anyone to share a pan with.

In college, though, Madison and I would bake and watch romantic comedies at least once a week.

Once I'm finished checking out and walking toward my car, my phone rings. I adjust the bags and answer, resting my phone between my ear and shoulder.

"Have you talked to Mom and Dad?" Graham asks. "They're not coming up today."

"I know. She called me earlier."

He pauses. "And you're okay with that?"

"They're with their friends, and it's not like we don't have the whole week. It's just one night." Next to my car, I shift the bags again to grab my keys from my purse. "What about you? Are you on your way?"

"That's what I'm calling you about. Since you're okay with them not coming…"

I stop fidgeting with the bags and freeze. "Graham, you *are* on your way, right?"

"No." The word holds more disappointment than a single syllable should.

I stare over my car at the empty parking lot. "What?"

"I'm sorry, sis, but I have to stay here. I have a few patients who really need to see me in the morning," Graham says. His sympathy and dedication ooze from every word. He cares for his patients as if they're family, which is what makes him a good physician. It's what makes us so proud of him, and it should be what keeps me from being too upset right now.

But I can't help the panic that seizes me. "Okay, but that means I'll be alone with Carter tonight."

"And that works out great. With him there, you won't be totally alone," he says, and I can hear keys clicking in the background like he's on the computer. "Isn't he great?"

"He's... something," I mumble.

Graham sighs, muffling the sound of scraping across the floor as if he's moving a chair. "I know he can come on too strong sometimes, but give him a chance. You two might even be friends. Or at the very least, cordial for the week. And then we can all go back to our lives."

"You sound oddly chipper about that." I furrow my brows, still standing in place by my car, a gentle chill in the air making me shiver. "You're not excited to hang out with your friend?"

"I am, but it's not like I don't see him every other week or so." Something like a groan escapes him. "Plus, it's your birthday, and it's tradition to spend it with family. You've seen what happens when *others* join."

I roll my eyes, knowing he's referring to Wyatt. "Oh yeah? Well, let's not forget the true winners you've brought over the years."

"Who? Bianca or Wendy?" He chuckles.

I crack a smile, peering down at my feet. "Bianca kept stealing my clothes, and Wendy never wanted to wear any clothes at all. Enough said."

His laugh is so loud I have to pull the phone back from my ear, but it makes me grin harder. I unlock my car and move to set the bags in the backseat as I say, "You're going to make it tomorrow, though, right?"

His voice falls when he says, "If all goes as planned."

Immediately, my stomach sinks.

"I'll do my best, okay? I have to run for now."

"Okay. That's fine." I look to the sky. "Love you, Graham."

"Right back at you, sis."

I settle into the driver's seat and toss my phone on the passenger side.

On the way home, I take a detour and pass by one of the parks Mom used to bring me and Graham to. At thirteen, Graham insisted he was too old to play on the monkey bars, but he did—for me. That's the kind of big brother he is. One with a heart bigger than his head.

I come to a rolling stop next to the sidewalk and lean over to peer out the window at the kids in thick jackets giggling and high-fiving each other like they just completed hurdles at the Olympics. I'm still smiling as I continue down memory lane and pass the gates to a familiar golf course. When Graham and I outgrew the playgrounds, Dad would take him there while Mom and I went to the nail salon for a girls' afternoon.

The flood of memories gets me excited for the week and ready to recreate some of the highlights. Brownies, frozen lasagna, and of course, French toast.

Movie and game nights.

Poker and whiskey.

Hiking and picnics.

The fun will really begin when they arrive.

As I make my way back toward the cabin, dark clouds roll in, hanging low in the sky, and thunder echoes in the distance like a gavel across the sky.

The first raindrop hits my cheek when I grab the bags from the backseat and rush inside as though it's pouring already.

What a fantastic and memorable birthday.

Bad weather. No parents or brother. Just an irritating asshole and me.

The cabin is not big enough to contain Carter's ego—or his dimpled grin. My God, the pictures online do not do him justice. His grin in person is almost too much to look at.

I'm not falling for it, or him, though. Graham hasn't told me much about their time together in college, but I've learned enough to know Carter Fields would cause me more grief than there are dollar signs in his bank account if I'm not careful.

Besides, we've done nothing but bicker since he got here. He doesn't see me as anything more than Graham's annoying little sister, anyway.

The one who called the sheriff on him.

No, I have nothing to worry about when it comes to him.

I open the cabin door, the bags rustling in my hands, and scan the living room but come up empty. "Carter?"

After a few seconds of silence, he emerges from one of the bedrooms. Wait… that's *my* room.

"What do you think you're doing?" I clutch the groceries to my chest like I'm using them collectively as a shield.

"I was going through your panty drawer. Duh." He shrugs.

"What?" I step toward him but stop when his face splits into a devilish grin.

"You're so gullible." He moves around the fireplace and takes the bags from me. He seems a lot less tense than he was earlier. What's his deal?

As I follow him into the kitchen, my gaze lands on the curve of his ass, and my stomach involuntarily flutters. *Traitor*.

When I reach toward a bag to put the items away, he smacks my hand. "You're not allowed to help."

I raise my eyebrows.

His grin is smug when he nods toward my room. "Come with me."

He grabs my hand and leads me out of the kitchen, past the front door, and around the couch, already comfortable despite having never been here before.

Pushing my door open, we cross the small space, his hand still intertwined with mine. It's strong. Confident. Surprisingly warm.

I find myself squeezing his hand back.

Opening the bathroom door, he sings in a low, gravelly voice, "Ta-da."

My mouth falls open. Inside, two red candles are lit, filling the small space with the smell of fall and cinnamon rolls. The flames sway as if they hear the soft melody playing from the Bluetooth speaker. Fresh flowers sit in a vase on the sink. He must've picked them from the front yard.

In the corner is the holy grail. A bubble bath.

I grip his hand more tightly and turn, but I don't realize we're still in the doorway. When I face him, our chests are one breath away from touching.

He peers down at me, and his tone is apologetic when he

says, "We got off on the wrong foot. On *many* wrong feet, actually."

My cheeks heat.

"Despite what you may think, I'm not here to sabotage your week. I want you to have a good birthday. You deserve it, and I want to try to make it better, not worse." A teasing tilt of his lips uncovers a dimple, drawing my attention there.

A lump forms in my throat, and when his hot breath fogs my glasses, I gulp. My skin tingles as the heat rolling off the rest of him wraps itself around my body.

"Consider this my apology." His eyes stop their dance as they lock on mine. "I'd like to start over."

His full lips, piercing gaze, and hard chest are distracting, and I have the urge to fan myself.

After a pause, I can only manage a nod.

His fingers cling around mine, and I surprise myself when I don't pull away. I'm still entranced by his eyes. The fire swimming among the hazel storm. The—is that desire?

I confuse myself again when the thought alone—the thought that this gorgeous man might *want* me—sends shivers down my spine.

He's not my type. I don't date enough to say I have a type at all, but Carter is not it.

Even if he has an endearing side.

I think I nod again to his proposal of a do-over, and I definitely hold my breath when he leans toward me like he's going to kiss my cheek. His scruffy beard tingles against my jawline as he continues moving his lips to my ear. "Enjoy," he whispers, then pulls back and winks.

I let out a strangled gasp, one of shock and confusion and arousal as he turns his back to me. I let go of him at the last possible second and snap out of this hypnosis only when he's out of sight.

Unusually flustered, I close the door, set my glasses on the sink with a light clink, and splash water on my face. After a few more deep breaths, I discard my clothes in a hurry, my body still humming.

But it's not because of the bath.

I'm about to step into the tub but stop myself. Carter gave up our differences too easily, right? It's only been a few hours, and I'm supposed to believe he cracked already?

I mean, he drew me a damn bubble bath. Who the hell does that for someone who almost got them arrested and has spent all day being less than hospitable, to put it gently?

This is most definitely a trap of some sort.

I grab my silk robe, slip it on, and make my way back to the living room. "Carter?"

He stands in the kitchen, his broad shoulders instantly tensing as he drops the flour and sugar onto the counter. With his back to me, he says, "It's not a trick. I didn't poison the water or some shit."

I breathe a sigh of relief, then cough to cover it up. I can't let him know that's exactly what I thought. "No, that's not it." I laugh nervously, waving him off.

He spins to face me and holds his hands out. "Please, God, tell me you want me to join you, then."

"No," I say, breathless. My eyes dart around the space between us—it's hard to look at him with his crooked grin sucking me in like a vortex, one I know will swallow me whole. "I was going to say…" I clear my throat and lick my lips when an idea hits me. "Feel free to sleep in Graham's room tonight. He won't make it in until tomorrow."

"He's won't?"

"He called me before I left the store." I toy with my robe and chew the inside of my cheek, suddenly nervous to be even this close to Carter.

And we have a whole damn evening alone.

"My parents won't be here, either," I add.

"Oh." He nods, then says, "Okay."

I exhale, stepping forward with my arms out. "I'm sorry I almost got you arrested earlier. I know it could've blown your cover and made things so much worse for you. I'm just… I'm sorry."

He pushes off the counter and stands tall. "Thanks for saying that," he says, each syllable enunciated like we're in a business meeting.

My heart rate picks up the longer I stand here, my feet like lead as I try to catch up on the turn we've taken. Scratching the side of my head, I ask, "How did you know I like baths?"

The tops of his shoulders barely lift as he shrugs. "Everyone loves baths."

Even though my vision is a tad blurred without my glasses, I can still note the way his eyes flash to mine like there's an underlying meaning of this conversation.

Is a bath supposed to be a metaphor for something?

He nods to my room. "You better get in there while the water's still warm."

Confused and oddly aroused, I back away and into the privacy of my bedroom again. My chest heaves as if I told him to sleep in my own room tonight.

What the hell is happening?

When I left for the store an hour ago, he had me fuming.

I was cursing his name and considering Googling ways to turn his *privates* green.

I even stooped so low on the maturity scale to plan on dipping his hand in water to make him piss himself while he slept on the couch.

Now, I'm hot all over because of the way he looked at me from across the room.

As I sink into the bath, the water already cooling, I pray I make it through the night with my sanity intact and clothes on.

It was one thing not to want Carter Fields, the irresponsible playboy billionaire, but another thing entirely to resist the hot, tender guy who drew me a bath and watched me like he'd never seen a woman before.

As I close my eyes and try to get comfortable, I imagine asking Bree for advice. She'd tell me to go for it. To let loose. To have fun. I'm up here to celebrate my birthday, but also to relax for the first time in forever. What better way to enjoy my break from reality than with a sexy guy?

No, no, no.

Bad idea.

Right?

EIGHT

Carter

Her fucking robe. Christ, is she trying to kill me with that thing?

I almost didn't hear anything she said—something about me sleeping in Graham's room tonight? I was too focused on the way the red silk of her robe clung to her curves. How she idly toyed with the tie holding the thin fabric together.

She was naked under there.

I didn't miss the way her nipples hardened the more we stared at each other. By the time she turned away from me, they were poking through the provocative silk, begging to be fondled.

Her glasses were gone too, revealing brilliant blue eyes. When they landed on me, I swear she could see right through me.

I can't decide if I like her glasses better on or off. On, I imagine her as a sexy professor who likes to fuck on her desk.

Off, I get a clearer view of her eyes and face with nothing for her to hide behind. Without her glasses, she appeared free and open. What would those eyes do if I kissed her? If I slipped my hand into that silk robe of hers, my fingers skating over her smooth skin—

"Damn it," I grumble under my breath.

Alone in the kitchen, I bite my knuckles. Why couldn't my best friend have a fucking brother? Why does he have to have a sexy sister?

My phone vibrates on the counter next to me, slapping me with a dose of reality better than a bucket of ice water.

Graham.

I wipe the dazed look off my face and swear under my breath again. He'd give me a swift kick to my dick if he knew I was fantasizing about his little sister.

Groaning, I check his text.

Graham: I don't know if Tessa told you, but I won't make it up tonight. Have to work in the morning, but I'll be up there tomorrow night. Sorry, dude.

I'm about to type out that I already know and that it would've been nice to have a heads-up.

It would've been even better if Tessa and I didn't have this confusing heat between us. Even when we're bickering, she has me ready to devour her.

This cabin is too small for us to be left alone… with her fucking robe.

At least until her parents and brother get here. Nothing's a more solid cockblock than the family. I'll be fine. I can keep my hands off her for a few more hours—that's nothing—

especially since I can't tell if she wants to straddle me or strangle me. Perhaps, both?

Now, there's an idea.

I smack my cheek, snapping myself out of this damn hold Tessa has on me, and grab the flour and sugar from the counter. I start to put them away but drop them again when I realize I have no clue where anything goes around here. With all the excitement of my arrival, I didn't ask for a tour or have time to snoop and find things for myself.

I do so now, opening and closing cabinets high and low.

Bubbles.

Her smooth body submerged in nothing but bubbles.

I shake my head to rid my mind of these dirty thoughts.

But every movement leads back to soapy water gliding between the valley of her bare and perky breasts, down her stomach to her—

Fuck.

Why did I have to draw her a bath? I could've easily given her the fresh flowers I picked. It would've been a kind enough gesture, especially since I reopened the gash on my thumb from a thorn in the process. I risked my well-being for her. We could've had a good laugh over it.

That could've been the end.

But no, no, no. I had to draw her a damn bubble bath that's conjuring too many dirty thoughts for me to function. I'm harder than a rock.

I open and close my fists at my sides and repeat my mantra.

Graham's sister.

She's Graham's sister.

All I wanted to do was call a truce. No matter how bad

this morning could've turned out for me, the root of my anger has nothing to do with Tessa.

It's about me.

I've had more time to myself today than I have all year put together. It's given me the opportunity to reflect, and even though I enjoy my rowdy lifestyle, I'm too reckless.

I've let the partying and trysts with a long line of women get out of hand. Ever since I started investing in more nightclubs than anything else, I've lost sight of my priorities, and it's all come crashing down on me lately.

As CEO of Fields Company, I'll have more responsibility and will need to be more careful of my reputation. No matter how much fun I'm having, I need to be more mindful of how I'm coming across to not just the world or even Tessa, but to my future staff.

I need balance.

My father's lectures over the last few months hit me like a freight train, and although I have the urge to roll my eyes, I stop myself because there's truth to them. I always knew it but didn't want to hear it.

I continue exploring the kitchen, my head clouded, and more thunder rolls in outside as the storm worsens. Almost an hour later, Tessa reenters the living room in a cropped sweatshirt and pajama pants, the thick drawstring tied just below her belly button. A large sliver of her stomach shows when she raises her arms to tousle her wet hair to the side.

Her glasses are back in place too.

My God, she's definitely going to kill me.

"It's raining!" I blurt.

She jumps back.

I drop my phone on the counter and point to the window.

"While you were nak—while you were in the bath, it started raining."

She nods and gives me a smile that reaches those gorgeous eyes. They're usually sparkling blue, but right now, they seem lighter. "Yes, it's crazy how water falls from the sky. I believe it even happens in Manhattan too."

Well played.

What the fuck is wrong with me? I've been voted New York City's Most Charming Man by more than one esteemed magazine over the last couple years, but after one day with Tessa, I'm suddenly tongue-tied. I'm saying all the wrong things and acting more nervous than an awkward teen at a middle school dance.

Chuckling, I scratch the back of my head and try to compose myself—and fail. Even though she's across the room, I can still smell the cinnamon on her.

It's suffocating.

"Carter, relax. Do you shut down like this every time it rains?" She points to the window but continues scrutinizing me.

"Let me try again." I grip the edge of the counter, hoping to God she can't see through me. "What do you normally do around here when it rains?"

"Well, it's dark, so we wouldn't go outside, anyway." She sways to the side.

"Touché."

"We can have dinner, though. Maybe a few sandwiches? I got turkey and stuff from the store, and it'll be easy." She meets me in the kitchen, and I stiffen, flattening the back of my legs and ass against the counter to put as much space between us as possible.

"Sounds… amazing, actually." I rub my stomach over my loose T-shirt, instantly realizing how hungry I am.

"You heard me say *sandwiches*, right? With deli meat, cheese, and maybe some mayo?" She quirks her eyebrow over her shoulder.

I narrow my gaze at her. "I heard you fine."

"Just checking." She giggles as she opens the fridge. When she reaches inside, she bends at the waist, pushing her ass out.

Her cropped shirt lifts, revealing more skin and… lacy pink panties.

They peek from the waistband of her pajama pants as if they're waving at me. Teasing me.

Jesus Christ.

"Hey, we may even get wild and add lettuce and tomato." She pops back up, produce in hand, and smirks sarcastically at me.

"For your information, I happen to enjoy sandwiches." I grab the bread from the counter behind me and get to work untwisting the knot in order to open it.

"I'm not saying you don't," Tessa says, laying out the spread by the stove. "I'm just surprised your reaction was normal instead of outraged. You know, like when I told you to sleep on the couch."

"Sandwiches don't cause backaches and stiff necks." I pull out four slices of bread and move toward the plastic plates.

"Okay, I'll give you that."

"Finally!" I slam the counter with my free hand, and my outburst makes her jump. "Sorry. It just felt really good to win one. Has anyone mentioned to you how argumentative you are?"

She dips her head and laughs, her hair falling forward and

hiding her face. When she stands upright again, she pushes her glasses higher on her nose, which scrunches up.

I join her as we continue our sandwich-building dance, our exchanges relaxed and fun, unlike the ones we had when I first arrived.

Turns out, she's easy to talk to and laugh with.

To my surprise, her smile calms every worry, making me forget all about why I'm here and what work I need to finish tonight and tomorrow morning.

With Tessa, it's easy to forget all the reasons I shouldn't make a move.

But she's off-limits, and contrary to what the world may think, I'm not childish. I'm not so immature to throw a tantrum and go after the shiny thing I can't have.

No, playing nice with her is for the good of her vacation. I want her to have a good time off with her family, that's all.

So, with a sandwich and an apple on my plate, I sit on one end of the couch, away from her, and eat.

I keep my hands to myself.

My thoughts inside my mind.

And the only taste I'm getting tonight is of turkey, cheese, and mayo—the most frustrating sandwich on the planet.

NINE

Tessa

I startle awake to phantom sounds of an alarm. Blinking a few times, I bring the ceiling fan in and out of focus as I recall that I don't have an alarm set. I'm just used to getting up early.

That, and I've been listening to Carter's mumbling words for half an hour now. From the sounds of it, he's been making work calls rather than social ones.

One right after another.

After a few minutes, it's silent, and I assume he's ended the call.

Without any hope of dozing off again, I throw the covers off myself and waddle in a sleep-induced state to the bathroom. When I emerge, I still don't hear Carter as I make my way to the coffee maker—it's calling out to me.

Much to my surprised delight, the smell of fresh brew hits me once I step into the living room. In the kitchen, hot coffee sits in the carafe, ready for me. *How thoughtful.*

I grab a mug and get to work filling it just the way I like—cream and sugar—then glance around for Carter. I spot movement outside and notice he's pacing the front yard, his phone to his ear.

Humming to myself, I watch him take slow, measured steps, his head dipping and falling back with each one. He's still in his pajamas, his plaid pants hung low on his narrow hips. As he spins to walk back in a straight line in front of the window, he stuffs his hand in his pocket and smiles.

But it's forced. Unlike the carefree one I received last night while we ate our sandwiches, this one appears unnatural. He seems angry and tense.

He was different last night, and it eased the tension between us. It even has me thinking this week won't be so bad after all.

I grip my mug between both hands and sip my coffee, studying him through the soft waves of steam rising from the liquid. I don't know how long I stand here—how long I appraise every inch of him as I bite my bottom lip. For reasons I can't explain or admit, Carter's captivating, even when he's taking a work call in his pajamas.

When he ends the call, he taps the phone to his chin, and I snap myself out of it, spinning in place as I search my surroundings like I forgot I'm in my family's cabin. As I turn from side to side, my coffee spills over, and its heat stings my wrist. "Shit," I mumble as the door swings open.

"What happened?" Carter steps inside, scanning the living room.

"Nothing." I laugh nervously, waving my free hand between us. "I spilled a bit of coffee on my hand."

"And here I thought it was a one-time thing yesterday." He tilts his head to the side. "I guess you're just clumsy, huh?"

Smiling, I set my mug on the counter and grab the hem of my shirt, lifting it up to show a two-inch scar over my ribs. "See this?"

Over my shoulder, Carter zeroes in on the spot I point to.

"It happened when some friends and I went whitewater rafting in Tennessee in college."

"That doesn't sound like you were clumsy." He furrows his brows.

"Let me back up." I lower my shirt and grab a napkin from the counter to wipe my hand. "We were walking to the raft when I tripped over my friend's backpack and fell on a rock. I never made it to the raft."

"Shit." He covers his mouth, but I can still see his grin.

I wave him off. "You can laugh. I did, even as blood ran down my stomach. It was a small wound, but it looked like I was attacked by a shark."

Carter lets his laugh out, the sound low and unfiltered. He seems more relaxed now, as if he's forgotten all about the stress of his calls this morning, and it makes me feel a little too good that I'm the one to thank.

"Everything okay?" I grab my mug again, the coffee at the perfect drinking temperature now.

He exhales, averting his gaze. "Just fine."

"I'd believe that if you didn't growl it." I offer him a sympathetic smile.

"I had every intention of working this morning to finish up some reports and answer emails. Instead, I've been reassuring clients and colleagues that I'm of sound mind and that our canceled meetings for the next two weeks are being rescheduled by my assistant as we speak." His voice is robotic, sounding as though he's reading a teleprompter for a press conference or something.

And I imagine whoever runs his PR advised him on wording for how to handle this situation.

He gives me a tight-lipped smile, then looks at his lit-up phone screen and curses. "Let's see how good I'm getting at damage control." He puts the phone to his ear and says, "Richard, how's the family?"

He grabs a blanket and steps outside, leaving me alone to resume my position by the window—the best view of him.

I should walk away. Take my coffee to the window seat and read my book. I didn't get any reading done last night like I'd wanted because I was too busy thinking about Carter asleep in the room next to mine.

I only met him yesterday, but Carter's all I've been able to think about since.

This new dynamic we share after all our bickering yesterday is nice.

And dangerous.

I'm getting more and more comfortable with him when I should be distancing myself.

Last night, thoughts of having *fun* with Carter consumed me, but they were crazy nonsense. Even if he wasn't so wrong for me, he's my brother's best friend, and I couldn't do that to Graham. It would be too weird for him, and I can't do anything to jeopardize my relationship with him. It was hard having so much distance between us when I was with Wyatt, and I won't have a repeat.

I can't risk Graham's friendship with Carter, either.

Not over something as silly as *fun*.

Besides, Carter has Ginger waiting for him back in the city. From what I can tell online, he doesn't get serious with anyone. On the contrary, he changes women on his arm like he does watches. But Ginger…

Ginger Myers has stuck around longer than the rest.

And she's a gorgeous supermodel who runs in the same circles as Carter. Those two make sense.

I run my sweaty palm down my pant leg and shuffle to my room for my book. All the romance and excitement I need are in those pages, and that'll have to be enough.

When I come back and turn the knob for the fireplace, the flames flickering to life, Carter still paces the driveway, his stress obvious in the lines on his forehead. As I settle into my reading spot, I pull a blanket over my legs and wrap the top around my waist like my mother did when I was a kid.

This is where she would read to me. The books she chose were a little more mature than what might've been appropriate for my age, but it didn't bother me. I'd cuddle into her side and listen to her enunciated words until I'd fall asleep.

As though she could hear my thoughts, her name pops up onto my phone with an incoming text.

Mom: At the gate. Can't wait to see you, sweetie!

Another text follows, containing an image of both my parents, my mom's arm slung around my father's shoulders.

Smiling, I text back that I'm excited and add more exclamation points than is necessary—I'm too damn happy to care.

It's been so long since we were all here together, and I'm craving time with my family in our most special place.

I've just pressed send when the door shuts, and Carter stands before me as if he's waiting for me to answer a question I never heard.

"Did you say something?" I ask, setting the phone in my lap.

He slips his own phone into his pocket and dips his head, then starts to turn but stops himself. "What're you smiling about over there?"

"Why?" I squint, studying the firm crease between his brows. "Jealous it might be another of my brother's friends out to annoy me during my birthday celebration?"

"Ha-ha." He narrows his eyes, a mischievous gleam shining in them.

"It was my mother," I confess. "No models or actors in my messages like *some* people."

"What?"

"I saw you smirking at your phone yesterday. Was it Ginger? Or Scarlett Johansson, perhaps?" I lean forward, tucking my covered knees to my chest and wrapping my arms around them, recalling the pictures of him with blonde actresses from a couple years ago.

During a brief pause, confusion washes over him, but then he grins. "Oh, that?" He points to the couch, obviously remembering when we sat on opposites sides of the living room yesterday. "That was Miles, my friend and personal trainer. He was sending me leg workout memes that were funny as hell."

"Oh," I whisper, releasing tension in my shoulders that I didn't realize was so strong.

"I'm sorry"—Carter wags his finger at me and leans on the door—"but do I sense jealousy? You thought it was a model, and you were jealous, weren't you? God, I love when women fight over me." His grin turns smug faster than a bear swipes a fish in the river.

I roll my eyes. "You're ridiculous."

"And you're blushing." He crosses his arms over his lean chest, his chuckle rumbling from deep in his throat.

Instinctively, I touch my cheeks with both hands to check, and they are warm, indeed.

He bursts into laughter, and I reach behind me for a throw pillow to launch at him.

"Ah!" I let my head fall back, and he laughs harder.

My giggle starts softly at first, then grows louder—I can't help myself. I played right into his hand, and he caught me.

As his laughter subsides, his shoulders falling, he rasps, "We're not together. You know that, right?"

For a moment—for a single stupid moment that I'll later berate myself for—I'm relieved to hear him explain, even though I have no right. I don't respond as my tongue feels too big for my mouth.

I'm still staring at him, too interested in his revelation than I care to admit, as he continues. "Ginger and I are not together. We're friends, who… *enjoy* each other's company on occasion. But that's all." His voice loses its humorous edge.

I gulp. "Why are you telling me this?"

He lifts his head as he shrugs. "It feels important for you to know."

TEN

Carter

For the next few hours, I take several more calls and answer even more emails. I expected to work—to vet properties on our list and approve last-minute details for the charity dinner—but instead, I'm fielding questions regarding my state of mind.

Fantastic.

Just what I fucking need.

In between assuring our clients and partners that I'm not losing my shit, I can't help but stare at Tessa curled on the window seat looking like she needs company, constantly asking myself the same question—what's going through her head?

She was jealous when she thought I was texting Ginger, when the truth is, she and I haven't spoken since she left my penthouse. I haven't even *wanted* to talk to her. That's not the kind of relationship we have. But even so, why the hell did I want Tessa to know that? Why did I feel an overwhelming need to explain to her that I'm not with Ginger?

And part of me celebrated when Tessa's lips parted—she was obviously relieved to know I'm single.

Why did that make me so wildly fucking happy?

I shouldn't be ecstatic that she cares. It shouldn't be a big deal, but it feels like I won the lottery.

After hours of practiced damage control, I'm standing alone in the living room. It's late in the afternoon when the rain starts again, worse than yesterday, the thunder loud and strong enough to feel like the cabin's rocking. I glance outside, taking in the dark sky and sideways rain angrily tapping against the glass window.

It appears to be ten o'clock at night when it's really only four in the afternoon.

Tessa emerges from her bedroom, her eyes glowing. She's in leggings and tall socks stretched to her knees.

I do a double-take, squinting at the little figures on her socks. "Are those *Family Guy* characters' heads?"

She inches toward me and props her foot on the edge of the couch, wiggling her toes. "Why, yes. Yes, they are."

I laugh. "I didn't take you for a fan."

"I'm not, but my friend Bree thinks that show is hilarious. Always gives me shit for thinking it's ridiculous, and she's hell-bent on making me a fan, starting with these socks."

"I like this friend of yours."

"Oh, God," she says, setting her foot back down and adjusting her cardigan around her. "She'd give her left arm to personally hear those words from you."

"Excuse me?"

"She'd be too much for even you. Trust me." Tessa giggles. Exhaling, she rubs her hands together and takes a seat, tucking one foot beneath her. "Everything okay at work?"

"Sure." I sit on the other end of the couch, my movements as unsteady as my breathing. After a brief pause, I throw my hands up, letting out my first easy breath of the day. "I finally said fuck it and had my calls forwarded to my office. I asked my assistant to take messages too and set up an automatic response for emails. I'll deal with it later."

"Wow. How will they feel about that?" She runs her fingers through her hair and blinks at me through her lenses, distracting me.

A strangled gurgle escapes me, and I try to cover it up with a cough. "They'll be… fine," I say hoarsely.

She squirms in her seat, resting her elbow on the back of the couch and angling her body to face me. "What's it like to have an assistant? I'd have them do my grocery shopping every week. That's one thing I'd love to rid my to-do list of. The lines at checkout, carts ramming into you like bumper cars, and rude bastards cutting in front of you? No, thanks."

"Not exactly what my assistant does for me," I say. "I need to give Whitney a massive fucking raise, though."

"And Whitney's your…" Tessa raises her voice at the end, leaving her question hanging in the air.

"Housekeeper." I clear my throat, averting my gaze from the way she licks her lips. It's innocent, but I have too many filthy thoughts as it is. "Although, Whitney is definitely more than that."

"A housekeeper and an assistant, huh?" She bites her lip. "Do you lend them to friends? Maybe a friend's sister who lets you crash her birthday?"

Her response catches me off guard, and my laugh bursts from me with vigor.

We talk and joke easily like this for a while, and her cardigan falls off her shoulder exactly three times, after which she lifts it back into place like it's no big deal.

Like I'm not three feet away struggling with images of that cardigan tossed to the ground with the rest of her clothes.

And then, there are her fucking glasses. They test me like they want me to pull them off her. I easily imagine leaving them to be the last item I remove from her before I slide my fingers over her shoulders and down her arched back to cup her bare ass.

God, Tessa makes me forget how to function. How does she do that?

At one point, her stomach growls loud enough to sound like a wild bobcat, and I jump out of my skin.

"Well, that was embarrassing." She laughs, clutching her stomach as she stands.

"You're hungry." I shrug, pushing myself up from the couch. "It's nothing compared to taking a shower at a frat house and someone stealing all your clothes *and* towel."

She snorts and covers her mouth with both hands.

"It wouldn't have been so bad running naked through the hall to my room if my mother hadn't decided to surprise me with a visit."

"No…"

"*With* her friend Cynthia and her daughter who were touring the school that week."

"Wow. A tour and a live show," Tessa teases.

I shake my head, then offer her my hand. "So, what's for dinner?"

She squeezes my hand in hers and leads the way to the kitchen, a little bounce in her step. If I wasn't watching her so closely, I might've missed it. Over her shoulder, she says, "I bought a ready-made lasagna from the store yesterday. It takes about an hour and a half to bake, so it should be done by the time my parents and Graham arrive. Plus, we'll have leftovers to eat over the next couple days."

"Smart." I force a smile in an attempt to cover my disappointment of our inevitable interruption. Once everyone else gets here, I won't have these moments alone with Tessa anymore.

In the short time since we met, I've grown accustomed to our talks. To her laugh. The way she scrunches her nose when she pushes her glasses up.

With a full cabin, I'll only be able to enjoy her from afar before she leaves altogether and I'm left alone.

"It's what my mom always does," Tessa continues as she turns the oven on to preheat, then faces me. "She's an amazing cook but admits even she can't beat this lasagna. There's something about the blend of cheeses. It's the right amount of each. The sauce, too, is—" She dips her head, sliding her palms down her leggings. "I'm sorry. I'm rambling about lasagna like I'm Martha Stewart or something."

Unable to stop myself, I move toward her and place both hands on her shoulders. "You can talk to me about anything you'd like. This lasagna. The rain outside. Hell, you can even tell me what color panties you're wearing. I'm equally okay with any of it."

She lifts her surprised gaze to me, but it's quickly replaced by mischief. "Who says I'm wearing any at all?"

I bend at my knees, exaggerating the effect she has on me, but in all honesty, my knees definitely weaken like I'm standing on land for the first time after weeks on a boat. I'm more pathetic now than I was at sixteen when I lost my virginity to an Olsen twin look-alike.

I wag my finger at her. "I know you're only kidding, but I'm going to pretend you're serious."

She playfully smacks me away and gets to work on the lasagna, pulling the clear wrap off the tray. When the oven dings, I try not to stare as she bends over to put the pan inside. I focus instead on how many steps it takes to resume my post by the counter.

Four.

With four excruciating steps, the edge of the counter hits my lower back, and I'm no longer within arm's length of her.

She sets the timer on the oven and spins to face me, crossing her arms and squinting like I'm a puzzle she can't figure out.

"Before you ask, no, I'm not a virgin." I shrug.

She throws her head back and laughs. It's raspy, like she spent all day screaming, and it echoes around the cabin. The sound reaches inside my chest and grabs hold.

I like getting a reaction out of her, whether she's yelling at me or I'm making her laugh. *I like it too much.*

She wipes at the corners of her eyes. Her face is free of makeup, her tan skin natural and glowing, and my fingers itch to touch her cheeks.

Tessa brings her slender fingers up to tuck her hair behind her ear, revealing three golden studs along her lobe. Her hand falls back to her side as if in slow motion, her fingers brushing her chest, then the side of her breast, until they rest on her hip.

We stand staring at each other like we're seeing each other for the first time. I almost prefer her spewing insults my way because the heated way she watches me now is dangerous.

For both of us.

"Games!" Her mouth falls open as though her outburst surprises her more than it does me. "We should play a game while this lasagna bakes."

"Strip poker?" My body hums at even the idea.

"No." She rolls her eyes and grabs my hand, leading me past the expansive window right when lightning strikes and thunder blasts. She jumps and comes to a screeching halt, but I don't stop in time. Instead, I bump into her, and my hand automatically flies to grip her hip.

My fingers curl around the waistband of her leggings, desperately wishing I was touching her skin, and I give her a tug until her back is flush against me.

I take one, two, three deep breaths in, enjoying her feminine scent.

Intoxicating is what she is.

"Carter," she whispers breathlessly as my gaze falls to the curve of her shoulder. Her sweater has slid down her arm, exposing her smooth skin, and her pink bra strap peeks out from her tank.

We should play strip poker.

The words are on the tip of my tongue. I even open my mouth to suggest it again, but her phone vibrates on the counter, pulling us from our trance.

She clears her throat and adjusts her cardigan, pulling the material back up to cover herself. Keeping her head low, she brushes past me to grab her phone from the kitchen. "Hello?" she answers, worrying her bottom lip between her teeth.

"You're still in the city?"

My attention snaps to hers.

Who is that? Graham? Her parents? Both?

For a moment, hope flashes through my chest, but it quickly disappears when I notice Tessa's frown.

"You promised." She sighs, turning away from me to pace across the kitchen floor until she finally comes to a stop again. Her disappointment radiates from her like steam.

"Okay." She uses her forefinger to idly draw circles on the counter. "Love you too."

She ends the call, clutches the phone to her chest, and looks up at me.

"Everything okay?" I ask, moving toward her, my feet unexpectedly heavy. Seeing her so crestfallen is my new least favorite image. After hearing her laugh for most of the afternoon, I can't stand seeing her upset like this.

I need her happy again.

She gives me a small smile, obviously attempting to put on a brave face when I know she's crushed. "That was Graham." She waves the phone to her side. "He's not going to make it tonight, either. He's still at work, but it's fine. I know he's busy. I'm used to a physician's schedule, anyway, given that's how I grew up: my dad rushing to the office and coming back at all hours of the evening, depending on his schedule and the emergencies. So… it's fine."

"I'm sorry," I offer.

She inhales, and her smile becomes genuine, although I still note a hint of sadness in her tone. "How about that game? And not strip poker." She pokes me in the chest, then brushes past me toward the living room.

I run my hand through my hair and roughly exhale,

following her lead. "Are you sure? *Vogue* magazine called my abs *delicious* last summer, so you'd be in for a real treat if we play."

"Ha!" She shakes her head and squats in front of the TV to rummage through the cabinets of the entertainment center. "A board game or cards. Don't tell me you don't like PG-rated games."

I sit on the armrest of the couch and say, "When I was six, my dad taught me how to play regular poker. Does that count?"

"Six?" She looks over her shoulder at me, raising her eyebrows.

I laugh, picking off a piece of lint from my sweatpants. "He and my mom had trouble conceiving. It took a few years and two miscarriages before she had a healthy pregnancy and gave birth to me. All my dad wanted was an heir—someone to pass his name and legacy onto. My sixth birthday was about as long as he could wait to start grooming me and teaching me his ways."

"That's sort of… sweet, in its own weird way. Hopefully, he at least waited until you were eighteen to give you a taste of whiskey." She stands, tossing her hair out of her face.

"Thirteen. Then again, that's around the time Europeans have their first sip of wine, so I was in good company."

"Oh, you're European?" She furrows her brows as she idly shuffles a deck of cards in front of her. "I don't recall that detail in any of your bios."

"I'm not, but my dad uses the Europeans to justify many of his actions. Says they're some of the happiest people he's ever dealt with, so they must be doing something right." I cross my arms and shift in my seat to fully face her, my lips twitching. "How many of my bios have you read exactly?"

Her deep blush appears faster than lightning. "Only, like, one or two."

"Uh-huh." I can't help my smug grin. "That's all?"

She huffs, jutting her hip out. "Are we playing poker or not?" She sets the cards on the coffee table between us, then reaches down for a tin can of various colored chips.

"Only if we make it interesting." I slide to the floor and scoot close to the coffee table.

She grabs two glasses and a bottle of whiskey from the bar in the corner.

"Now we're talking." I pour us both a drink, nearly salivating for the amber liquid, while she turns the knob on the fireplace to get it going. The flames roar to life, filling the space with warmth and static background noise.

Tessa sits cross-legged on the floor on the other side of the table and distributes chips. "What do you mean by *interesting?*"

"If I win, you have to tell me why you didn't give me your number at the coffee shop yesterday morning."

A chip falls out of her hand and lands with a loud clink between us. She freezes, her face angled away from me, but I can still see the soft glow from the fire illuminating her surprise. After a moment, she clears her throat and says, "Okay, fine, but what do I get *when* I win?"

Her self-assurance makes me chuckle. Did she not hear me say I've been playing since I was six? "If you win, I'll take my shirt off for you."

"What?" I imagine if she'd taken a sip of anything, she would've spit it out.

"I've seen you checking me out. I'll make it easier for you and simply show you. Maybe I'll even let you touch my *delicious* abs."

"I haven't… I'm not…" She shakes her head, stumbling over her words. "You're so obnoxious."

"All part of the charm."

She rolls her eyes, then meets my gaze with newfound confidence as if she's already won. "If I win, you have to tell me about Trixie from college."

Now, I actually spit part of my whiskey and use the back of my hand to wipe my chin. "Deal."

"Texas Hold'em okay?"

I nod. "Hit me."

In silence, she passes out an even number of chips, then deals the cards for each of us. Once she's finished, I carefully pick up my two cards as if they're bombs. This may be just a little game, but I have a lot riding on it.

She scratches her nose.

I place my bet, and she calls, after which she tosses the top card to the side and flips three new ones over. She scratches her nose again, and I raise the bet.

She calls.

When we get to the river, the final card, I mentally fist bump the air, especially when she reveals she has two pairs.

"A straight," I say, revealing my hand. "Get ready to confess, gorgeous."

"That was one round. Best three out of five?" She tilts her head, smirking in challenge. "The lasagna should be done by then."

"Fun and efficient—my style." I chuckle, but my body is tense. Immediately, I tap my ankle with my thumb while she deals our cards, my nerves suddenly shot.

I didn't realize how badly I needed to know the reasoning behind her rejection until now.

It's at my fingertips.

After the first round, I know her tell—scratching her

nose—and I plan to use it to my advantage.

I lick my bottom lip, and I can almost taste victory as I pick up the new cards. A nine and ten of hearts—this has to end well.

Except it doesn't.

Thunder booms outside with vigor as Tessa swoops in with a damn clutch and wins the second round, then the third, her *tell* not so helpful anymore, and I start sweating. She fucking tricked me.

I laugh to myself and take a drink. Even I can appreciate her devious tactics.

When I win the next round, bringing us to a tie, I slap my knee with excitement.

The moment of truth.

"You nervous?" I eye her.

"About as much as I was when I crashed my car into a mailbox. Oh, wait…" She quirks her eyebrow, making me throw my head back and laugh.

"I see how it is." I finger my two cards, flipping the corners up to get a good look.

"Well?" She leans on her heels, bringing herself to sit taller, her expression unreadable.

I use one hand to push my bet to the center while I make a grumbling noise and motion with my other hand like I'm pulling a lever. "That's my bulldozer shoveling my chips in—I'm all in."

She breaks her steely gaze and dips her head, giggling, her wispy hair falling over one eye.

I glance at my cards one more time and wait on pins and needles.

When she calls my bet, her expression is back to indecipherable—a bluff more airtight than a Ziploc bag.

By the end of the round, we're both leaning forward, and my cards are sticking to my sweaty palms.

My competitive nature has me on edge. But the truth is, my need to win this goes far beyond my natural hunger to come out on top. Deep down, I need to know her answer.

Seconds pass as we stare at each other, waiting for the other to break.

The fireplace goes off, set on a timer.

And then…

"Full house." She spreads her cards in front of her and breaks her stone-cold exterior.

"Fuck." I turn my cards over, revealing a pathetic three of a kind, and hang my head.

"Bathroom break." She stands, waving her arms in the air. "When I get back, I need a full glass of whiskey and all the Trixie details."

She hums as she skips to the bathroom.

I underestimated her. I should've known she wouldn't give her tell so easily. Stroking my chin, I'm unable to stop my lips from curling. *Damn, I was so close.*

Disappointment racing through my veins, I fill her drink and top mine off before she returns and plops down across from me.

She squirms on her spot on the floor, getting comfortable. "I'm ready."

I lick the whiskey from my bottom lip and start. "It was right after Graham's twenty-first birthday."

Tessa tucks her socked feet under her and holds her glass between her slender fingers, her pink nails more suitable for a Cosmo than a Crown Royal neat.

"I wanted to do something special, and because I'm such

a kind and generous friend, I took Graham out to a strip club. It was his first time."

"How very thoughtful of you," she says sarcastically.

"I bought him his first lap dance because, like I said, I'm a nice guy." I wink. "It was a woman named Trixie."

She nods as understanding dawns, and she continues sipping her whiskey without flinching.

"Trixie was nice. Big tits. Round ass. Teasing smile." I pause for dramatic effect. "Long and sneaky fingers too. She stole Graham's wallet while he was too busy fiddling with his drink and groping her ass."

Tessa snorts. "Oh my God."

"Yep. To her defense, Graham left it out beside him and made it too easy for her."

"What else could she do but steal from a preppy Harvard student?"

"Which is what I told Trixie, but she denied it. Next thing I knew, Big Tito came out of the back and insisted his girlfriend *ain't no thief*, but I insisted harder that she was." I pause again, but this time it's because Tessa's mouth has fallen open, completely captivated by my story as if it's a fairy tale instead of an anecdote of two ridiculous college kids.

It's adorable and sexy.

"Well? What happened?" she presses.

I chuckle under my breath, swirling the whiskey in my glass. "You know the scar on Graham's left cheek? The small, barely noticeable one under his eye?"

"Yes…" Her eyes widen.

"It was courtesy of Big Tito."

She spits a couple drops of whiskey onto the table and covers her mouth.

"Yep. A solid right hook to his *pretty face*—as he said before he veered back for a second punch. Which, by the way, landed on my shoulder when I jumped in front of Graham because…" I wave my hand for her.

She doesn't miss a beat and finishes, "Because you're such a nice guy."

"Exactly."

"And the wallet?"

"Found it empty and ripped in half in the parking lot. But hey, I saved your brother's life, okay? It was better than saving the wallet."

She smiles, and I laugh into my glass before I toss back the drink, enjoying the burning bliss of my favorite alcohol. But I'm enjoying the company better—better than I have any female company in a long time.

Tessa's real. She's funny and smart and fucking *real*. She's also my best friend's sister, and I can't have her, as I've repeatedly tried to convince myself.

No matter how damn badly I want our situation to be different, it isn't. And I can't do that to Graham—I can't cross that line.

Given my track record of dating, I'll only end up hurting Tessa if anything were to happen between us. Which would be enough for Graham to blacklist me and kick my ass worse than Big Tito ever did.

I can't risk it.

I can't risk Tessa's heart or Graham's trust.

My eyes lock on hers as our laughter subsides, and even though we're only separated by two feet of coffee table, she feels farther away.

The oven timer dings, but it sounds muffled from the

blood rushing to my ears as I try to focus.

"Want to eat me?" she asks, rising.

I cough—no way did I hear her correctly. "Excuse me?"

"Want to eat with me?" she repeats, pointing to the kitchen behind me. "The lasagna is ready."

"Right." I stand, adjusting my dick as I follow her to the kitchen. "Let's do it."

She's just finished piling the pasta onto two plates when her phone rings. "Hey, Mom. You almost here? I'm just now getting the lasagna out of the oven." She balances the phone between her ear and shoulder and licks tomato sauce from her thumb.

Good God.

I clench my jaw, purposely remaining on the other side of the counter. It'll hide my embarrassing stiffy since my sweatpants are more useless than mittens on a deer.

"You're in Chicago?" Tessa drops the large spoon, sprinkling flecks of red sauce across the counter in front of her.

I stiffen when she grows silent for a beat. The fire roars back to life in the living room, mixing with the sound of rain outside, and then, she exclaims, "Tomorrow?" *Pause.* "I didn't realize it was storming so badly out there." *Another pause.* "Okay, okay. I'll see you guys tomorrow, then. Be safe. Love you too."

Hanging up, she sighs as she stares at the lasagna, but it doesn't seem like she really sees it.

"Tessa?" I ask, my voice hesitant. She doesn't immediately respond, and I have the urge to look away, feeling as though I'm intruding on a private moment.

But I can't leave her.

Not when she's troubled like this.

I may not understand why it's so important to her that her family be here—I've never had big family to-dos for birthdays myself—but it means a lot to her. And I have an overwhelming need to help.

"Tessa, is everything okay?" I try again as the tension fills the space between us.

"Hmm?" She glances up this time and backs away like she suddenly remembers what the conversation was about. "My parents are stuck in Chicago until the storm clears. They're on a flight out first thing in the morning and are driving a rental down. So…"

"So, it's just you and me for another night, then?"

"Just you and me." Her nostrils flare, but I can't tell what it means to her. Is she upset by her family's absence or that she's stuck with me?

I can't do anything about the former—with a storm like this, I couldn't even send a jet—but I can't change the latter, either. At least, I don't want to.

I can't leave her here by herself. I don't want to leave Tessa, period, but I definitely can't abandon her here.

So, we're spending another night in this cabin… alone.

I grind my teeth as I accept my plate, thank her, and follow her into the living room again.

We eat in relative silence. Noise from the TV filters between us as we sit on opposite ends of the couch, as far away as we can be from each other. She only speaks to ask me how I like the food, and all I can muster is a nod and thumbs-up like a fucking idiot.

Once we're finished, I help her with the dishes, sidling up next to her in front of the sink. If Whitney could see me now, she'd cackle herself into a coma.

Not because I'm incapable of doing basic chores like this, but washing dishes is the type of thing other people have done for me for years.

But the weirdest thing happens: Tessa makes me *want* to scrub marinara off plates, especially when we ease back into comfortable conversation about this area, her friends, and my philanthropic endeavors.

In any case, I don't mind doing dishes. I like it better than laundry, which I do know how to do, contrary to what Tessa might think. Her brother is the one who taught me when we were in college. I hate to admit it now, but back then, I had absolutely no desire for responsibility, only the next keg party and smoking weed.

I was losing control, but Graham grounded me with menial tasks like washing my car and even basic cooking. When I complained, he'd deepen his voice—I called it his dad voice—and command I learn how to do these things, because what if I woke up tomorrow entirely broke?

The thought alone gave me nightmares.

With a new perspective, I listened when he helped me become a decent human, and for that, I owe him more than all the money and material items in my possession.

Tessa and being here in their family's cabin, even without Graham, is reminding me of all that.

We fall silent as I hand her a rinsed-off, squeaky clean plate to dry. During the exchange, our fingers brush against each other. We remain quiet, with only the muffled sounds from a sitcom on TV filtering between us, but at the small contact, I swear I hear a small, feminine gasp.

I suppress a groan.

Something's shifted between us over the course of the

evening, especially in the last hour—ever since her mother called.

But there's more to this shift.

My instincts—the same ones that have garnered the company many seemingly impossible deals—tell me it's something more.

Tessa's acting different. Quiet and tense like she's bracing herself for… what exactly?

"It's been a long day. I think I'll go to bed." Her arms sway at her sides as she sashays out of the kitchen. She stops at her door, her hand curled around the knob, and faces me. I lean forward when she opens her mouth, but then, she closes it without another word.

"Good night." I give her a tight-lipped smile from where I'm still standing in the kitchen.

She nods and disappears behind the door.

Once she's out of sight, I rest both elbows on the counter and bury my face in my hands, cursing into my palms.

I don't think I've ever been in the same room with a beautiful and perfect and *single* woman for longer than thirty minutes without making my move. Yet here I am, two whole days later, without even a taste of Tessa. My self-restraint should go down in history because I've definitely set some sort of record.

But this is only day two.

Day. Fucking. *Two*.

She's going to be here for the rest of the week, after which she'll leave with her family, giving me the place to myself.

How the hell am I supposed to resist Tessa for another day, let alone the whole week?

ELEVEN

Tessa

I should be asleep.

I've been buried underneath my warm covers listening to the wind outside and the trickling rain tapping against my window for almost an hour, but I couldn't be wider awake even if I'd raided a Monster energy drink fridge.

Sighing, I throw my bare feet over the edge of the bed and creep to the door. I slowly pull it open and step up to place my hand on the back of the fireplace as I poke my head around it to peer into the living room.

Carter sits upright in the middle of the couch, his attention glued to his phone, which illuminates his wild hair and beard. His brows are furrowed as he runs the tip of his finger along his bottom lip, idly tracing the curve of it.

My lips part, hanging open as if I'm hypnotized.

He roughly exhales, sinking into the couch and stretching his arm across the back like he's inviting me to come sit with him.

To snuggle into his side and breathe in his expensive, manly scent.

Instead, I cross my arms and lean a hip against the cobblestone. "You're really opposed to marriage?"

He jolts in his seat, dropping his phone to the floor with a thud. "Jesus Christ! I thought you were asleep."

I shrug, entering the living room and sitting down with my legs crossed by the fire. "I can't sleep."

"So you thought you'd come in here like a ghost and scare the shit out of me?"

"Relax." I wave him off. "You're still breathing, aren't you? Besides, if I were a ghost, there are plenty more interesting people I'd haunt. Like Chris Pratt." I wiggle my eyebrows, wrapping my arms around my bent knees and hugging them to my chest.

"Chris? That's who you'd pick?" He raises his eyebrow and sinks to the floor on the other side of the coffee table from me, much like we were while we played poker.

"Well, I'd start there, then make my way around Hollywood, to Sebastian Stan, Ryan Gosling—"

"Okay, I get it," Carter snaps.

"Wow. Not a night owl, I guess," I say sarcastically.

Is that jealousy I sense? Because I find celebrities hot?

I uncross my legs and hook them behind me, uneasy under his stare. *Why did I even come in here?* "Oh! My question."

"About marriage?"

"Marriage, companionship, love. You're opposed to it all?"

"Whoa." He eases up as a teasing smile plays across his ample lips. "I usually wait until the tenth date for this sort of discussion."

I roll my eyes, starting to hoist myself up. "Why did I even bother?"

He reaches out to stop me, scooting across the floor toward me, his hand gentle on my arm. "Me and marriage go together about as well as expensive French wine and Spam. One ruins the taste of the other, right?"

"I'm surprised you even know what Spam is," I joke.

He chuckles, narrowing his hazel eyes like he has a secret. "I thought a metaphor would be more appropriate and helpful to explain my relationship with marriage, okay?" He takes his hand back and taps his chin. "Or is it a simile? An analogy? I was better at math, not English."

"It's an analogy."

"I'll take your word for it." His smile spreads slowly, but it soon falls again. It takes with it the warmth and humor from the air as he asks in a low voice, "How many happy marriages do you know of?"

Suddenly, a chill sneaks down my neck as I sink back into my spot on the plush rug, chewing the inside of my cheek. I'm taken aback by his question, mostly because it's a real one. A real and scary and sad one. He asked it as though he already knows the answer and is disappointed by it.

He toys with his thumbs as his expression further sobers, leaving no trace of his previous amusement. "Because I'm not convinced there is such a thing. I know too many people, especially in my world, who are married, yet feel more alone when they're together than if they were apart."

The gravity melts through his words like fire through wood, and it causes knots to form in my stomach. It's obvious he feels so hopeless when it comes to long-lasting love.

"That might be the case for some couples, yes, but not for everyone," I whisper, my eyes glued to him.

"Maybe, but it's true for everyone around me. My parents are the prime example." A dark shadow dampens his usually bright and animated features. "They've been married for over thirty years, but they haven't been in love for… I don't know how long. To be honest, I didn't want to accept it until recently. I'm not sure I do even now."

My body tenses.

"I don't know when they gave up on each other." He lets out a humorless laugh, one that feels like sandpaper against my skin, and his dejected gaze meets mine. "They go to therapy once a week."

"That's good. It means they're trying," I offer, instinctively leaning forward and squeezing his hand on the coffee table.

"That's what I thought too when they started years ago." He gives me another crooked smile, but there's no joy in it. "Didn't take long to realize it's a pretense. A way to show their friends and our company's board that we're a traditional family, whole and happy. But even without the company or their stuck-up friends, I think they'd still see Dr. Hubbert because they've been doing it for so long. It's part of their routine. The appointments are scheduled in their planners in permanent marker, even."

I sit back on my heels, saddened by his revelations. "It must be difficult for you to see them like that."

He nods, absentmindedly running his thumb over my knuckles. "Not everyone is like your parents, Tessa. Not everyone's love is so strong it can be seen through a picture." He waves around the room, referring to the frames on the walls.

My heart is caught in my throat, and a strange urge to

convince him I'm right—that there are other kinds of couples out there—overcomes me. "They're in love, but it hasn't always been easy." I lick my dry lips and drag myself across the floor, scooting closer to Carter until our knees are touching. "My parents' jobs were demanding. They had very busy, and often clashing, schedules for years. For my entire childhood and beyond. It was difficult to carve out time for romance, but they persisted. Date nights to a gallery opening, the theater, or dinner just the two of them. We'd have family getaways too, especially after they bought this place, but they made time for their marriage, even if it wasn't every week that they went out. It was in the everyday too. The small touches in the kitchen. Their hugs when they got home."

Carter grumbles something under his breath.

"They'd argue over small things, sure. The right way to load the dishwasher or if the toilet paper should be over or under. They—"

"Over is the correct way." He lets go of my hand and holds a finger up, then waves for me to continue.

"I don't agree, but one argument at a time." I glare at him, then sigh, tracing circles with the tip of my finger on the coffee table, losing myself in the idea of love. I didn't realize it until now, but I need to convince myself more than Carter of its existence. "No one said marriage is easy, but if you're with the right person, the fight is worth it. My parents aren't perfect, but they've always loved each other. It's why they've never given up, and I think that's important. To be so in love that giving up just isn't an option."

His Adam's apple bobs as he swallows, drawing my attention there. He's silent for several seconds before he finally says, "You've never been in love, then?"

I slowly shake my head, oddly feeling like I'm on display as his intense gaze rakes over my face, his hazel eyes glowing with the flames from the fireplace. "I thought I was once. But as it turns out, it was too easy for me to give up. Guess I haven't met the right person yet."

"Right. The perfect guy," he says in an understanding tone.

"What?"

"Yesterday morning, you mentioned you'd never met the perfect guy."

"Ah." I dip my head, recalling our run-in at the coffee shop. It's hard to believe he and I met less than two days ago, and yet, I feel like I've known him for years.

I would know him better if Graham's plans for us to meet would've worked out over the last few years, or if Graham talked about Carter in more detail. But Graham hasn't said much about him lately.

"Do you think he exists? This perfect guy?" He lifts one eyebrow, his finger tracing circles dangerously close to mine. Our hands are an inch apart, and the proximity alone sends shivers down my spine, drying my throat.

"No, but I meant perfect as in perfect *for me*. Not necessarily perfect in the general sense: guy with a sense of humor, who is good-looking and respectful."

"Well, if you want perfect in the general sense, then don't worry, sweetheart"—he gives me a smug grin—"I'm here."

"I'm sorry… what?" I blink, my finger stopping with the tip on the wood close to his.

"You literally just described me."

"You are everything I don't want." I huff, and the blush spreading across my cheeks is almost too much to bear.

Smoothing my shirt down over my sleep shorts, I stand. "That's enough excitement for one night. I'm going to sleep."

"Right behind you."

"What?" I choke out.

He stands, pointing in the direction of Graham's room. "I'll be sleeping in Graham's room again since he won't be here until tomorrow."

"Oh, of course." I run my suddenly sweaty palms down the thin cotton of my shirt. Why does the thought of sharing a wall with him make me nervous?

We did it last night and I was fine.

Well, *fine* is a relative term. I was restless, but fine, nonetheless.

That was also before I got to know Carter better. Before I was pressed against his front when the crackling thunder scared the crap out of me, and I practically jumped onto him. For a brief moment, I could feel his body heat. The strength of his round pecs against the back of my shoulders. His minty breath in my ear.

And the way he gripped my hip like he didn't want to let go left me—I was panting.

After what should've been an innocent run-in with him, I was left breathless like a dehydrated runner after a marathon.

I expect another sleepless night awaits.

He rounds the coffee table toward me, his warmth emanating as if his arms are wrapped around me.

Holding me.

His delectable lips nipping at my neck.

What the friction between his beard and skin would make me—

"Good night," he says, tearing me from my damning thoughts.

I place my hand on my doorknob, and he does the same to Graham's bedroom door on the other side, facing me. We're a few feet away from each other, but it still feels intimate somehow. The way he watches me feels like he's peering into my mind and soul, reading the filthy thoughts going through my head.

What is he thinking?

I adjust my glasses in hopes of seeing him better, but it's no use. I can't read his expression, let alone his thoughts.

Giving me a tight-lipped smile, he's the first to open the door, but I reach my arm out to stop him, rushing toward him. His eyes widen, taking on something headier.

Anything but innocent.

Now *that* I can read, and it makes my knees weak.

"Thanks for…" I clear my throat. "I'm glad you're here. Otherwise, I would've been totally alone, and that would've sucked."

Carter's nostrils flare, but the movement is small.

"So, what I'm trying to say is, thank you for wrecking your car and needing somewhere to hide." I peek up at him, forcing a smile, my cheeks flushed.

His lips twitch, and he nods, his gaze intensifying the longer we stand toe to toe like this. In each other's space. Breathing the same air.

His presence is intoxicating.

I lean up onto my tiptoes—just a fraction—and tilt my head to the side, ready to lose myself in this palpable heat between us. But at the same time as I do so, Carter leans back, opening the door.

It's hard to swallow, my throat thick with disappointment and humiliation. What did I expect? For Carter Fields to take me in his arms, maybe push me against the wall, and have his way with me?

His friend's little sister?

Sighing, I run my hand through my short hair and turn on my heel. I need the safety of my own room.

My own bed.

Alone.

That's the smart thing to do, anyway, even if it stings.

Even if I wasn't so disappointed by always doing the smart thing.

TWELVE

Carter

I should've kissed her.

She practically begged me for it, and I'm not one to leave a sexy woman wanting.

I may not be marriage material, but I'm well versed enough in the female language to know even sweet little Tessa would let me take her for a ride.

I smirk in the silence of Graham's room, but it quickly slides off.

It's wrong.

Dangerous.

But it could be heaven.

I flip onto my side, pulling the covers tighter around me, and stare at the wall. On the other side, Tessa lies in her own bed. *So close…*

Groaning, I toss onto my other side, turning my back toward the wall, when my phone rings, buzzing on the nightstand near my head.

Thank fuck—a distraction.

"Hey, Dad," I answer, unsurprised he's calling me this late. Although the reasons for his late-night check-ins are always varied, it's nothing out of the ordinary. He works late just like me.

Before Tessa scared the shit out of me, I was on the couch answering emails from the Director of Business Development and from Ava, my event coordinator. She had questions about the menu for the charity dinner in a couple weeks, and if there's one thing I enjoy talking about more than real estate, it's food.

"How you holding up?" my dad asks like I'm in prison, the sadness in his voice obvious.

"Fine, especially considering it's only been a couple days. I can do anything for forty-eight hours, including abstaining from getting drunk, eating desserts, calling models—"

"All right, all right." His raspy chuckle echoes through the line.

I flip onto my back, clutching the phone to my ear. "What's up?"

"I wanted to let you know Shanty's brokering the Heiderman deal."

I growl, sitting up so fast I nearly pop a rib out of place. "What the hell?"

"He's got connections with Heiderman. That was the tipping point for them to go through with the sale."

"Connections? Give me a break," I sneer. "Shanty probably bumped into Charlie Heiderman at a bar by accident and never even spoke to him."

"It's a good thing we have Shanty on our side. Otherwise, the deal would be dead, son," he insists.

I throw my legs over the edge of the bed. Pacing, I blow out a frustrated breath.

"Don't be so sour. What have I taught you? Personal grudges and vendettas have no place in business."

I freeze. "What're you talking about?"

"Landon Shanty's new fiancée? I know about your history with her."

I wince like he's pricked at a wound. "Emmy—I mean, Emmeline? She has nothing to do with this. Shanty's an ass, and that's all there is to it. He's a one-man show, and Fields Company is a team. Which is why I never wanted to offer him a position with us in the first place."

"As you've said many times."

"It has nothing to do with Emmeline," I argue.

My father gives me one of his dreadful sighs, and I want to punch a wall.

"I'm serious," I bite out. "Emmeline and I went out for drinks a couple times—it wasn't like we were on the verge of getting married and Shanty stole her away from me. Christ, there's nothing to hold a grudge over."

I sound defensive even to my own ears, but it's the truth, nonetheless. All I want is for him to believe me for once when it comes to my personal life.

Emmy and I danced around each other for months, attending the same galas and events. As a wealthy socialite, she makes an appearance at many of the same functions I do, and we were bound to get close.

After a few winks, drinks, and laughs, we fell into bed together.

We had chemistry between the sheets too, but when the sun came up, the extent of our conversations covered favorite breakfast foods. While it is the most important meal of the day, it's not too exciting to spend an hour breaking down croissants, layer by flaky fucking layer.

We both agreed that the chase was more exciting than the morning after, so we decided to remain friends. End of fucking story. Why the hell is my father bringing this up now?

"You're better off without the drama, anyway, son. You don't need to fight a man for a girl. It's tacky. The right woman will come to you, like your mother and me."

I brush off his comment—it's nothing I haven't heard before. "Gee, thanks for the pep talk. I didn't realize I was chasing after her. I've spent the last six months pining after Emmy and scribbling her name in my notebooks, you know."

"Is this part of your meltdown? Do I need to come get you from wherever you are?"

"No, Dad, but I appreciate your concern for my well-being. Truly, it's touching." I snicker, actually shocked he doesn't know my location. The only person I told was Whitney, but I guess she's loyal to me and not him, as I'd thought the morning I left.

In any other case, my father would know every detail about me. It's how he stays a few steps ahead while I'm busy balancing work and having a life outside the office, unlike him.

But not even his overbearing detective skills foresaw my accidents this month.

"Is that Carter you're talking to?" my mother's muffled voice sounds from the background. "Tell him Francine's niece has his number. She'll be calling him when he gets back."

"Please tell me Francine's niece is a decorator who wants to redo my penthouse. Or a hair stylist who wants to cut my hair. Anything but—"

"She'd love to go out sometime," my mother calls out.

Exactly what I was afraid of.

I squeeze my eyes closed, the urge to yell creeping up my throat.

"Tell him, okay?" Mom says to my dad. "I don't hear you telling him, Victor."

"I will. After we're finished discussing the important matters."

"What's more important than helping our son settle down? He's going to run the company without a woman by his side? Without a woman to make him look good in public? Someone to—"

My father scoffs. "I said I'd tell him. What more do you want?"

"Well, this doesn't sound like it involves me, so I'll be going," I say sarcastically, itching to end this torturous phone call.

"Wait, she's gone. We can talk freely." He sighs… again.

"We can talk freely with Mom around. We are a family, after all."

"You and your smartass comments."

I bite my tongue from telling him it's one of the many qualities I inherited from him, reminding myself this is my father. There's a line between joking and disrespect, and I always try to tread that balance.

"Oh, hell. Brandon's calling me. I'll call later this week to check in again, son."

After he ends the call, I smack the edge of my phone to

my forehead, then toss it to the floor, uncaring if it breaks.

As I fall into bed, my parents' exchange nags at me, especially in light of my conversation with Tessa earlier tonight. They're always mouthing off to each other, but what my mother said…

A woman to make him look good in public.

Is that what she thinks? Is that why she stays around? Because she thinks she's part of some twisted business deal?

I spiral down a rabbit hole, mentally running through all the dinners and fundraisers I've overseen and organized on behalf of Fields Company. The lavish meals and fancy champagne. The musical guests to entertain donors into leaving the venue thousands of dollars lighter.

Donors love seeing a complete and wholesome family, but it's not all they're looking for. They donate to charitable causes because they believe in the good they're doing, and they have more money than they know what to do with.

My mom's always been the life of those parties, working the room like she owns it. I used to believe she simply enjoyed doing so, but does she? Or does she feel like it's her duty?

Is it another part of their elaborate but monotonous routine?

These are the questions I keep contemplating as I roll around in bed. I should be going over the contracts I need to have drawn up, the deals we're making in Europe to grow our presence over there, the buyers I need to schmooze when I get back to the city.

Instead, I'm picturing my parents' marriage like I'm seeing it for the first time.

THIRTEEN

Tessa

The coffee maker beeps, signaling it's finished. Inhaling, I let a big whiff of the fresh brew, along with the soft glow from the sunrise filtering through the curtains, calm me.

There's not a cloud in sight, unlike the last couple days.

I did all I could not to get up this early—the sun hasn't even fully risen yet—but nothing worked. No counting sheep, snuggling deeper into the comforter, or practicing my breathing.

I'm so used to waking up at six every morning for work, it's hard for me to sleep in anymore, even during vacation. Carter, on the other hand, has no qualms about it this morning. I could hear his snores well before I cracked an eye open.

Then again, I'm not sure what time he went to sleep last

night. It was likely much later than me. As I grab the handle of the carafe, I recall his muffled voice through our shared wall like he was on the phone.

Who could it have been so late at night?

I have one thought—a woman—but I can't dwell on it.

It's none of my business, no matter what a strong connection I believe Carter and I share. He's not mine, nor do I want him to be.

At least, that's what I keep telling myself.

I finish pouring myself a cup, add cream and sugar, and smile at the steam billowing from the liquid as if it's a newborn child. Ah, the hope they both offer.

Mug in hand, I make my way out of the kitchen, grab a blanket from the couch, and leave out the front door. On the porch, I place my drink on the table between the rocking chairs and wrap the blanket around me before I sit, causing the chair to sway backward like I'm on a ship.

I blow on the hot liquid and take a sip, humming. The crisp morning air, the pink glow of twilight above the trees, the coffee—it's all exactly what I need after a long night of tossing and turning. For the second night in a row, all I could think about was… Carter.

His laugh.

The way his eyes dance.

His firm grip on my shoulders.

When he walked me to my bedroom door, I half expected him to kiss me goodnight and stand back like a gentleman.

As if we'd been on a freaking date.

It all came crashing down when I heard him on the phone. They'd talked for a while, although I couldn't hear what they were saying.

I squeeze my eyes closed. I'm being ridiculous. He's not my type, and I'm not his, either. Even if I wasn't his best friend's sister, he wouldn't be interested. Carter goes for models named Ginger and attends parties at New York and Paris's most exclusive clubs.

He's a billionaire. To him, I'm… average. Unexciting. Dull.

I rest the back of my head against the chair, rocking gently so I don't spill my coffee. What am I even thinking? Starting something with him would be stupid for many reasons.

He'd crumple me up like a piece of paper.

On top of that, he's Graham's best friend. Graham would be pissed at us both, and I couldn't take it if he shot me one of his disapproving glares.

It's worse than Dad's.

I couldn't take it if I lost him because of a guy again.

"There you are," a gruff voice sounds to my side. I didn't even hear Carter open the door. He squints at me, his hair a wild mess of short curls, and the crease on his cheek from where he slept makes me smile.

It's pretty adorable—and very hot. The perfect mix.

"Hey," I breathe as though he asked me to kiss him.

Get a grip.

"No glasses today?" He frowns, confusing me.

"Oh," I say, touching my face. "I don't wear them all the time. Just when I'm too lazy to put contacts in, but today is not a lazy day."

"Clearly. What're you doing out here? It's freezing." He wraps his hands around his curved biceps. His thin white tee, low hung pajama pants, and bare feet are not enough to shield him from the cold.

"That's why I have these." I hold up my blanket and steaming coffee.

"Hang on." He closes the door, then reappears with a beanie on his head, a hoodie, and shoes. In his hands, he also has a cup of coffee and a blanket. Sitting next to me, he asks over his mug, the waves of steam partly concealing his lips, "How's this? Am I doing it right?"

"Doing what right, exactly?"

"Early morning meditation. Isn't that what you're doing? Why else would you be up at this hour while on vacation?" He twists his lips.

I giggle. "You were up earlier than this yesterday."

He swallows his sip. "I was on the phone. Big difference than whatever this is," he says, glancing between me and the driveway, beyond which rows of trees line the road for miles.

"I'm enjoying the sunrise. It's peaceful." I shrug, licking drops of sweet liquid off my lip.

"Why someone would get up this early *on purpose* is beyond me. If it's not for work, it's not worth it." He scoffs and leans back in his chair, wiggling in his seat while pulling the blanket tighter around him.

"Why are *you* up?" I manage, itching to crawl under the blanket with him. "Were you working?"

He shakes his head. "Couldn't sleep. You were snoring, and the walls are pretty thin."

I glare at him. "Those were *your* snores. Kept me up half the night. You sounded like a mix between Chewbacca and Big Foot."

"Lies." He grins around the rim of his mug and takes another sip, peeking at me through one opened eye, then lets out a soft and satisfied *ah*.

"It's easy to sleep as hard as you obviously were after the late-night booty call," I blurt. Clamping my mouth closed, I raise my horrified gaze to meet his. I just can't keep my damn mouth shut around him, can I?

He sets the mug in his lap and stares back at me, eyebrow lifted. There's more smug amusement in the hint of dimples on each side of his face than he's shown for the last two days. "Not that I owe you an explanation for my late-night *conversations*, but it was my father who called last night. We were discussing a business deal."

"Oh." My cheeks heat.

He leans forward, angling his body toward me, and rests his elbows on his knees with his drink clutched between them. "You don't like being wrong, do you?"

"Pfft." I shake my head, forcing a smile. "I can admit when I make a mistake, and I did. But I don't care if it was your dad or a model. Or the princess of England, for that matter. Makes no difference." I finger the edge of the blanket, staring anywhere but at him.

"Keep telling yourself that." In my periphery, I catch him wink as he leans his back against the chair.

I exhale, my heart thundering in my ears.

How embarrassing.

After a heavy pause, I point to his coffee and jut my chin out. "Drink up and rest while you can because we have a big morning planned."

He tilts his head, his eyes widening in panic as if I said we'd be reading romance all day.

"This is probably your first time getting up this early on a regular non-workday since high school. We have to make the most of it and show you what the day before noon looks like outside of an office."

He groans. "Okay, but don't make me have too much fun. I can't afford to make this a habit on my days off. That's just wrong."

"How do you not like this?" I wave to our tranquil surroundings, the sun now high in the sky, beaming down on us like it's shining a spotlight in our faces.

"This is great, but it's nothing like Manhattan. Getting up this early just to stare at rows of skyscrapers is torture."

I giggle and shrug in agreement—he's not wrong.

"As CEO of the company, I'm even thinking of instituting a rule: no meetings before eleven o'clock. That way, people won't be subjected to the headache of loud horns, angry menaces of Wall Street, and air pumped full of pollution instead of this freshness." He laughs, but his humor quickly fades as he looks out into the woods.

I follow his gaze, my ears perking up to listen for any mysterious sounds he might've heard. A deer, perhaps, or a racoon. But I find nothing.

I turn back toward him and sip my coffee, then take a wild guess. "Not looking forward to taking over the company?"

"I am." He sighs, and his voice takes on a graver tone than I'm used to from him when he says, "Contrary to popular belief, company included"—he quips, glaring at me—"my dad has prepared me well for the role. All my life, he's trained me for this. I know the business and markets better than I know my wines and expensive watches. I'm the one who's taken lead on our expansion into Europe, even." He runs his large hand over his beanie. "I'm fully equipped to do the job and am beyond ready to take on more responsibility. It's just…"

I wait for his response, engrossed in his confession. He

jokes a lot, and while that's fun, I like this serious side of him equally as much. I'm swallowing it up like a glass of fine wine—or cheap wine. Unlike Carter, I wouldn't know the difference.

"It's obviously hard for my father to step down, so he keeps lecturing me and asking me if I really want this. Sometimes, I want to tell him I don't just so he'll stop asking."

"But you really do."

He adjusts the blanket around his shoulders. "I really do. Even though it'll be hard and it'll require early mornings." He gives me a sly smile. "I have no problem losing sleep for a greater purpose."

"Spoken like a true leader." I nod, my lips curling upward.

He grows somber again, giving me a sad, shy smile. "I'll have big shoes to fill. My dad's good at what he does, and everyone loves him. They respect him and his authority, but I'm afraid that won't transfer to me."

I furrow my brows.

"I'm professional, but I joke a lot." He tilts his head, and I nod back to him in agreement and understanding. "People see me as the fun guy, which I didn't care about until now. Until I realized our team might not take me seriously. My three accidents this month didn't help."

"I don't imagine they did." I chew the inside of my cheek.

He squints at me in sarcasm. "I screw up in my personal life—who doesn't? But when it comes to business, I'm a closer. When I want something, I go for it." His gaze flicks down to my lips, sucking the peaceful air from around us. Clearing his throat, he averts his gaze and mutters, "When it's a smart move, anyway."

I gulp, blinking away my instant disappointment. He's probably not even talking about me.

Carter sits taller as he clenches and unclenches his jaw like a fist. "Our colleagues and clients find me persuasive and charming, so it's mainly the co-workers I'll have to win over."

I make a gagging noise, teasing him and breaking the brief moment of tension.

He throws his free hand up, chuckling. "It's just what I hear."

Once our laughter subsides, I offer the best advice I can think of. After all, I have plenty of experience when it comes to people's insecurities about their jobs. "Don't be so hard on yourself. Let people get to know you as a leader, and soon, they'll forget about the guy who crashed into a mailbox." I lick my lips. "Like I tell my clients, there's always a learning curve at the beginning. As long as you take note of your mistakes *and* your strengths in order to keep growing, you'll be fine."

"Wow." His jaw drops as he searches the porch. "I don't have a bucket, but hang on."

"What're you talking about?"

"You're being nice to me." A taunting grin splits his cheeks. "You must need to puke now, but I don't have a bucket for you."

Understanding dawns, and I shove him as his laughter echoes through the silence. "You make it really hard to be nice to you," I manage.

"Okay, okay." He holds his hands up. "Truthfully, that was good advice." He raises his mug, and I glare at him as I lean over to clink mine against his. "What clients?"

"I'm a career counselor."

"No shit?"

"No shit," I confirm, holding my head high with pride. "I worked at a college for about a year after grad school, then moved to a center in Brooklyn where I'm expanding my reach and diversifying my clientele."

He nods. "Do you miss the school?"

I bite my bottom lip and catch Carter following the movement. Running my palm down my pant leg inside my blanket, I shudder at the combination of his attention and the chill in the air. "Sometimes," I say, my voice unsteady. "It was fun working with students who were on the cusp of the beginning of their lives. Career choices are difficult, and college is a vulnerable time, no matter if the students are in their twenties, thirties, or forties. But working at the center, I get to help people from the very start of their journey. From scratch, like a pan of homemade brownies."

He hums, listening to me intently.

"I like being able to assist people who are starting over too. Single moms transitioning careers to better themselves and the future for their kids. Veterans reentering the world from their tours. I still help college students as well, so changing jobs has been a win-win for me." I shrug, my grin so wide, my cheeks are sore.

"Sounds very fulfilling," he says.

"It is." I hold his gaze. "My parents are an inspiration to Graham and me. They worked hard in their careers because it satisfied their need to help people, and it's what Graham and I always wanted to do, albeit in different ways."

"It's nice that your family is so close." Carter clenches his jaw, peering down at his nearly empty mug. When he meets my gaze again, the shining sun illuminates his softening features. "If I couldn't tell by the way you talk about them or from the brief time I've spent with them in the past, I'd get it from the number of pictures inside."

"There are a lot."

"I like them."

I raise my eyebrow. "You don't feel like we're watching you at all times?"

"No, that hadn't occurred to me." He chuckles, narrowing his eyes at me, mischief consuming them like fireflies in the night. "I particularly like the one where you're dressed as a bumblebee."

I throw my head back and burst with laughter.

"You had the stinger, black cheeks, and the whole shebang. Love bees much?"

"Listen," I say, my voice hoarse and scratchy, "I was really into bees. I cut out pictures of them from magazines and anything else I could find when my mom wouldn't get me any more stickers. She did get me a bee costume for Halloween, except I wanted to be a bee year-round."

His mouth opens as understanding dawns. "That explains why you're a bee at the beach in one picture."

"Yes, and you can tease all you want, but I was happy." I ease into my chair as the memories flood. "I pretended to sting Graham every time he came near me with his skateboard."

Carter's laugh rumbles from his chest, and the sound echoes across the quiet space again. It's becoming familiar, just like these conversations, and it's all tearing the walls I've built around my heart. "He never mentioned he was a skater."

"Probably because he was pretty terrible at it. The worst in the neighborhood." I drink the last of my coffee that's gotten cold since I've been lost in conversation with Carter.

Lost in his eyes.

The deep sound of his gruff morning voice.

His eyes clearing of their sleepy haze.

"What made you stop dressing like a bee?"

"Besides growing up?" I smile. "I got stung by one and it hurt so bad, I cursed every bee to Hell for eternity. I cast a spell and everything—I was really into *Sabrina the Teenage Witch* at the time."

He chokes on his coffee, covering his mouth with one large hand as he chuckles.

The sound reverberates in my own chest as if I can feel it—and him—there.

Clearing my throat, I stand, nervous for the direction my feelings are headed. It's too much, too fast.

The way Carter makes me feel is dizzying, like whiplash or standing from a seat too quickly, and I need to put an end to it—now. "On that note, ready for a hike?"

"A hike?" He peers out toward the woods.

"Don't worry. The paparazzi won't find you in there, and the woodland creatures don't care about your celebrity status."

"Are you sure? Because on the drive up here, a passing deer looked at me funny." He rises out of his chair and follows me, his laugh echoing down to my toes.

Damn it.

Why couldn't he continue being the asshole I pegged him as from the start? I was so wrong about him, and as I change into hiking gear, the guiltier I feel about the way I judged him without even knowing the guy.

Although Carter's still an arrogant playboy—a handsome one too—he's more than all that. He's funny, genuine, and hardworking.

The more I get to know him, the harder it becomes to remember all the reasons I should resist him.

FOURTEEN

Tessa

"**W**hat would your assessment of me be?" Carter asks as we walk out of the cabin and across the street, my shoulder to his bicep. "What job would I be good at?"

"Hmm." I give him a once-over, silently appreciating that he still hasn't shaved. I enjoy his stubble and hoodie better than his clean jaw and suits—even if I like it a little too much. So much that I went to bed last night regretting my decision not to accept his offer to take his shirt off if he lost at poker. "You're arrogant, too eager for a good time, and have very few special skills."

He straightens his back.

"I'd say your current job is perfect for you—a playboy billionaire." I crack a smile.

He tsks, shaking his finger at me. "Well played, Rollins. Well fucking played, but I'll get you back."

"Oh? Should we play another round of poker, or is your ego still bruised from last night?"

"You hustled me, you damn minx." His dimpled smile is brighter than the sun. "How'd you get so good, anyway?"

"Nana Hope was an excellent poker player, and she taught Graham and me everything she knew."

"Ha!" Carter nudges my shoulder with his. "No, no, no. Graham's poker game is shit. What's the truth?"

Pursing my lips, I toy with the straps of my backpack, agreeing that Graham sucks at poker. I've always been better at it than him.

Although I'm telling the truth—Nana did teach me to play—the other part of the truth is… I got lucky. Nana used to say playing poker well takes practice and skill, but there's nothing better than luck. Luck will surprise and carry you, or it can destroy you.

I'm a decent poker player, but luck definitely helped me last night, especially against someone like Carter, who learned to play when he was six, evidently.

"I'll never give away my secrets." I narrow my eyes at him in challenge, playing coy.

He shakes his head, his fingertips barely brushing against me as we walk. "I'll figure it out. Mark my words, I'll figure *you* out, Tessa."

I shrug, smiling down at my shoes as if they're hilarious, but in truth, it's Carter. He makes me feel lighter. His presence instantly calms me. Conversations with him just *flow* like they never have with anyone else.

I pull my backpack up with both hands, adjusting the

straps on my shoulders. It's heavier than I intended, but I'm stuck with it now.

"Are you sure you don't want me to carry that for you?" Carter extends his hand toward me, but I swat at it.

I've already refused his offer twice and giving in now will only mean I admit defeat, but my competitive edge won't allow me to do that.

"I appreciate you offering, but I can handle it."

"You *really* hate admitting you need my help. That you're glad I'm here, and that I make you laugh." He watches me as he says in a smartass singsong tone, "But you do. I know you do."

And that right there is why I refuse—I will not give his ego any more of a boost.

I skip ahead to hide my amusement as we reach the trail in the woods. I lead Carter down to our right, through the tall trees full of red and yellow leaves.

During the next few moments of silence, I take in our surroundings, the chirping birds sounding almost as excited as I am that the sun has finally broken through the dark clouds. Other than the slight chill in the air left from the storm, it's a perfect day to be outside.

As we pass tree after tree, the birds' tunes echoing around us, I say to Carter, "To answer your earlier question properly, though, I'd have to give you more than a simple aptitude test."

He blinks.

"You asked me what job I'd suggest for you," I clarify.

"Oh, right."

"My role requires more one-on-one conversations about goals, daily life, resources, and interests. It's more than figuring out what each person is good at. It's nailing down where they see themselves in five or ten years and helping them get there. I sometimes lead group sessions too, which is always fascinating. People like to encourage each other, and it creates this amazing sense of community where people see they're not alone."

Carter remains silent for a few minutes as he peers down at each step he takes, his strides much longer than mine. "I bet you're good at what you do. You seem to really care about people. Not high-maintenance billionaires, but *other* people."

I laugh and glance over my shoulder in the direction his voice came from. He's a few feet behind me, so I stop and wait for him to catch up. "When was the last time you went hiking?"

"Somewhere around the year nineteen-ninety, give or take a decade." His chest heaves as he reaches me. "Listen, I jog and lift weights several times a week in an air-controlled gym. There's too much elevation and fresh air out here. My spoiled lungs can't take it."

"I'll slow down for you." I wink.

"How generous," he says.

We climb up a couple hills and continue down the path. I hoist my backpack into place, and as we walk, I lean my head back to admire the tall trees and their trunks' varying widths. The glow of the sun cascades through the branches like waterfalls down each trunk. Every now and then, I make sure to look down so I can skirt around the puddles that are scattered across the trail from last night's storm.

Exhaling, I muse, "Graham and I hike this trail when we're both up here and the weather cooperates."

"I'm glad to hear it. I know I should've asked you back at the cabin if you know where we're going, but apparently, I trust you more than I thought."

I smile and continue trudging through the woods, feeling like I'm reunited with old friends among these trees. I miss doing this with Graham, but it's a different kind of special to hike this trail with someone new. With Carter, this place feels fresh, like I'm seeing it for the first time, and I'm enjoying pointing out memorable spots.

I stop and point to a clearing in the trees. "When Graham was fourteen, he thought it'd be funny to take me down this pathway, hide me behind a tree, and run down the main trail toward our parents, pretending he'd lost me. Even at seven, I knew it was a horrible idea."

"I can't imagine your parents disagreed with you." He inhales a lungful of air, his chest expanding as he rests his hands on his hips.

I cover my giggle. "No. But I defended Graham when our father gave him a stern lecture."

"You're close," he whispers, but it's more of a statement instead of a question.

Although it's not the reaction I expected, I'm not surprised by his observation. He's known Graham for a while, after all. Even when he was in college, Graham called to talk to me multiple times a week, asking me about my dance recitals or what book I was reading.

As I grew up, I appreciated his efforts more and more, especially when I realized why he did it. Our parents have always been involved as much as possible, but they frequently worked late. Graham wanted to make sure I didn't feel alone when they did and I had to stay with a babysitter. I didn't have him in the house to keep me occupied anymore, but he made sure I felt his presence.

"We are," I say.

Carter scratches the back of his head and tightens his jaw, seemingly disappointed, but I don't ask him about it.

In silence, we come to a stop at an overlook toward the end of the trail. Moving toward the edge, I take in the orange and brown colors of the landscape, admiring the gentle hills surrounded by scattered crop fields. The stunning view, coupled with the stronger breeze this high up, sends goosebumps down my arms.

"The torture is definitely worth this view." Carter stands beside me, his arm brushing against mine and his breathing labored.

Mine is too at this point. Unlike him, I don't spend time at the gym like I used to. I normally settle for walks and short distance jogs, so this hike was a challenge. Although somewhere around the second mile, I decided I'm going to get back into yoga with Erin when I'm home. Maybe I'll join a gym too, but one thing at a time.

I pull my backpack off and grab two waters. "Rest for a bit?"

"I'm way ahead of you." He leads the way toward a bench and spreads his legs out.

"Make room for me."

He pats his lap. "I saved you the best spot."

I roll my eyes, but I have to admit, I like the sound of his suggestion.

He scoots over but leaves his arm outstretched across the back of the bench, so when I sit, his fingers graze my shoulders.

Tease.

"Hungry?" With tingling fingers, I offer him a turkey sandwich and protein bar that I packed for our outing.

He accepts both, thanking me in the process, and we stare

out at the scene in front of us. Among the trees, Heublein Tower stands tall in the distance like a beacon. Graham and I had hiked to the historic tower once, and the panoramic view from the top was even more spectacular than this one.

This trip has been full of memories already, and my family's not even here.

The one person I should've met years ago is, on the other hand.

I pull my leg up and tuck my foot underneath my other knee, facing Carter. "Is it strange we've never met before? You're one of Graham's best friends, and you've met my parents. Yet, I didn't even recognize you the other day."

"I'm still hurt, by the way." He clutches his chest and exaggerates being heartbroken.

"I'm sure you're wrecked," I tease around a bite of my sandwich. "The three of us were supposed to have dinner a few times, but Graham always canceled at the last minute."

"He does that a lot, doesn't he?"

I nod. "It's his job, though, so it's understandable."

"That's Graham. Out to save the world." His tone might hold a hint of sarcasm, but his smile is genuine, making the corners of his eyes crinkle.

I laugh. "He certainly has a God complex, which he got from our dad."

"What did you get from your parents?"

"I'm an angel, of course." I shrug, and with the last couple words, a few pieces of food fly from my mouth. I slap my hand over it, then wipe my chin. "Oops."

"What other angels do you know who eat so sloppily?"

I make a show of swallowing before I say, "One time. I'm sloppy this *once*."

"Actually, the lasagna last night…"

"What?" I feel the blood drain from my cheeks.

"I didn't want to say anything, but you had cheese hanging from your nose for about an hour." He tears a large bite of his sandwich between his perfectly straight teeth.

I start to respond but stop when he bursts into laughter. "I knew it couldn't be true." I nudge him away, but he doesn't let go.

On the contrary, Carter's grip on my bicep tightens as he tucks me into his side. My hand instinctively goes to his chest, where I splay my fingers over his pec. His jacket is too thick for me to feel him, but based on what I've seen at the cabin, I imagine my fingers digging into the lean muscle there.

My laughter gets caught in my throat.

Carter's large hand drops to curl around my bent elbow, wrapping me up.

He smells of the woods—fresh and spicy.

His bearded chin scratches the top of my head, and I'm on the verge of a dreamy sigh.

This feels too good. Too natural. Too hot for an innocent hug.

But with a view like this, alone as we are, it's hard not to succumb to the romance of it all. It feels like we're the only two people in the world.

When he peers down at me, his eyes intense and unwavering, I see my feelings mirrored back at me, and I'm starting to think this is where I belong.

With Carter Fields, the consequences be damned.

FIFTEEN

Carter

"**D**irt is in my nostril." I exhale through my nose, attempting to rid myself of the offending soil. "The last time I was around this much dirt was in Talladega. Actually, that was the last time I was around this much nature, period."

"Alabama?" She raises her eyebrows, surprised.

I nod, wiping at my nose as the wind picks up, swirling more loose dirt around us. "It was for the NASCAR race when Graham and I were in college. It's also the first and only time I've ever seen a grown man piss his pants."

"No way! Graham did *not* piss his pants." Tessa brings her hands up to cover her face.

I burst into laughter. "No, not Graham. A total stranger." I settle back into my spot on the bench, shifting on the uncomfortable wood. "Although, if it was Graham, that would've made for a very different story. To be honest, I don't think our friendship would've survived the humiliation."

"I don't blame you. I might've had to disown him myself." Snorting, Tessa brings her legs up and crosses them, her body facing me. She rests her elbow on the back of the bench, then leans her head in her hand, and I almost forget what we're joking about.

Wisps of hair blow around her face. Her cheeks are rosy, and her smile is easy.

Tessa's fucking gorgeous.

More breathtaking than this damn view, and the fact that she's off-limits hasn't hurt as much as it does in this moment.

I try to swallow the sudden lump in my throat.

"You have to back up and tell me the real story—from the beginning." She smiles up at me, watching my lips move as I tell her about the trip the guys and I took years ago.

She's probably the only woman I've met who would rather hear about a random drunk pissing himself or a stripper stealing her brother's wallet than a clean, fluffy tale of cute squirrels eating nuts in the forest.

It's refreshing and sexy as hell.

"Remember, you asked for this." I squirm in my seat again as I let my mind drift back to what feels like a different lifetime. "It was Graham's idea to go to the race. I had a private jet at my disposal. Getting there and back in a blink was no issue."

"Of course." She swipes the unruly hair from her forehead and places it behind her ear.

"I also had no issue buying us a few rooms at a nice hotel, but Graham insisted we do Talladega *the right way*. I only wish I knew what he'd meant before I agreed," I say, dragging my hand down my face. "He'd heard of campgrounds and how rowdy people tended to get. He wanted to experience it like a civilian, so I went along with it. We all did."

"How many of you were there?"

"Five of us." I take a sip of water, then lap up the droplets on my bottom lip and continue. "We got to these campgrounds, which were just piles of dirt surrounded by trees."

She startles me with her high-pitched laughter.

"That's not even the funny part," I say over her. "What the hell are you laughing at?"

"You… You're so…" Her whole body shakes as she continues cracking up. "What did you think campgrounds were? A stadium people drove their RVs and campers into that had electricity and air conditioning?"

I clutch my chest. "No…"

She only laughs harder at my obvious attempt to sound offended, but we both know I did, in fact, believe at the time that campgrounds weren't so archaic.

To my defense, up until college, I didn't know much about the real world, campgrounds included.

"Anyway, Drake, the asshole, didn't lock the *lovely* porta potty we'd rented once he was finished, and some grizzly lumberjack wandered into it one night in a drunken haze. And left with piss down the front of his pants like a Neanderthal."

"Oh my God!" She covers half her face again with her hands.

"And if that wasn't bad enough, while we were dealing with him, the guy's dog snuck into our camper and ran off with our hot dogs." She opens her mouth to say something, but I hold my finger up and use my best TV commercial impression when I say, "But wait! There's more."

"Please, no more."

I nod, my cheeks sore. "During the excitement, none other than—can you take a guess what creature then graced us with its presence?"

"A fox?" She shrugs, leaning forward for the rest of the story.

"A skunk." I spread my arms as I stand to take a bow. "A skunk wandered up undetected and sprayed us all. I have yet to take enough showers to get rid of that smell."

Her face turns red from laughing so hard, and I join her, enjoying this stroll down memory lane. It's been a while since I last recalled this trip, even though it's probably the most ridiculous experience of my life. Still, it was almost fifteen years ago, and so much has happened since then.

Talking about it and remembering all the fun times we had back then makes me realize how different things are now. How much more pressure I feel with work and the media. How much I miss the shenanigans the guys and I would get into. I still see some of them every now and then, but it's not the same.

We're different people now.

"What did you do afterward?" Tessa asks, drawing me back into the conversation.

"I promptly herded everyone out of the camper, called a car, and booked us the best suite at a five-star hotel. I bought everyone new stuff too—I had to get the fuck out of there."

"I wouldn't blame you if you set the camper on fire." Her smile lingers in the tilt of her lips as we continue talking.

"Believe me, I wanted to." I throw my hands up. "I mean, I could've rented out the entire speedway seven times over, but Graham wanted the real experience. He even got me excited for it, and I thought it would be humbling—Graham was good at that." I rub my chin, a grin spreading.

"Sounds like it worked, then."

"Nah. I found out the truth later on." I shake my head, peering back out at the view as another gust of wind rushes between us, and the birds caw above us.

"Oh?"

"The dick wanted me to suffer because I hit on Diana Shipley, the girl he was trying to date." Tessa snickers beside me, and I lean toward her. "Before you make your snarky remark, let me be clear. I had no idea he was into Diana because he never told me, so *I* was the casualty here."

"Poor Carter. Didn't get the girl or the fancy weekend."

"Who said I didn't get the girl?" I smirk.

She eyes me, a glimmer there that radiates to her blushing cheeks. Her hair's halfway up in a ponytail on her head, and her glasses were left behind in the cabin, giving me a full view of her face.

Her plump lips and button nose.

The slender column of her neck.

Even decked in hiking gear and without a stitch of makeup, she's stunning.

When she moves to gather our things—the wind is relentless—her pert ass is hard to ignore as she bends down for the backpack.

I take a deep breath of fresh air and avert my gaze anywhere but on her—I need to get a fucking grip.

We start the trek back to the cabin, much to my dismay. I liked holding Tessa while we sat on the bench.

Which is shocking in itself—I don't normally like the cuddly, mushy shit romantic comedies feed society. But with

Tessa, holding her while we talked felt natural and special, even.

Even through her jacket, I could feel the heat of her when she was in my arms.

I'm fucking drowning in her.

"You and I might never have met before this, but Graham talked about you a lot." I peek down at Tessa as we walk side by side back the way we came.

"He talked about you a little too, although I'm not sure you want to know what he said."

"I can pretty much guarantee you I don't want to know." I chuckle.

She nudges me with her shoulder. "I'm kidding. He actually has a few nice things to say about you."

"I'll have Whitney send him a thank-you card when I get back."

She hums, gripping the backpack straps with both hands. I offered to carry the bag when we left the cabin, but she insisted she could handle it. She even seemed outraged that I might've suggested she couldn't, when I really just wanted to help. I consider offering again now, but the thought of the glare she gave me earlier stops me.

"Dare I ask what my big brother has to say about me?" She bites her lip.

"You were young when we were in college, so he mostly talked about you making the volleyball team and honor roll."

I slow my steps as I recall more and more of what Graham said. I'd forgotten most of it until this week. Until Tessa stood before me. Although he always had only good things to say about her, they didn't do her justice.

She's better than he let on.

I swallow the lump in my throat that only grows larger

the more time I spend with her from knowing I can't act on this attraction between us. "At our alumni reunion a couple years ago, it was different. He was still proud of you, but everything he said was to warn us against you."

"What do you mean?" She comes to an abrupt stop in front of me, leaving only a foot between us.

Her mouth hangs open just a little, and she watches me with more curiosity than a museum curator would a sculpture.

"A friend of ours was recently divorced at the time. He had a few drinks and cracked a joke about getting your number from Graham, who kneed him in the balls without a second thought."

"At least Graham's discreet." She laughs softly, but it doesn't do much to change the intensity in her pursed lips or stance.

My gaze bores into hers, all kidding aside. "He was right, though. You're too good for any of us assholes. None of us deserve you."

Least of all me.

The words are on the tip of my tongue, but I'm suddenly struggling to form coherent thoughts, let alone full phrases.

She swallows, but it appears in slow motion like it's difficult for her.

I inch forward, coming toe to toe with her, and cup her chilled cheek as the cool day continues around us. "You are too good," I repeat in a whisper, my voice thick with overwhelming emotion as my fingertips find their way to the slope of her neck. I grip her there, fisting a small handful of wavy hair.

Her lips part as if she's inviting me to lean down. Like she wants me to kiss her.

My God, do I want to fucking kiss her.

A single taste wouldn't hurt, right?

I angle her head back.

That's all. Only a taste.

I dip down toward her, licking my lips, already imagining what hers will feel like against mine. We're wrapped in each other's arms in the middle of the woods. There's nothing standing between us.

This is our chance.

I'm so close to capturing her lips in mine when a loud bird caws above us, echoing like it's screaming. It might as well hold a megaphone.

We jump apart, panting as we stare at each other.

Her hand flies to her chest, and I run my hand over my beanie as I blink our surroundings back into focus.

When I turn to her again, her expression is unreadable, and instead of moving toward me, she steps backward.

The moment has passed.

I swallow my disappointment as we hike back to the cabin in silence. All the while, with every new step, I try to convince myself it's for the best.

I wouldn't be able to stop myself at a single taste, anyway.

I'd want to claim all of her.

That's the thing about someone like Tessa. She's the kind of woman I wouldn't be able to get enough of once I started, like an addict.

I'd become addicted to my best friend's sister.

Fuck.

SIXTEEN

Carter

We haven't spoken since we returned to the cabin. Even though my body was numb from the fall chill outside, I took a cold shower to tamp down my urges, the drops stinging the horniness right out of me.

I've never wanted anyone so badly, and I've only known her for a few days. Although, Graham's talked about her enough over the years, making me feel like I've known her longer.

She has this way about her too. This inherent light and comfort she offers to those around her, and instead of being blinded by it, it's more like the glow at the end of a dark tunnel.

She's my way out.

Out of what, though?

I've never needed anyone for longer than a night. Ginger and I have an understanding that works for both of us. One that allows me the satisfaction of a warm bed for a few hours. Otherwise, she and I would've parted ways already. Instead, we enjoy each other's company for a night here and there, and when it's time to leave, there are no hard feelings.

Her job is demanding, and I'm wrapped up in the company and don't want the commitment of a relationship.

I've never even been in a relationship.

At this point, I don't know what the word even means.

But Tessa is the commitment type. She's not the kind of girl to settle for a fling—the only thing I can offer.

I push off the dresser, my jaw clenched.

There's too much working against us.

When I emerge from my room, damp hair curling at my forehead and tickling me, I find Tessa bouncing around the kitchen, her movements as carefree as her loose hair. Her wet locks are wavy and tousled over to one side, and she's in a large tee, the front of which is tied in a knot at the waistband of her leggings.

She's wearing her glasses again too.

The square ones that make her look like a sexy professor.

Wild thoughts of her in a pencil skirt and those glasses fill my head. I'd hike the tight material up over her hips and bend her over an office desk while I stood behind her and—

I grind my teeth, shaking myself out of it.

I'm just wound up, is all. I almost had her lips on mine barely two hours ago, and I'm tense. I'll be fine. I can admire her from here, and it'll have to be enough.

Light rain has started again, ticking against the glass windows in soft knocks, and the gray clouds dim the space in here. It's only midafternoon, yet with the dark sky through the large windows, it seems like it's much later.

None of it stops Tessa's positive mood, though.

I lean against the doorframe as she cracks an egg into a mixing bowl while singing quietly. She doesn't seem to notice I'm here and proceeds to measure sugar into a cup, her lips still moving and her hips swaying.

When she turns to grab another ingredient, she lifts her gaze to lock on mine and stops. "How long have you been standing there?"

"Long enough to know your rendition of 'Watermelon Sugar' is much better than Harry's." I wink, pushing off the door.

"How do you even know that song?" Her curious eyes travel from my socked feet up to my face. "You seem like more of a classic rock fan."

"Harry's a friend, but you're correct in your assessment." I round the corner of the counter and meet her in the kitchen, rubbing my hands together. "What can I help with?"

She drags a bag of flour toward her and measures it with a cup, shaving off the top with the smooth edge of a knife. "I'm making brownies for Sheriff Thompson and his wife. Almost finished with the mix, but I can use help cleaning up."

I survey the kitchen, and I now realize it looks like a tornado of baked goods blew through here. Measuring cups and spoons litter the stove and counter, along with a couple of baking pans. A carton of eggs is opened by the refrigerator, and sugar granules are sprinkled across the black countertop like salt on the roads during winter. When she pushes the flour out of the way, she leaves a trail of it in front of her as well.

"What happened? Did you use every single item in this kitchen for one pan of brownies?"

She follows my horrified gaze around the mess and shrugs. "It's a special recipe and requires ultimate focus. Besides, it's for *three* pans—one for the Thompsons, another for our neighbors, and the third for us."

"Fair enough." I get to work, putting up the items and cups she's finished with. As we work, I ask her over my shoulder, "Have you heard from Graham or your parents?"

She takes a spoon to the sink and grabs a spatula. "Graham texted me while you were in the shower. He got stuck at work—something about flu season giving him a hard time—but promises to head up early in the morning."

"And your parents?" I slow my movements, rest my hip against the sink, and clench my jaw, equally dreading and excited for her answer, no matter what she says.

"They boarded their flight this morning as planned, but I haven't heard from them since." She pulls out her phone, then drops it with a sigh.

I set the dishes in the sink and turn toward her, taking in her frown. "Hey, they'll be here."

She leans against the counter opposite me, her normally bright features shadowed with disappointment. "It sounds so silly, being upset that my family's not here to celebrate my birthday. It's not like I'm five years old or something."

I cross the small kitchen in a couple of strides and rub her upper arms, lowering my voice when I say, "Not silly at all. It's tradition, and it's important."

"Exactly." She fully faces me, her body relaxing and obviously relieved. "I haven't been up here in forever, and we always used to spend our birthdays here. I guess I always knew we'd eventually get caught up with work and life and that we wouldn't get to keep this up forever. I just didn't figure it would happen so soon. I've been feeling like I'm losing them and part of myself without these trips up here, and I thought I could get some semblance of peace with it all this week."

I nod, beginning to understand. Simply reminiscing about the college days with her earlier had me itching to text the guys for a reunion soon. I can only imagine how excited Tessa has been for this getaway with her family, a trip they've made for years before everyone grew up.

I grip her arms, hating that she's so heartbroken. I've come to enjoy her laughter too much, and I need it back. "What can I do?"

"Today helped," she says, peeking up at me through long lashes, and her pout gives way to a hint of a smile. After a short pause, she hesitantly says, "It was a, um, good distraction."

"Right. That's what I'm good at—distractions."

"Thanks." She shimmies out of my grasp and grabs the hand mixer to blend the brownie concoction.

It starts with a low buzz, and a small cloud of powder from the flour and cocoa floats out of the bowl until the mix becomes dark and smooth. When she's done, and the kitchen grows quiet again, she uses the back of her hand to wipe her forehead. Next, she carries the mixing bowl and pours its contents into a nonstick baking pan, then puts it in the preheated oven.

We don't speak.

The thick tension from our hike back to the cabin only grows with every passing minute. Each exchange. Every glance.

My heart thunders as she leans over the stove to set the timer, the hem of her shirt rising with the movement.

The curve of her ass stares me in the face, and I tremble to dig my fingers into that flesh. To grip her hips and hoist her onto this counter, then settle between her legs.

I can't fucking take it anymore.

I need her.

"I'm not a distraction, am I?" I ask, my voice low and deliberate as I enunciate each syllable.

She stands upright, her fingers curling around the bar on the oven door as if she needs it for support.

"We simply had fun, right? Or was it just me?" I ask, barely above the sound of rain outside and thunder rumbling in the distance.

She turns around slowly, her eyes squeezed closed. "It was fun," she whispers, her eyelids fluttering open again.

"You wanted me to kiss you." This time, it's not a question or a request, but a statement. One I know to be true. I can see it in her eyes when they meet mine. The wild desire there. The lust for me.

The truth of her hunger lies in wait in those eyes.

"I *want* you to kiss me," she says with firm conviction, and my knees buckle.

The earth shatters around me, leaving me alone with Tessa.

Nothing outside of these walls matters.

"Come here." It's an assertive growl, somewhere between a caveman and a businessman.

She steps forward, and I meet her halfway, my hand flying to grip the back of her neck. I guide her head up toward mine while I press my hips into her, earning me a whimper from those perfect lips. Dipping my head to run my nose along her jaw, I breathe in her sweet smell.

Her lips are parted and waiting.

For me.

She's ready for me.

I brush my lips against hers like I'm afraid of capturing them all at once. Like I already know she's going to destroy me, and I need to take this first kiss in stride.

I spread my fingers on the back of her neck up to her hair, tangling them in her strands, then use my thumb to caress her flushed cheek. My other hand remains on her hip, pulling her closely as I suck her top lip between my teeth, teasing her.

The moment the tip of my tongue reaches the inside of her lip, she lets out a breathy moan that shoots blood down south faster than the lightning striking outside.

Without breaking the kiss, she snakes her hands up my chest, around my neck, and pulls me down like I'm not close enough.

I move to her bottom lip, nipping at it, and when Tessa's tongue darts out to meet mine, I fucking lose it.

Completely surrendering to her and this intense connection between us, I crush my mouth to hers—tasting, sucking, ravaging her mouth like I'm punishing it. As if it's the reason we haven't been doing this from the moment we arrived.

Her body sags against mine as she meets me in a push and pull dance I never want to end.

Our kiss becomes frantic. Hungry. It's urgent, as though the timer on the oven is for us and not the brownies.

Her hands shoot to my hair until her fingers dig into my scalp, making me growl in her mouth, and she swallows the sound like it's oxygen.

She pants, rocking her hips into mine, and I devour every sound, tug, and nip.

I plan to devour *her*.

Gripping her hips, I lift her onto the counter and spread

her legs open for me, much like I imagined moments ago, but the real deal is a thousand times better. I soak in her gasps as her hands grow more eager, clawing at my shoulders and bunching my shirt in her hands.

She needs me as much as I need her.

I help her with my tee, yanking it up and over my head.

Her hands explore the hills of my pecs, down the ridges of my abs, then up again and around to my back. She wraps her legs around my waist and traps me as though I had any intention of running away.

Not a chance.

"I want you," I whisper against her mouth, sucking her bottom lip between my teeth, earning me a moan. "Fuck, I *need* you."

"Take me, Carter," she pants. "Take me."

The way she says my name—it's a plea and a command wrapped in one.

The two syllables leave her pretty mouth as smoothly and sweetly as honey.

Jesus.

I cradle her head in my large palm and kiss her, my tongue finding its way back inside her appreciative mouth, swirling with hers in a mix of pleasure and lust.

"Now," she murmurs against me, squeezing her legs around me.

I tear my lips from hers and undo the knot of her T-shirt, then roughly pull it over her head like the fabric offends me. She hops off the counter and wiggles out of her leggings while I shove my pants, along with my boxers, down.

Our breaths quicken, filling the kitchen and mixing with the smell of chocolate.

Sweet fucking bliss.

Raking her gaze over my bare body, she pauses when she takes in my hard cock and licks her lips. She hops back onto the counter, her tits bouncing with the movement, ready to be cupped, nipped at, and sucked on.

Tessa is a damn wet dream.

"Hold on," I say, my voice strangled and hoarse. I force myself away from her, rushing to the other room for my wallet and fish out a condom. Faster than a damn cheetah, I make it back to a needy Tessa, who's spread out like a goddess before me.

"Come here." She scoots to the edge of the counter, giving me a beautiful view of her wet heat.

It's glistening, practically begging for me to bury myself inside her.

My cock screams at me to hurry as I sheath myself with shaking fingers.

My entire body hums, buzzing with anticipation and hunger for Tessa.

I only met her in person for the first time a couple days ago, but it feels like I've been waiting for this moment for years.

Stepping back into my place between her legs, I thread my fingers through her hair and kiss her. My nose is smashed against hers, tilting her glasses up, which reminds me…

"Off." I lift the glasses off her face and place them on the counter away from us. "I need to see all of you." I fist myself with my hand and line up to her entrance, groaning when her wetness covers my tip.

She moans with pleasure, encouraging me forward as she scoots her hips toward me, her eyes a darker blue than I've ever seen them.

As I kiss her again, I slide into her, fitting myself into her tight fucking heat.

Exquisite.

She throws her head back, allowing me access to trail kisses down her throat. I seize the opportunity, reveling in the way her breasts are pushed up at this angle as she wraps her arms around my neck.

Once I fill her to the hilt, my cock suctioned like a glove, I pull out. Cupping her breast and pinching her hard nipple between my thumb and forefinger, I plunge back inside her, eliciting a strangled gasp. Her faint cinnamon smell and feminine whimpers urge me to move faster and deeper, rolling my hips into hers like I'm a poet, feeling the beat of each line's rhythm as I rock into her at a purposeful pace.

"Oh, God, yes," she rasps, her grip on my neck tightening, and I savor the sting of her nails on my skin.

Her face reddens as she takes me over and over again, holding on to me for dear life as I roll my hips into her, my abs clenching as I struggle to hang on.

Her legs tighten around me, meeting my thrusts with wild abandon, seeking her climax.

And I'm happy to oblige.

My heart racing, I pump in and out of her with one goal—to make Tessa come all over my dick and this kitchen floor while she screams my name.

I need it more than my own release.

I quicken my pace, increasing the friction between us— sparks not even science can explain.

Her tits bounce, rising close to my chin. I lean down and take one in my mouth, pumping faster and harder until she clenches around me, crying out, "Yes, yes, yes."

Her eyes are wide and brilliant as she explodes in my arms in a mess of satisfied quivers and moans.

Slowing my pace, I let her ride out her climax, then pull out completely and yank her onto her feet. I spin her around so her back is against my front. Splaying my hand across her lower stomach, my fingers dangerously close to the sweet spot between her legs, I let my stiff length run along her cheeks as my heart races.

My length drips with her climax, aching to plunge back inside her.

She gasps and leans over the counter in front of her, her breasts smearing the leftover flour she'd used moments ago. In this position, she pushes her ass harder into me, and I bite out a curse. Keeping one hand on her stomach while the other travels up her arm, over the curve of her shoulder, and up the column of her neck, I angle her chin upward.

I capture her lips in an open-mouthed kiss, and it makes me throb with need, my dick rigid, the direct opposite of her soft body melting against me. Gripping her chin to hold her in place, I deepen the kiss, delving my tongue inside her welcoming mouth, and she whimpers more loudly this time.

She trembles in my hold, and my breathing quickens the longer she rubs her ass against the front of me.

Tessa makes me fucking crazy.

I guide her hands to grip the edge of the counter, smooth her hair to the side, and bring my lips to her ear, whispering, "Hold on, baby."

Shivering, she gives me an incoherent, dazed response, which makes me smirk. I tug her ass back to me and drive into her with one quick movement, pumping, sliding, fucking.

Her knuckles turn white from holding onto the counter, and she moves her hips to the rhythm of my thrusts.

I move in and out of her like I'm trying to beat a personal record, reveling in her tightness.

How snug I fit inside her.

The friction we create.

With a deep grunt, my release comes fast and hard, taking my energy with it and making me jolt forward to rest on her arched back.

"Shit," I rasp, my heaving chest slick with a small line of sweat.

"Oh my God," she whispers, her voice full of awe, the grooves of her spine meeting the swell of my stomach as I grapple to take deep breaths.

The timer on the oven dings, jolting us upright like we've been caught.

I squeeze her hand and notice the streaks of flour across her chest and shoulder. Tessa's unraveled and sated, her lips taking on a lazy tilt in the corners.

I did that to her.

I put that glow in her cheeks.

Her attention stays on me.

And we both smile.

SEVENTEEN

Holy fucking hell almighty.

I had sex with Carter Fields.

Mind-blowing kitchen sex, at that.

And now, we're sitting on the living room floor, giggling and eating brownies like we're high. I almost forget about my birthday. About my family's absence. Our lives outside of these walls.

All I see is Carter, but not the clean-cut and unattainable face of all the gossip magazines. Instead, I see the guy in sweatpants hung low on his hips, sans shirt.

His lean and sculpted muscles on display for my perusal.

His hair a mess from where I ran my fingers through it.

I'm wrapped up in him, smiling and squirming at the way

he groans with each bite of brownie like it's the last baked good he'll ever have.

Every now and then, he curls his fingers into the collar of my shirt, pulls it to the side, and nips at my shoulder in a loving way that melts my heart.

We're in a state of sugared bliss, and I never want to leave.

"Okay, maybe now I feel like your family's staring at me from the pictures." Carter side-eyes the ones on the fireplace mantel, exaggerating a shudder.

I pull him to me by his cheek and lick the chocolate from the corner of his mouth, giggling against him.

"Shit, I think Graham just growled for me to stay away from you." Carter points to the picture in the corner of Graham holding up a red box by a Christmas tree.

I start to make a joke, but my ringing phone stops me. Reaching for it, I see my mom's face on the screen. "Hang on," I say to Carter and answer my mom's call. "Hello, Mom? How close are you?"

"Honey, you'll never believe the day we've had," my mom says, her voice filled with exhaustion.

"What happened?"

"We're in Chicago."

"What?" I drop my half-eaten brownie onto the shared plate between Carter and me.

"We were about to board our flight, like I texted you this morning, and your father tripped over a suitcase and sprained his ankle. He fell on his knee too, and it's already bruising like a peach."

"Is he okay?" I stand and pace behind the couch, my heart pounding.

I hear Dad in the background, reassuring me he's felt

worse, especially during high school football. It puts me at ease, but I'm still worried. Spraining his ankle at his age is nothing like the hits he took at sixteen.

"I'm sorry, honey, but we're not going to make it tonight. Your father needs to rest and put ice on his knee and ankle before they get any worse. We already have a new flight booked for tomorrow morning, though. We'll be at the cabin by noon, I promise. I'll wrap your father up in packing tape if I have to."

Even though I'm still concerned about my dad, my mom comforts me.

"We spoke to Graham too. He's not there yet, either?" she asks.

I sigh. "No. He had to work."

"Oh, honey, I'm so sorry to ruin your birthday like this, but I promise we'll make it up to you. I'll fix an extra special plate of French toast. How does that sound?"

"That sounds great, Mom, but really"—I turn toward a concerned Carter, who sits on the edge of the couch, his arms crossed over his chest—"it's okay. Take care of Dad and get some rest. Both of you."

"Will do, sweetie. See you tomorrow."

After I hang up, the disappointment that they still won't be here quickly vanishes when I take in Carter. His hair is tousled, and his bare chest is strong and tan like he spends his days alternating between the gym and the beach instead of his office.

Suddenly, more time alone with him is exactly what I want.

"We have another night to ourselves," I say, a devious smile spreading with each step I take toward him.

"You're saying you're stuck with me?" The tip of his tongue

darts out to lick his lips like he's ready to pounce the second I give him the green-light.

"I can think of worse things." I round the armrest of the couch and jump on him, straddle his lap, and push against his chest so he'll lie back.

Running my hands through his hair, I kiss him, tasting chocolate on his lips.

So delicious.

He fingers the hem of my shirt, barely grazing the skin of my stomach, and it drives me wild.

"Stop teasing me," I murmur, wiggling on top of him, sensing he's as ready as I am.

He's rock hard, a steel pipe against my lower stomach, right above a bundle of nerves that could use some attention.

His attention.

"Your wish"—Carter flips me onto my back, making me yelp—"is my command."

I bite my lip, enjoying his playful seduction, and reach up to remove my glasses. Before I can, he stops me. "Leave them on this time. You'll be a sexy librarian, and I'm the naughty guy who brings in a stack of books past their due date. How will you punish me?" He licks his twitching lips, his dimples appearing like fluttering eyelids, a flirty peek here and there.

Sinking into the cushions, I grip his ass with both hands and drop my voice to a husky whisper. "You're in big trouble, Mister Fields."

He groans, nuzzling his nose in the crook of my neck. "Call me *mister* again and I might fucking come in my pants."

I grin, my cheek pressed against the side of his head. Scooting myself lower on the couch, I slide against his hard body until my lips reach his ear, then whisper, "*Mister* Fields…"

"Jesus," he growls and crushes his mouth to mine, pinning me in place with both his hands on either side of my face.

Guess I'll be the one punished.

Leaning his body weight on me so that I'm covered in Carter, he continues kissing me, and I slump farther into the couch, happily ready to make this my residence if it means I get to have Carter like this.

His tongue makes slow, languid swirls against mine, and I move my hands to cup his face, keeping him here. His kiss is addictive, sensual, and deliberate, like he's making love to my mouth, and I'm overcome with the need for him to run his expert tongue in… *other*… places.

He leans his forehead against mine and sucks in a sharp breath as he runs his hand up my inner thigh to toy with my panties.

It sends heat through my core and up to my nipples, hardening them, pointing toward him like a magnet.

I gulp, my nostrils flaring, and I study every inch of his hungry expression. In the kitchen earlier, he was a tad blurry since he removed my glasses, which I have to admit was freaking hot. I felt his heated touch just a little more heavily. His pants in my ear shot tingles down to my toes. Without my clear vision, I relied instead on my other senses, and with Carter, it was like I was being touched for the very first time.

Now, I can see him so clearly. Every vivid detail of his lust and desire for me is in his furrowed brows and cloudy hazel eyes that appear mostly whiskey brown right now.

This image of him is its own kind of special.

As if reading my mind, he says in a ragged voice, "I want to taste you this time. To make you squirm. To make you fucking scream. Do you want that too, Tessa?" He fingers the edge of my panties, a whisper away from my soaked center.

From where I need him the most.

"Tell me that's what you want," he says, his voice firm, yet full of something else.

A plea.

A needy gasp rips from my throat as goosebumps erupt down my legs.

"I'll take that as a yes." He shifts his weight and moves my panties to the side, inserting a finger inside me, making me nearly launch myself from the couch.

"Yes, yes," I pant, my eyes rolling into the back of my head.

"You're so damn beautiful," he whispers against my neck, placing open-mouthed kisses along my skin, down to my chest over my T-shirt.

I dig my fingers into his back, the couch, anywhere I can hold onto as he continues working me. My breathy moans mix with the quiet crackling of the fireplace as I squirm beneath the weight of him.

The tension builds as he takes me higher, but right before I explode, he pulls his finger out and slides down my body.

I blink, a protest locked and loaded on the tip of my tongue, but he doesn't give me the chance.

Because I see what he's doing, and oh…

Oh, dear God.

Carter freaking Fields is about to go down on me.

He pulls my panties off, and for every inch of me that he exposes, his eyes widen more and more. Once he chucks them to the side, he clenches his jaw like he can't contain himself.

He's about to devour me.

And maybe even… ruin me.

He slides onto the floor, pulling and maneuvering my legs off the couch and onto his shoulders so I'm sitting upright. Digging his fingers into my hips, he scoots me to the edge of the couch, much like he did with the counter before, and I'm at his mercy, more than ecstatic to be here.

He grunts and mumbles, but I can barely hear him over my labored pants and thundering heart.

My eyes closed, I feel his tongue lick up the seam of me, and I buck my hips off the couch, my trembling foot slipping.

He bends my leg and places my foot back on his shoulder, holding me in place with both hands, and I feel him smirk as he resumes swirling his tongue between my legs.

Carter's a cocky bastard, but he has every right to be.

His tongue knows more than most guys' should, like he's single-handedly bringing back a dead language with it.

It's magic.

I arch my back, slowly rocking my hips to his rhythm.

He alternates between licking and sucking at just the right spots, for the exact right amount of time to drive me toward the ledge, then gives me the right amount of space, leaving me wanting and begging.

Writhing.

I'm writhing under his touch, gripping the couch cushions, pillows, and blankets in a frenzy.

"Oh, right there," I say, breathless.

Heat creeps down my neck, spine, and to my core, waking every nerve ending on its way. I lift my hips the higher he takes me, searching for a mix of relief and pleasure.

At this angle and pace, his beard rubs against my sensitive skin, creating even more heady friction, and I can't freaking take it anymore.

"That's it," he murmurs, his deep voice reverberating through my pulsing heat.

I think I gasp.

Maybe scream.

I know I cry out his name at the same time I see each letter written in stars across a black canvas behind my eyelids.

"Oh my God, oh my God," I repeat several more times, riding out the waves of my blissful release.

It's the kind of climax that makes me wonder if I'm still alive.

If I'm breathing or dreaming.

The kind that scares and excites me.

Carter unhooks my ankles—*when did I lock my legs around his head?*—and sets my feet on the floor. He stands, licking his lips, leaving a glistening sheen across them, and it makes my own mouth water, especially when my gaze travels over his dimples, down to the solid V that disappears into his pants, which tent between his legs.

He's hard.

And I don't even think I can walk, let alone do anything else.

"Come here." Carter offers me his hand, a mischievous gleam in his eyes.

Or is it smug?

Either way, I don't care. He can gloat all he wants because we obviously both won.

I shake my head, my lungs working overtime to inhale and exhale. "Carter, I don't think… I can't…"

He bends down and takes my hands, hoisting me up. "You know what happens next, don't you?" He wiggles his brows, his lips twitching.

My eyelids flutter open, meeting his piercing gaze as his length pokes my stomach, making my posture straighten.

The girth of this man.

He nips at my lips and murmurs against them, "Now, you take a hot shower, and come back in here for more brownies and games."

I smile against him, kissing him more deeply and wrapping my arms around him. "On one condition."

He hums against me, running his hands up and down my sides, leaving me shuddering.

"You join me in the shower."

In a blink, he squats, circles his arms around my thighs, and tosses me over his shoulder. "I thought you'd never ask."

He spanks me before he sets me down on the tiled floor of my bathroom and gets to work on the water.

We discard the rest of our clothes, pulling them off each other like we can't survive otherwise, and for the rest of the evening, we make excellent use of our time alone.

Shower sex.

Strip poker, much to both our delights.

Fucking over the dining table, which will need to be bleached and possibly burned, much like the kitchen counter.

But I don't care about any of it.

I haven't been sexed up like this since… ever.

I'm too sated and elated to think clearly.

Long after the sun has set, and even the crickets have stopped singing, I fall asleep in Carter's arms with the biggest smile on my face, completely satisfied and spent.

This week hasn't been at all what I expected, but it's been a pleasant surprise.

Carter has been a pleasant surprise.

EIGHTEEN

Carter

"Turn to the left here, and their house is the second one on the right." Tessa points her slender, manicured finger toward a modest, single story home.

I pull my car into the driveway, coming to a stop close to a group of—are those *gnomes*? I squint at the tiny statues and their discolored hats and cheeks.

"Recognize some friends?" Tessa quirks her brow, smoothing her palms over her jean-clad thighs.

Thighs I spent the better part of yesterday and last night nipping and sucking on before burying myself between them.

I've never known such fucking paradise, and I've spent time on many islands, private and public. Nothing, not even the crystal blue waters of Greece and the fine wines of France and Italy, compares to having Tessa bare beneath me.

I tsk at her. "You know I have a strict code. I don't have friends with less than a few million dollars in their accounts. Sleepy and Happy over there probably only have a couple hundred."

She throws her head against the back of her seat, her petite frame shaking with laughter.

The sound, coupled with the sweet chocolatey smell of the pan of brownies in her lap, are almost too much to bear. It's all very… domestic.

On top of that, I'm sitting in my Maserati next to a few discolored gnomes, about to hand-deliver said brownies to the town's sheriff and his wife.

At their home.

Who even am I?

I meet Tessa around the car, grab the brownies from her, and offer my arm.

She thanks me, and once she's steady on both feet, she adjusts her sweater and spreads her hands out for the pan.

"No, no, no." I hold it out of her reach. "You wouldn't let me carry your backpack on our hike yesterday, so please let me do this today."

She chews the inside of her cheek and nods, then leads me up to the porch, walking so close our arms bump into each other.

I feel eyes on me and stare back at the lawn gnomes, whose gazes follow me to the front door. After Tessa knocks, I take in the weathered bricks surrounding the off-white door and turn toward the yard. "I've never seen any gnomes before in real life. Are they supposed to be this creepy?"

"Well, only if they're haunted." Tessa turns, following my gaze to the mini dwarfs by my car. "Judging by their level of creep factor, I'd say they're haunted by three-hundred-year-old ghosts with no nose or ears."

She snorts as the door swings open, revealing a woman around Tessa's height. Her plain straight hair sways as she pulls Tessa in for a hug, swinging her from side to side.

I stand back, furrowing my brows, suddenly concerned that I'm intruding.

Tessa squeals, hugging the woman back like this is a sorority sister reunion, but the woman seems to be thirty years older than Tessa, if not more.

"Oh my goodness, Tessa, you get prettier and prettier every time I see you," the woman gushes, her New Britain accent immediately distinctive when she says "prettier" without enunciating the Ts. "Come on in. I want to know everything. How are your parents? And Graham—has he settled down with a nice girl yet, or are we going to have to call in the big guns?"

We cross the threshold, and I find myself laughing at what could possibly be the meaning of *big guns*.

Tessa pulls me toward the couch, and before I sit, I offer the kind woman the pan of brownies.

"You two are such sweethearts." She gives me a once-over like she's noticing me for the first time, and her lips tilt in one corner. "And who might you be?"

"Mrs. Thompson, meet Carter. He's staying with us at the cabin for a few days." Tessa waves toward me.

"Glad to meet you." I take her free hand in mine and give it a gentle shake.

"Likewise. Please, call me Trina, as I've told her to do many times." She winks at Tessa, who remains quiet in her spot on the couch. "I'll be right back with drinks. Soda all right? I have some white wine from the vineyard down south. Eugene and Kyle brought it when they came to visit last weekend. Haven't even opened it yet."

I scan the living room, finding pictures of two men on the walls and scattered on the shelves of the entertainment center. From the looks of it, Eugene and Kyle are their sons.

Tessa waves her hands. "Absolutely not necessary. Soda would be great. Do you need any help?"

Trina makes her way to the kitchen, calling over her shoulder, "No, no. Make yourselves comfortable."

I sit next to Tessa, my knee bumping hers, and once Trina is out of sight and earshot, I lean over to kiss Tessa's cheek, taking in her sweet perfume. "You smell like roses."

"And you're practically inhaling me." Her breath is warm on my chin, and it reminds me of all the ways I made her pant yesterday and this morning.

I grasp her thigh, reveling in the mental images of her soft, bare curves.

My jaw tightens as I grind out, "I'll haul you right back to the cabin to do—"

"There are the kids," Sheriff Thompson announces, spreading his arms.

Tessa and I jump apart, and I glimpse her blushing cheeks. "Sheriff, hi. Good to see you again," she says in a throaty voice.

He takes a seat across from us in a recliner that nearly swallows his lanky frame, and he wears the same uniform he had on when Tessa called him the other day. "It's better to see you two under these circumstances instead of the last time." His chuckle is deep and raspy, and if I had to guess, I'd say he's a smoker.

We join in his laughter before Tessa introduces me, and Trina reenters with a tray of drinks for us all, along with a small plate of brownies, which she places on the coffee table between us. "Help yourselves."

"You didn't have to do all this," Tessa gushes as if we're receiving Dom Pérignon in crystal flutes.

It's one of the things I've come to enjoy and appreciate about Tessa. As I've said from the beginning, she's real and genuine.

She's down-to-earth, yet… *more*. Her heart is pure fucking gold.

"It's been a while since I've had these," the sheriff beams as he heaves himself forward like he's never done an ab crunch in his life, his face red as he grabs a brownie from the tray. "So, what do you do, son?"

Tessa pats me on the back and says, "He's a billionaire. Poses for a few pictures. Cuts a few ribbons. Holds a few babies."

I stare at her in horror and start to do some damage control when Trina lets out a high-pitched giggle. "I knew you looked familiar!"

Tessa's face reddens until she finally explodes in a fit of laughter.

I rub my chin, and my leg bounces, suddenly nervous. I've been part of meetings with the richest people in the world, yet I'm squirrely meeting two people in a town I didn't even know existed before today. In the recesses of my mind, I know it's because these people are important to Tessa, and making a good impression is important.

I don't want to mess this up.

"Well played," I mumble to Tessa, shaking my head.

Trina and Sheriff Thompson ask questions of my travels, the number of private jets I own, and even how many suits are hanging in my closet. I'm especially relieved that they don't ask about the less than stellar media attention I've received lately.

Instead, the Thompsons ask general questions of my life that aren't the kind I'm asked when interviewed by the likes of *Good Morning America*, and it's oddly refreshing.

As we chat, I settle into my seat on their fabric couch, more comfortable than I was when I first sat down, but more than that—I'm having fun.

When I arrived at the cabin a few days ago, I didn't know how I'd manage without my cars, clubs, and office, but Tessa's made everything—even baking—fun.

In fact, I've barely checked my email in the last day. I don't think I've gone this long without doing so since the beginning of the millennium.

Tessa sets her half-empty glass of soda down and asks, "How are Eugene and Kyle? I haven't seen them in ages."

"Oh!" Trina grabs a picture from the end table and passes it to us. "Look at this. They went to Niagara Falls last month, and they absolutely loved it. Isn't it wonderful?"

I take the picture from Tessa. The same two men from the other pictures stare back at me. They stand on a boat with their arms around each other's shoulders, and behind them is a cloud of mist, through which I can make out a waterfall.

When I look more closely, I notice one of the men's features—almond-shaped eyes and round face. He's shorter than the other man too, but at the same time, they're physically similar. Pale skin tone, light brown hair, and bright smile.

"This is great," Tessa beams, pointing at the photo. "I've lived in New York all my life, and I've never been to Niagara Falls. I'm so jealous."

"Oh, you should definitely do it. I'll have the kids give you their tips when you do."

"If only I can find the time. Isn't that always how it goes?" Tessa jokes as she hands Trina back the picture frame.

"Don't I know it. With this one's crazy schedule"—she nudges the sheriff—"we never can seem to do anything fun outside the city limits. Thankfully, we get to live vicariously through the boys. They love their travels."

"They're doing it right, making time for trips and each other." Tessa swallows, then dips her head, but not before I glimpse her forced smile.

Fuck.

This week was supposed to be spent with her family, continuing traditions and having uninterrupted quality time.

Instead, they're running out of days to spend together.

And they're not the only ones running out of time.

Trina checks her dainty wristwatch and stands. "Heavens. Harry, you need to be at the station in thirty minutes."

"Already?" Sheriff stands, smoothing his hands over his uniform, and shuffles away, calling his goodbyes over his shoulder.

"We should be going as well. My brother is supposed to be arriving soon, as are my parents." Tessa and I both smile at Trina and thank her for the pleasant visit.

I walk back to my car in a daze, confused with how drastically my life's changed over the last few days. But when I glance at Tessa in my passenger seat, I'm not hating this version of it.

In fact, I'm growing extremely fond of it.

By the time we return to the confines of the cabin, though, my stomach is in knots.

Graham and their parents should be arriving today. We won't be alone anymore. Where does that leave us?

NINETEEN

Carter

"**I** haven't even given you a birthday present," I say from behind Tessa as I close the door to the cabin twenty minutes after we left Trina's.

She spins around to face me, tapping her chin. "That's right. You haven't. What the hell? You only using me for my body?"

"It's only fair, since that's what you're doing with me." I narrow my gaze, smirking.

I step toward her, engulf her in my embrace, and plant my mouth on hers—I've been dying to do so all morning. Against her lips, I murmur, "I think I know how to make it up to you, though."

I slide my hands down to her ass and squeeze, making her yelp.

Her body jolts into me like it can't help but be flush against me.

Right when I'm about to slide my hand up her shirt, a ringing phone pulls us apart, the vibrations buzzing against my leg from her purse. She opens the flap to retrieve it and holds the screen out toward me. "It's Graham."

As she answers the call, I move toward the fireplace and turn the knobs. Once it comes to life, hot flames warming my cheeks, I look over my shoulder, and Tessa watches me from the kitchen with appreciation.

She doesn't seem to be paying any attention to the phone call.

Idly, I scratch my chest, underneath which my heart beats rapidly.

"Yes. Hi. I'm listening," she says into the phone, then clears her throat, blinking. "What? Nothing."

I stretch my arms over my head as I make my way toward her, my hands itching to touch her. As I move closer, her bulging eyes travel down to my stomach. Once I reach her, I weave my arms around her waist and hold on tight, like we're about to freefall out of a plane.

Resting my cheek on her shoulder, I hear Graham's voice through the speaker. "How's Carter treating you? He's not so bad, right?"

Tessa relaxes into me, her body warm and tantalizing, and I glimpse the soft smile playing on her perfect lips. I don't miss the blush on her cheeks, either, as I await her response.

"He's, um… fine," she croaks.

I nip at her shoulder, and in the back of my mind, I know I should step away out of respect. But Graham is miles away.

I've known him long and well enough to sense he wouldn't be calling if he were close.

It's still just Tessa and me. No prying eyes or responsibilities here. No room for who I am outside these walls.

Here, I'm a new man.

"What about you? Are you on your way?" Tessa asks into the phone as she runs the tip of her finger up my forearm while I place kisses on her neck, breathing her in.

I feel her shoulders deflate when Graham's sigh echoes loud and clear from the speaker—as I suspected.

I stand upright but don't remove my hands from her as she says, "Graham, you promised."

His response is muffled, and I work my jaw back and forth, waiting for her to confirm what I'm predicting.

She takes a deep breath. "Do what you need to do." Pause. "All right." Another pause. "Sure."

Once she ends the call, she tosses her phone onto the counter with a thud and sags against me, her back to my front.

"What's going on?" I whisper in her hair, fingering the hem of her sweater, her skin smooth and hot underneath.

She makes a sound somewhere between a hum and moan as I dip my fingers into the waistband of her jeans, finding the top of her cotton panties.

Before I even reach any lower, I know she's soaked for me.

That's Tessa—insatiable.

"Anything I can do to replace that frown with a smile?" I ask, my voice hoarse as I slip my fingers inside her panties, and she shudders against me.

With the tip of one finger, I draw circles on the tight bundle of nerves between her legs, and she wiggles her ass against me, my name a plea on her lips.

When her tongue darts out to run across her pouty bottom lip, it occurs in slow motion. Like she's savoring this thing between us, just as I am.

She raises her arm up and over her head to thread her fingers through my thick hair, her whimpers soft and melodious.

"You're already doing it." Her sigh is content and full of desire, her voice a heady whisper.

I turn her in my arms and capture her lips with mine, cupping her cheek in my large palm. Sucking her bottom lip between my teeth, I revel in the sweet taste of her, gripping the back of her neck tighter.

She opens for me to delve my tongue inside to explore hers.

And I lose myself there.

By early afternoon, I'm wrapped around Tessa in more ways than one.

Her leg is tossed over both of mine, and her arm is draped over my midsection. She's tucked into my side like there's nowhere else she'd rather be, and I know the feeling.

It blooms in my chest like the fucking rose bushes outside.

Even more terrifying than me, Carter Fields, thinking about flowers, is that I want to keep her here. With me. Something I've never wanted before in all my adult life.

"Tell me more about the sheriff and his family. What are their sons like?" I ask, staring at the ceiling of Tessa's room as I absentmindedly run my fingers through her hair. I barely graze her shoulder when I reach the ends and start over again.

She smiles against my chest, obviously happy to talk about their sons. "They're good people, and I don't mean just kind and generous. They're an honest family with hearts the size of New York."

I nod. "I could tell from the moment she opened the door."

I feel her smile grow wider against my hot skin. "Their sons, Kyle and Eugene, are twins. Kyle was born with Down Syndrome, but Eugene wasn't." She leans up on her elbow, resting her cheek in her palm. "They're adopted too."

"Really?" I tilt my head to the side to get a better look at her.

"Trina's told us the story. She and Harry found out they couldn't have kids early in their marriage, and they agreed on adoption. They were on a waitlist for years before they were put in contact with a nonprofit organization that seeks loving homes for orphaned kids with Down Syndrome. They raise money and offer grants to the families too and organize a lot of really admirable events and campaigns to raise awareness."

"That's amazing." I sit up too, excited energy coursing through me—such an organization is exactly in my area of expertise.

"It is." She gulps, her smile growing watery. "Trina and Harry adopted Kyle and Eugene with the assistance of the nonprofit, and they never looked back. It's really... I don't know. *Heartwarming* isn't a strong enough word."

"I agree," I whisper and meet her gaze.

The longer we stare at each other, an idea forms in my head, and I have one of those *Aha!* moments.

"Do you remember the name of the nonprofit they worked with?" I ask.

"Darby's Dreamers," she answers immediately. "It's run by a family who adopted Darby when she was three. She'd lost her parents in an accident a year before that and didn't have extended family to take her in. She was in foster care until the Loffley couple found her. They started the organization a couple years after that to help other families like theirs."

The wheels in my head turn, stirring up a plan, and my mind races to mentally create flow charts and to-do lists.

When Tessa gets up to use the restroom, I pull up my email on my phone, skipping over the numerous new ones I'll have to pour over soon, and send a quick one to my assistant to research Darby's Dreamers. I add a note for her to find contact information for the Loffleys as well. Yara immediately responds that she'll have everything ready, and we can go over it when I get back to the city.

The city.

I stare into space in the direction Tessa disappeared, and a wave of nausea overcomes me.

I should be excited to get back home where a chef prepares my meals, Trevor brings the car around for me, and Whitney washes my dishes.

Instead, I dread not eating cheap frozen lasagna and scrubbing off tomato sauce from tacky floral plates at the sink with Tessa.

She lives in the city, though. I'll still see her. We can remain friends.

Right?

I sit back, resting my head on the pillow, and my stomach sinks worse than it did the time I had to run my first meeting for the company at twenty-two years old.

I was a confident—more like *arrogant*—twenty-two-year-old, but when I stood in front of a group of adults in a million-dollar conference room, I was reduced to a ball of nerves.

"What's that look for?" Tessa tiptoes back into the room like she'll spook me otherwise.

I shake my head, a sudden lump in my throat clogging the words I need to say.

Stay with me.

Be with me.

Love me.

Even though we still have her brother to worry about.

Even though I'm not equipped or in a position to have a real relationship, especially with someone as unique and special as Tessa.

But how can I risk destroying something so fucking good?

"Nothing," I croak. "Come here."

TWENTY

Tessa

I blink awake, half my view blocked by a floral comforter.

A strong arm is wrapped around my bare stomach.

I crane my neck toward the ceiling and squirm onto my side, watching Carter next to me.

The glow of the flames from the fireplace next to us illuminate his sleeping form.

His slow breaths are even and carefree, strangely comforting me. He grumbles but stays asleep, his nose twitching like I'm tickling him with a feather.

The sight makes my heart flutter.

I glance around—how did we end up on the floor of the living room? And when did we grab the comforter and sheets from my bedroom? We're tangled up in them, sprawled on the floor in a heaping pile of sexy chaos.

I sigh, fully waking myself. When was the last time I took a nap? Or felt this relaxed and rejuvenated?

When was the last time I took a nap with a guy I really liked?

My abs clench as I pull myself up, grab my glasses from the coffee table, and rest my back against it, recalling how wild Carter was for me earlier. It all rushes back to me.

We started in my bedroom.

His firm, yet tender fistfuls of my ass in his palms.

The way he sucked on my nipples as if it was his mission in life to ruin me for any other man.

We rattled the metal headboard so hard, I eventually pulled us onto the floor to avoid putting a hole through the wall.

Then, we switched it up for round two, landing in a hot mess of kisses on the floor of the living room, wrapped in the comforter and each other.

After quenching our needs, we promptly passed out.

I touch my swollen lips as I watch him sleep.

Even recalling his caress puts me at ease, and I lose myself to thoughts of the last couple days.

His sleeping form is peaceful, sending any lingering distress flying from my mind like a twig in a tornado.

It's what Carter is. He appeared in my life seemingly out of thin air and took over my mind and body, slowly breaking into my heart without my permission.

After Graham called to say he'd be late again, I was barely upset. All I could think was that his and my parents' delayed arrival meant more time alone with Carter.

The truth is, I would've been more pissed about their absence had things not *worked out* between Carter and me. Instead, I've been enjoying my birthday in ways I never expected.

What I'm not enjoying is the nagging thought of what happens when Graham and my parents actually get here. What happens to Carter and me once our bubble bursts from the needle of reality?

Carter comes to, squinting up at me, his back muscles flexing as he raises his head. "Where are we? What day is it? And what did you give me?"

"What did I give you?" I repeat, tilting my head and holding the sheet around my naked chest.

"Yes. I'm too weak and exhausted to have only been sexed up. You had to have given me some kind of drug."

"Funny because I was going to say the same about you." I shimmy down and bite his bare shoulder, smiling around it as I peek up at him.

"Kinky." He hums. "I can be into that. Maybe bite my ass? Smack me a little?"

I roll my eyes and am about to respond when my phone buzzes on the coffee table behind my head. Reaching for it, I exhale, then answer.

"We're in Connecticut!" Mom squeals, and instead of reciprocating her enthusiasm, my chest sinks.

"Oh, that's… great." I avert my gaze from Carter and shift, clutching the sheet tighter around me like it's a wall. A barrier between me and his piercing gaze.

But it's a fragile attempt.

I can feel his gaze on me, following every small move I make.

"There was a mix-up with our rental car. They canceled our reservation after the debacle with the flights, and they don't have anything available until this evening. Don't worry, though, because your father is handling it."

I gulp. "How is Dad?"

"Well, the flight and air pressure increased the swelling of his knee and ankle, but we iced it immediately upon landing. He's managing."

"Oh my gosh. What can I do?" I furrow my brows, holding my hand out like she's in front of me.

"Nothing, sweetie. Just hang tight. We'll be driving a shiny Honda in no time and will be there soon."

"Okay. Be safe."

I hang up and stare out the window, focusing on nothing in particular as my mind drifts.

"Hey," Carter says, his voice soothing. There's shuffling behind me as he rises up and kisses my shoulder.

I close my eyes, committing his touch to memory.

I'm sore in all the right places.

Satisfied.

Yet, knowing we're about to be bombarded by more people in this cabin makes me feel like none of it's enough. Like I need to make the next couple hours count before it all comes crashing down.

I shift to my knees and crawl down between his legs, licking my lips, needing him again.

"Tessa…" He sucks in a sharp breath, then lets out a strangled growl.

I tug his boxers down, freeing his hard length, and wrap my lips around it, taking him until his head reaches the back of my throat.

My eyes sting with tears as I lick my way back up his shaft and take him again.

Carter makes a noise, something between a surprised shudder and a pleased groan, as I bob my head up and down at a comfortable pace, enjoying the taste of him.

Roughly exhaling, he fists my hair, and it drives me to suck him harder, grazing his tender skin with my teeth.

His hips jolt upward, making me moan, enjoying this as much as he seems to be.

I let go of him with a pop and trace my tongue up his shaft again like I would an ice cream cone, leaving his body trembling.

"You're going to kill me, Tessa." His gruff voice is strangled and hot and sexy.

"That's the plan." I wink, then wrap my lips around his thick head once again, reveling in this effect I have on him. Having a man like Carter at my mercy gives me power I've never known.

I feel drunk.

Addicted.

He tightens his hold on my hair as I continue going down on him, my saliva covering his length and making it glisten.

It's the kind of girth romance novels are made of.

Panting, he thrusts his hips upward until his abs tighten, and he pulls me off him with a slight nudge to my shoulder. "I'm not coming until you do."

I gasp when he puts both his hands under my arms and hoists me up to straddle his narrow waist.

His eyes are ablaze and even brighter with the fireplace turned on behind me.

The warmth licks my back, adding to the heat of Carter's touch as he rubs my bare thighs on either side of him.

Eyes locked on mine, Carter reaches over to the scattered condoms on the floor and hands me one.

Once he's sheathed, I position him at my entrance, sink down, and take him until he's nestled deep inside me.

"Jesus," he hisses, then reaches up to tuck my hair behind my ears. "I want to see you."

I'm trembling—the way he's looking at me makes me tremble with need and pleasure.

"You are so fucking beautiful, Tessa," he whispers. "Inside and out."

I lick my lips, still tasting him there, and let his words sink in as he grips my hips.

Unable to wait any longer, I move, lifting up and crashing down with a vigorous rhythm. I bounce, taking him over and over again until my vision becomes spotty, my glasses fogging up.

I yank them off and toss them aside as I continue riding him, my leg muscles burning with purpose.

At one point, we're moving so fiercely I bite the tip of my tongue, but I don't stop. I can't, not with Carter, and instead, I merely let the sting fuel my movements.

I'm wild.

If I thought going down on him gave me power before, this is on a different level. The way he keeps his attention on me without blinking—it's electric.

Small beads of sweat trail down my back, and heat from the fireplace warms me further.

It's too much. This connection is unlike anything I've ever experienced, and I'm about to combust.

"Carter!" I draw out his name at a decibel I didn't think my voice could reach as my climax rips through me with sudden voracity.

His fingers dig into my hips as he takes over, thrusting upward and chasing his own release. His pants come out in small puffs until his abs and leg muscles flex beneath me, followed by a string of curses that sound more like praise as he finds his own bliss.

Wiping the corners of my mouth, I'm spent and throw myself onto the floor, unable to sit up any longer. I tuck myself into his side as he lets out a deep and satisfied exhale.

"Good morning," I whisper, nipping at his earlobe.

"If every morning started like this, I'd be a lot happier about being up so early." He turns toward the window, squinting seemingly at the soft glow of the setting sun. "Also, it's not morning."

I giggle. "No, but I feel like our nap was a whole night's worth. I'm exhausted."

"You're welcome." He smirks.

"So arrogant," I tease right when my stomach growls. "Oh my God, I need food."

"You're not stuffed? I figured I would've been enough to—"

"There you go again." I stand, unable to stop the giggle that escapes me. "Come on. My family will be here soon. I need to eat, change, and straighten up the living room. We tore through there like the F train."

He groans, his head lulling to the side, then points down at his filthy state. "I need to clean up, but I'll meet you in the kitchen in six minutes on the dot."

"That's specific." I study him.

He shrugs, his narrowed eyes full of mischief. "*Six* sounds a lot like *sex*, so…"

I throw my head back. "See? This is why I called you a man-child, and I'm never taking it back."

He reaches up and grabs my sides, pulling me down to the floor again, where he tickles my stomach. "Take it back, or else."

"No!" I manage over my high-pitched squeals, my face surely red from laughing so hard.

"I won't stop until you apologize." His fingers dig into my sides, tickling the life out of me. I'm ten times louder than if he'd tickled the Pillsbury Doughboy.

"Okay, okay!" I smack at him, struggling to breathe. "I'm sorry! You're so mature and not at all childish."

"Much better." He withdraws his fingers, sitting back with a smug expression.

"Ass," I mutter as I stand to locate my glasses, which earns me a spank on my own ass. I yelp, spinning in place to flip him off, but I pause.

Sliding my glasses onto my nose, my breath catches as I take in his current state on the floor. The sheets are rumpled around him, barely covering his body. The veins running alongside the V down to his cock, which stands at attention, tenting the sheets there.

My gaze travels up from there to his droolworthy abs to where his bent arm rests behind his head. The best parts? His twinkling hazel eyes zeroed in on me and his twitching lips.

It's a dreamy expression that makes my heart flutter.

Inhaling to steady my voice, I say, "I'm timing you, and if you're late, I can't promise there will be any food left for you."

"I'm on it." He jumps up, revealing his entire naked body, and rushes to the bathroom while I stare after him, mouth agape.

Carter Fields knows how to make a girl blush.

And scream.

My cheeks flushed, I grab his T-shirt from the edge of the couch and pull it over my head before I ball the sheets and comforter up from the floor, then take them to my room. The shower sounds from my bathroom as I fling the sheets onto my bed, followed by the comforter. Once I smooth them all out, I return to the important task of feeding us.

I make it three feet across the living room when the front door of the cabin swings open.

"Graham!" I come to a stumbling stop in front of my smiling, oblivious brother.

"Hey, sis." He shuts the door behind him, cutting off the cold air from outside, and sets a duffel bag beside his feet. "I left earlier than planned so I wouldn't get stuck at work all day again. I know how important this is to you, and it is to me too. I sent you a text…" His voice trails off when he takes in my appearance.

Oh my God.

I tug at the hem of Carter's shirt, embarrassed I'm only wearing panties underneath. Red panties that are visible through this white T-shirt.

Red panties that Graham's best friend tossed aside before he—

Oh. My. God.

Graham furrows his brows, blinking at me like he doesn't recognize me.

I put my arms out and explain. "Okay, listen, Carter and I got to talking, and we just—please don't be mad."

He blinks faster, and it seems like he doesn't even see me at all.

"Graham?" I wave my hand in front of his face, but it's followed by silence.

Silence that stretches for what feels like hours.

"Graham, stop overthinking this." I step toward him. "Carter and I—"

"Baby, want me to make you a drink—" When Carter sees Graham, he jumps like he's been electrocuted. "Hey… man… What's up, bro?" He fidgets with his stance, his hands moving from his hips up to cross over his bare chest and back down to his hips.

I grimace, pulling my shirt down again. I don't think I've ever been this embarrassed in my life. Not even Julie Carlisle pulling up my skirt during my Christmas pageant solo when I was nine was this humiliating.

Graham doesn't take his eyes off me—his now unblinking eyes.

I hold my hands up, my words coming out in one breath when I say, "Graham, we didn't plan this, and we don't want this to be weird for you, but Carter and I are adults. We hit it off, and one thing led to another."

"What the fuck?" Graham turns his lethal glare toward Carter. "This is my *sister*." He seethes, pointing at me like Carter might not know who I am.

"I know, and like she said, we didn't plan this. It happened. I really like her."

"Oh, you like her? Well, I sure hope so since you *slept* with her. Then again, how can I believe you when you fuck people you don't even know all the time?" Graham lets out an incredulous laugh that makes me cringe. It sounds nothing like him.

I clutch my stomach as nausea rolls through it like waves of the ocean and turn toward Carter.

"It's not like that with Tessa." He steps in front of me, facing Graham.

"Then, what is this? What does this mean?" Graham points between us, his tone stern as though he's giving us a pop quiz that we better not fail.

"We haven't decided on…" My voice trails off as my nerves get the best of me. I shake myself out of it and square my shoulders. "We haven't discussed it yet."

"Yeah. We haven't had a chance. A little busy—"

I smack Carter in the side, glaring at him. "What are you doing?" I hiss, stepping around him to face Graham.

"Fantastic," Graham says, his sarcasm dripping like the rain outside as he turns to Carter. "How could you do this? My own sister. What part of *she's off-limits* did you not understand? Because at our reunion, I was definitely talking to you. Not the rest of the guys. *You.*"

"What?" Carter frowns, standing back.

Graham puts his hands on his hips and turns toward me, his chest heaving. "And you. It took, what, a few days to fall for his bullshit? You're smarter than that. It's why you left that asshole Wyatt. I thought you wanted someone for the long haul, and that's not Carter. Trust me."

My chest sinks as the reality I've tried to block out slowly settles in, crushing my heart. "You don't know what you're talking about," I say weakly.

"Oh? From where I'm standing, I'm the only one who knows what the fuck I'm talking about." He grabs me by the shoulders and gives me a little shake. "Open your eyes. Carter's not going to give a shit about you the second he leaves this cabin, and you deserve better than that."

"I do care about you, Tessa, and that's the truth." Carter attempts to step between us, but Graham shrugs him off.

"Okay, then, Mr. Boyfriend of the Year," Graham snaps at him. "Tell us, how many girlfriends did you have last year? Or ever? And I do mean, *actual* girlfriends. Women you dated for longer than a couple hours. When was the last monogamous relationship you had with a real woman and not just hook-ups whose names you don't even remember the next day?"

I place both my hands over my aching chest like I'm trying to keep my heart from leaping out. It's pumping so quickly that it might just flop to the floor in a pile of mush.

Carter holds Graham's stare for a tense moment before he hangs his head. "I may have never been in a relationship before, but fuck, Graham, give me some credit. I would never do anything to betray your trust, but I really like her."

Graham scoffs, pinching the bridge of his nose. "This is why I never wanted you two to meet. I knew. I just fucking *knew* you wouldn't keep your grubby hands off her. You always want what you can't have. The shiny new thing. The shiny *good* thing. And Tessa? She's way too damn good for you."

"Wait. Back up," I say at the same time Carter asks, "What do you mean?"

I hold my hands up, then point at my brother. "You didn't want us to meet?"

Graham turns his hurt expression toward me, and I drown in the knots in my stomach. "No. I purposely dodged any dinner we were supposed to have in order to protect you, sis. Carter's a good friend—he *was*, anyway." He grips the back of his neck. "But I knew you'd get your heart broken. I couldn't stop Wyatt from hurting you, but I did everything I could to keep it from happening again."

I try to take a deep breath, but the lump in my throat gets in the way, making me choke.

I sit on the couch, trying to gather my thoughts, and Carter moves toward me. Two steps and Graham places a hand on his chest to stop him. "Tessa, please, let me—"

The front door swings open, hitting Graham in the back and causing him to lurch forward.

"Oh my goodness!" My mom fumbles with her bags, trying to close the door again. "Are you okay, sweetie? I'm so sorry."

"What's going on?" my dad's voice sounds from behind her. "I'm getting soaked. What's blocking the door?"

"Of course. Sorry, dear." Mom whacks Carter in the back of his knees with her bag as she spins out. "Oh! Sorry."

"Graham? What're you just standing there for?" my dad asks. "Help your mother."

"I'm trying to," Graham grinds out as Mom continues in circles, elbowing his arm in the process like she's stuck in a tight sweater. "Mom… Mom… Please stop moving."

Carter moves toward Graham's bedroom, and when he returns, he has a shirt on. I bury my face in my hands and sink into the couch—at this point, I'd make it worse if I tried to assist.

My dad finally enters the living room, the door shut behind him and his coat dripping onto the forest green rug. He lets out something between a sigh and a grunt. "Ah, this place never changes, and I love it. This will be yours someday, you know, kids?"

I push the hair out of my face and glare at Graham, whose fists are balled at his sides. When he stares back at me, I expect to find anger in his expression, but I'm surprised to find remorse.

For what? For Carter and I sleeping together, or for not trying hard enough to keep us apart?

Because the truth is, he's right. I don't know what I'm doing with Carter, and I don't know his intentions, either. I didn't ask or care because I chased the connection we formed the moment I ran into him at the coffee shop, before I even knew who he was.

I did the same with Wyatt.

I jumped headfirst into a relationship with him and got clobbered because I ignored all logic and followed my heart.

Did I do it again? Was I so naïve to believe Carter's different?

I've convinced myself he is, but at the end of the day, Carter Fields is Manhattan's notorious billionaire playboy. I'm Tessa Rollins, Brooklynite career counselor. Although I'm doing well for myself, I'm nowhere near Carter's league.

This cabin has been our safety net.

The real world of Manhattan would chew us up and spit us out.

My mind is foggy and confused, and dread fills every crevice of my body.

"Happy birthday, sweetie!" Mom lets Graham take her bags, and he pushes them to rest against the wall. Free of luggage, she holds her arms out to me.

I drag my feet toward her and fall into her embrace, my gaze meeting Carter's hooded one over her shoulder.

The last few days had to have been real... right?

"Thanks, Mom," I say in a robotic tone.

"Let me get a good look at you." She squeezes both my arms, studying me up and down like she hasn't seen me all year, even though we had lunch two weeks ago. Her smile is warm and proud, seemingly uncaring that I'm only in a T-shirt and panties as long as I'm healthy.

Some of her therapist colleagues whom I've met over the years are a bit cold and guarded, always assessing and analyzing people like they're on the clock twenty-four-seven. A handful of their kids are essentially robots with a pulse, much like Sheldon of *The Big Bang Theory*.

Not my mom, though. When she walked through the doors of our home every evening, she was kind and loving and generous. We baked homemade pizzas every Thursday night.

Had ice cream every Sunday.

Planned trips to the park when weekends were sunny, and the museums when it was raining.

Right now, though, her comfort and understanding aren't enough to put me at ease.

The tension in the room is suffocating, especially when my dad nods to Carter. "Good to see you again, son."

My mom turns around and opens her arms for him. "Carter! It's so lovely to see you again, and I look forward to catching up this week."

"Don't bother," Graham practically growls. "He's not staying."

"What?" My dad finishes putting his drenched coat on the rack by the door and faces us, hands on his hips. "I heard you're a good poker player and was hoping to find out for myself."

Carter grimaces. "Maybe next time, sir."

"He really should be going." Graham crosses his arms like he's a cheesy bodyguard about ready to throw him out and bark at him to *stay out*.

"We should talk," Carter says to me, his tone soft and pleading.

"Haven't you done enough?" Graham steps forward, but I place my hand on his chest to keep him from going any farther.

"Would you let up? I can handle myself just fine. This isn't elementary school." I nod to my mom, whose mouth hangs open, and I force a smile for my dad.

Carter tightens his jaw, and I pull his arm into Graham's room, where Carter's clothes litter the bed and floor. We were too busy to clean the mess we made in just about every room.

I was going to straighten up before everyone arrived, but I got distracted—by Carter and the way he makes me feel.

But has it been real?

That's the question I keep asking myself, and I don't have an answer. How do two people like us make it beyond the walls of this cabin?

"Tessa, you have to believe me. These last few days meant something to me. I wasn't just passing the time. You're more than just a good time. Please believe me."

"I do." I twiddle my thumbs in front of me.

His shoulders sag with relief.

"Do you still want to know why I didn't give you my phone number at the coffee shop the other day?" I whisper.

"What? What does that have to do with this?"

"Everything." I give him a sad smile. "There was something about you. A familiarity that went beyond any pictures I found on the internet. Beyond anything Graham told me about you. We had a connection."

He nods like he knows exactly what I'm talking about.

"I had a similar feeling with someone before. I was swept off my feet like this. But it was too good to be true." I lift my teary gaze to meet his. "It was because of what I thought was a special connection that I kept taking Wyatt back after he'd screw up. He'd have a new girl's number in his phone every other day and claim it was an Uber driver or a new co-worker.

He'd forget we made plans and stand me up repeatedly. I kept making excuses for him, dating him on and off for a year until I realized we were merely wrong for each other. All we had was a moment in time, seduced by the fantasy of it all."

"I'm not Wyatt."

"I know that." I grimace. "This is harder and more complicated."

Carter curses under his breath, spinning in place before he stills in front of me again, his eyes anguished.

And I'm so close to yanking my glasses off so I don't have such a clear picture of his pain. It's too much.

My voice is watery when I say, "You and I are too different. I mean, what happens when we leave here? When you go back to your life in New York and date supermodels? How will this thing between us be enough?"

He shakes his head, laughing, but there's no trace of humor in it. "So, that's what this is about. It has nothing to do with *us*, and everything to do with *me*."

"That's not what I'm saying." I step forward, but he holds up his hand.

"No, I get it. I'm a player. I'm too much of a loose cannon. I'm no good for you—got it."

I exhale, but it does nothing to calm the frustration bubbling up my throat, causing tears to sting the corners of my eyes.

"You're right. Graham's right." He brushes past me and picks his bag up off the floor. "I'll get my stuff and be out of here before I taint any more of your life."

"Carter, stop!"

"You know"—he spins toward me—"you might've felt a connection like this before, but I haven't." He points between us, his lips a thin line.

"What're you saying, then? Huh?" I raise my voice as a tear escapes down my cheek, and I swipe at it angrily. "You want to date me? You want to do the whole bit—dating, marriage, kids? Is that what you want? Because if it is, tell me now, and I'll deal with Graham."

Carter stares back at me, pain flashing across his unusually dark expression.

My nerves get the best of me, and I shove him back, my palms on his warm chest—the same chest I trailed my fingertips down just moments ago before all hell broke loose.

"Is it what you want?" I push him again. "Tell me!"

Standing back and my arms falling to my sides, I hold my breath for his response.

An answer I receive with his silence.

I back away, emotions clogging my throat. "That's what I thought."

I spin on my heel to hide the second tear slipping down my cheek, and without another word or glance backward, I leave his room. Keeping my head ducked down, I disappear into my own room, leaving pieces of my heart with Carter.

A few minutes later, I hear muffled voices in the living room, followed by the door slamming shut.

He's gone.

Carter Fields stormed into my life in a blink and left just as quickly. But it was enough.

It was enough to leave a lasting impression. One I don't know how I'll shake myself of.

Even though I don't want to rid myself of him. Of the warmth he left in my heart. It's why I was prepared to fight for him and for us.

I was going to stand tall in front of Graham and tell him

he wouldn't be the reason Carter and I wouldn't have a future.

As it turns out, Graham wasn't the problem this entire time. It was us.

And that devastating realization is what has me curling into a ball on my disheveled bed, alone and crushed.

TWENTY-ONE

Carter

"**M**ore juice?" Cousin Daisy holds up a bottle of grape juice, and I stare laser beams through it, wishing like hell I could turn it into wine. "I'm sorry it's not wine."

Did I say that out loud? I couldn't have. My mouth is stuffed with French toast.

"We're not drinkers." She points to herself and her husband, Gary, on the other side of the table. "Plus, having two kids in the house who wander makes it hard to keep alcohol out of reach."

"Of course," I manage around the enormous bite I took in order to be done with this torturous brunch.

Not because of Daisy and Gary, who's just finished describing to me the parts of a boat.

My sour mood is because of the French toast.

Tessa said her mom makes the best and that it's a staple of their cabin visits.

But I'll never know the taste of them.

It's been three days since I left the cabin, and I want the damn French toast.

Gary points at me, drawing my attention back to the table. "Carter, have you been fishing lately? Try any new spots since I last saw you?"

Daisy and Gary are the closest relatives to me, yet I rarely ever see them.

The last time would've been Christmas almost two years ago when my parents hosted the holiday dinner at their estate in Martha's Vineyard.

I wipe my mouth with a napkin, debating whether I should tell him I switched fishing for golf years ago, but I decide against crushing his spirit. "I haven't been in a while."

His grin spreads slowly, like he's stepping up to bat with a joke. "I bet you're a MacDaddy lure kind of guy. Am I right? I'm the same. I can tell a fellow Daddy when I see one."

I open my mouth to respond, although I'm not sure how, when their kids appear by my side, asking for more juice.

They hold their cups out at the same time.

Once Daisy refills them, they retreat to the living room again.

I scoot my chair back across the rug and stand. "I'm going to get some air, if that's all right."

"Of course. Take your time. When you get back, I have an interesting fact to share about estuaries. You're the kind of guy who'd appreciate it." Gary winks.

I force a smile and thank Daisy for brunch.

On my way out, I pass the kids, who sit at a play table in the corner of the living room. They look up to me at the same time and wave in sync.

It's like they're one person.

Furrowing my brows, I walk through the front door and pace the porch, then drop down the steps and round the house to the back.

Their house stands tall at three stories, turrets on both sides of the front, much like a modern castle. My mother helped them pick this house out years ago as a favor to her sister, Daisy's mother, who lives in Ireland with husband number five.

I've only met him once and didn't bother remembering his name since he likely wouldn't be around for long.

I reach the back of the house and pull out a chair by the pool, the wind blowing through my hair. The flower beds and landscaping are immaculate, and the heated pool is the perfect shade of deep blue—I expect nothing less from them. They take pride in that sort of thing.

I'm only surprised they don't have a pond in their backyard where Gary can live with the fish.

I pull my phone out, and my stomach instantly lurches when I don't see anything from Graham or Tessa. Not that they'd reach out, but I keep holding onto hope that they will.

I can't get Tessa's dejected expression out of my head. When I close my eyes at night, all I see are her quivering bottom lip and crushing disappointment in every feature.

Each cell in my body wanted to say yes.

When she asked if I wanted the whole shebang with her, I wanted to scream that I did, then take her in my arms and kiss her until there was no question left about my feelings for her.

But what are my feelings?

How is it possible to fall for someone in only a few days? Especially for someone like me.

No matter how big of an asshole Graham was about it, and I hate to admit it to myself, he was right.

The bastard.

I can't fault Graham for speaking the truth or for trying to protect his little sister. I'd do the same in his shoes, but it doesn't fucking sting any less.

As the breeze sweeps by, causing ripples over the water in the pool, my fingers tremble, itching to make a call. I surprise myself when I dial the number, like I'm floating outside my own body.

When there's an answer, a lump forms in my throat, making it difficult to speak.

"Son?" my father's voice rings out. "Son? You there?"

"Yes," I croak.

"I was just going to call you. I invited Landon Shanty to the charity dinner next weekend. He's a big proponent for a good cause. Did you know he's spent many hours volunteering for organizations who box food to be sent to North Africa and wants to—"

I barely hear what he says. "Why have you and Mom stayed married?" I blurt.

"What?" My father isn't often caught off guard. He's meticulous and prepared. He does his research before he goes anywhere, whether it's a meeting, lunch, or new country.

But I've surprised him.

The single syllable he utters is full of shock.

"You and Mom. Your marriage. When did it fall apart? And why do you both insist on keeping up pretenses?"

There's silence on his end, but I know he's listening.

"Dad, why do you insist *I* keep up the pretense?"

For the last week, since meeting Tessa, I've come to realize how much pretending has cost me. I've always known the connection between my parents wasn't the strongest or most ideal, but I pretended.

That they were in love.

A team.

Shared a special bond.

Even though I knew deep down that none of it was real.

It's the only example of a relationship I've ever been exposed to. Most of my Harvard friends' parents were divorced, separated, or openly having affairs. My parents and Graham's were the only ones still together, and I thought they had it figured out, although they weren't the same at all. I'd only met Graham's father a couple times before, but it was enough to know he and my father are nothing alike.

My parents' marriage is nothing like theirs, either.

But again, I pretended because I didn't want my world to implode, and it's all caught up to me now.

"Why, Dad?" I press, uncaring that I might not like the answer. I don't care that it might upset him, either, or that he might give me more of his exasperating sighs.

This is no longer just about him.

"This isn't a conversation we should be having over the phone, son."

"How else would we talk? The phone seems to be our only means of communication lately. Even when I'm at the office, down the hall from you, you call me to discuss business matters or what we're having for lunch. Like you can't look me in the eye anymore." I whisper the last part.

I didn't mean to say it.

I hadn't been thinking it.

It just came out.

A phone rings on his end—he's in his office. "I need to go, Carter. We'll talk soon."

I'm the one who sighs this time before I end the call, disappointed and frustrated.

I've never been one to place blame on others for my shortcomings—I know I'm screwed up, and I own up to my mistakes—but at this moment, I blame him. My father and my mother both. I blame them for my fucked-up notions of love and commitment.

Graham's brutal truth and Tessa's sad eyes flash through my mind for the millionth time.

I'm not good enough for his sister, and Graham will probably never forgive me, which is what I was afraid of all along.

But when I entered the living room the other day—when Graham caught us—a sense of relief settled inside me. Like seeing sunshine after days of rain. Graham knew about us. Tessa and I didn't have to hide like we did at the sheriff's house. We didn't have to be locked in that cabin.

And I was fucking happy.

Something in that split second told me everything would be okay, but I'm not sure I believe it anymore. Even if I could get my head out of my ass and wrap my mind around the feelings in my chest, I wouldn't know where to go from here.

TWENTY-TWO

Tessa

"I haven't seen you in forever." Bree sits at the table across from me, sipping her drink. Once she swallows, she forces out, "Spill."

I push my salad aside and adjust my glasses farther up on my nose. "It's only been a week."

"Yes, which is enough time for us to have switched toner suppliers at the office, for me to have gained three and a half pounds, and oh—Erin is now a vegetarian."

I drop my hands on the table with a thud. "No way. She eats cheeseburgers like they're chips."

"I know, but this guy she went out with over the weekend kept on and on about how terribly cows are treated and how unhealthy red meat is. She didn't sleep with him—he had a weird foot fetish—but she took his lecture to heart."

"Wow." I shake my head.

She wiggles her eyebrows. "I mean, he's not wrong, but I like meat too much, especially a man's—"

"Okay, I get it." I snort, glancing around the small café. "No need to give me visuals."

She holds her hands up in surrender. "Now, we only have thirty-two minutes left for our lunch break. When are you going to tell me about Carter Fields?"

"You can call him Carter. No need to double name him every time, you know." I try to smile, but it feels more like a grimace.

I'm back to reality, eating lunch with Bree at this rustic chic café, where we come at least twice a week. The pink flowers outside that are visible through the large windows used to make me smile before my trip to the cabin.

I haven't seen or talked to Carter since he left a week ago.

Graham hasn't mentioned him, and our parents didn't ask questions—not immediately, anyway. The day after their arrival, my mom cornered me in my room to ask me what happened, offering me a plate of warm and delicious French toast as a bribe.

I'd come out of the bathroom, a towel on my head, to find her sitting on my bed, her back against the headboard. She was all too comfortable and ready to spend hours discussing Carter.

And it didn't take long for me to crack.

I told my mom I have feelings for Carter. That he and I share something special, and I might even be falling for him.

I told her about Graham's harsh outburst and how Carter left soon after. That he didn't have the gall to look me in the eye before he did so, either.

It was a relief to get it all off my chest and talk to my mom, but not even three plates of French toast and her mature advice to be patient with Carter helped.

I'm freaking hopeless.

I'm still raw and vulnerable as I relay the bulleted version of the quick but painful story to Bree, who leans forward, leaving her salad untouched. She nods and gasps at all the expected moments and lets me ramble on for what feels like hours.

By the end, I'm deflated—and I still have half a day of work to get through.

"He hasn't even drunkenly called or texted you?" Bree purses her lips.

"No." I toy with my nearly empty glass of water, drawing circles in the dew with the tip of my finger. "It's like I didn't mean anything to him."

Her face falls, and next to our plates on the table, her phone pings with a notification. "Shit, I thought I turned this off. Let me—oh my God."

"What?" I crane my neck to get a better look, but she swipes it off the table like it's a grenade.

"It's just… My trainer is on me about getting my steps in. Did I tell you? I joined a gym. Not for the guys or anything. My trainer's a woman, actually." Bree brushes her hair aside and pulls her salad in front of her, then takes an unusually large bite.

"What's going on?" I move to check my own phone to make sure I haven't missed an update from work or anything, but Bree's hand shoots out and snatches it too.

"Do you know how awful phones are? The brightness of our screens is so bad on our retinas. It's like staring at the sun. It's what vegetarian dude told Erin, and you know what? I believe him." She shrugs, still keeping her focus off me.

"Bree?" I frown.

She sighs. "Listen, it's probably not as bad as it looks. The media haven't even let up since he's been in hiding. You know how ruthless they can be, so let's not get ahead of ourselves."

I put my hand out, palm up, and she places my phone back in my hand.

Before I can open my browser, she sticks her screen in my face and says, "No need. I have my notifications on for all Carter updates, although I wish I didn't."

I skim the headline and image underneath, my stomach sinking with every brutal detail I study.

"Like I said, there's probably more to the story, and—"

"I need to go," I whisper. "I'm sorry."

"Tess, please stay and talk to me."

I stand, squaring my shoulders. "I should get back to work. I'm already behind from missing last week, so I have plenty to keep me busy."

She searches my expression, and after a moment, she gives in. "Okay, but promise to call if you need anything?"

I manage to nod while I put the lid back onto my salad and grab my purse. Waving over my shoulder, I emerge onto the sidewalk and start my walk back to the center.

On the way, I pass the pink flowers, but I don't stop to admire their fresh petals as I normally do. All they do now is remind me of the flowers Carter picked for me when he drew me a bath.

He was so freaking romantic before we ever even kissed.

I zip my jacket and wait for the light to change before crossing the street as thoughts of the news race through me like a bad stomach bug.

Model Behavior: Billionaire Enjoys Drinks with Model Girlfriend

That's what the article said, and it included pictures of Carter with his arm slung around Ginger's shoulders.

Him whispering in her ear.

Them kissing at an outdoor patio during a nice lunch.

The first line read "Sources say the couple is getting serious."

Maybe Bree's right—maybe they're lies, or maybe there's an explanation for this. But what would it change?

Carter's free to do whatever the hell he wants.

He's not mine, and I don't control him.

It would be different if Carter felt enough for me to stay—to tell me he wants to try to be a real couple—but he didn't.

Besides, how could I have asked someone like him commit to me after a few short days? It's unreasonable.

I know deep down that it's not logical for me, either, to commit the rest of my life to someone after such a short time of knowing them. But the disappointment of how it all ended lingers like a dull ache.

It's especially hard at night when I'm alone in my apartment with thoughts of him. His touch. His laugh. His quirky jokes.

The more time that passes, though, the more I try to convince myself our connection was a ruse. A momentary attraction that led to lust, which led to a handful of amazing nights living out a fantasy.

But the nagging thoughts that I'm wrong rear their ugly heads around every corner, making me miss him. It makes me wish even harder that things will turn around.

I've just entered my apartment when my phone rings.

Carter.

I stare at it, studying every letter to make sure, but it's definitely him. The guy I've thought about all day. Not even my numerous appointments or files to organize were enough to keep my mind off him today.

I swipe to answer and bring it to my ear, but when I open my mouth, nothing comes out.

"They were old pictures," he says.

Immediately, his voice washes over me like a warm bath, and I relax. I don't even fully register what he says—hell, he could've said he has an extra toe, and I would've had the same reaction.

Because it feels too good to have him on the other line after so many days of silence.

Too good to have any contact at all, making memories of us flood my mind.

Our naked limbs tangled in the sheets.

Hot open-mouthed kisses.

Sweet, blissful caresses.

I blink, bringing my apartment into focus. I'm alone. Carter's not here. There won't be any more kisses or heated touches.

I have to guard my heart.

"Why are you calling?" I ask, my voice shaking.

"The pictures in the press today—the ones of Ginger and me—they're old pictures. They were taken before you and I even met."

I close and lock the door behind me, resting against it like I need it for strength to get through this phone call.

Because his words are too much. They relax and comfort

me when they shouldn't. I shouldn't care what he does in his free time, but I can't deny how relieved I am to hear there was, in fact, another side of the story.

Sighing, I clutch the phone to my ear and say, "You don't owe me an explanation, Carter."

"Of course," he strains. "I just… needed you to know."

He seems to be having too much difficulty getting the words out. This is a new side of him. An unsure, hesitant, and dare I say, even regretful side?

There's a brief pause before he says, "I assume Graham's still pissed? He hasn't returned any of my calls or texts, or a *thank you* for the Jets box seat tickets."

"Yeah," I say on a laugh, my knees wobbly. "He tried to get back at me during a poker game last week, but it blew up in his face. He lost his Mercedes, so if you see a young blonde woman driving around in a cool-ass ride, just know I didn't steal it."

He chuckles. "Why did he bother? He sucks so bad. He could never even beat newbies when we were in college."

"Obviously, he was so furious with me he couldn't think clearly." My giggle gets caught in my throat. I didn't mean to remind us both of what happened last week, but it slipped.

"Give him time. He'll come around," Carter offers.

"I wish I could say the same for you," I blurt again. *What is wrong with me?* "I mean, I wish he'd come around and forgive you, but I don't see him doing that anytime soon. You know how he is, and…" My voice trails off, unsure of where I'm going with it.

There's a long pause, and it's an unusual one for us. I shift on my feet, itching to get out of these shoes and work clothes.

All I want is to sink into a hot bath and drown in a glass of wine.

Especially when his voice sounds again, his words squeezing my chest with each passing second. "I'm sorry I can't give you what you want. I don't know how."

I can hear the defeat and disappointment echoing through each word. He believes what he just said, and the certainty in his voice makes me ache.

"No one knows how to be with someone. They just are because…" I struggle to find the right words. Exhaling, the rest of the sentence floods out of me like water through a broken levee. "They're together because they don't know how to be without each other."

I hold my breath, although I'm not sure what I'm hoping for. I don't expect to change his mind or for him to tell me he's actually outside, waiting for me to jump into his arms, although I have to admit I'd love the latter.

But whatever it is I'm waiting for, I don't get it.

All I receive in return is silence, and when I pull the phone back, I notice he's ended the call.

I clutch the phone over my chest, underneath which, my heart flutters.

Is this what's become of us? Reduced to a few anxious minutes over the phone?

His call made me realize just how much I miss our easy banter. The jokes. The late-night chats at the cabin.

They breathed new life into my days.

Will I ever even see him in person again, or will all I get of him now be pictures in the media without knowing if they're old or new?

TWENTY-THREE

"**H**e called you to explain it was an old picture?" Bree sets her margarita down and quirks her brow, indicating she means business.

She doesn't put her margarita down for just anyone or anything.

I shift in my seat at the table, bumping my shoulder into Madison by accident, and when I glance around our table, Bree, Madison, and Erin all wear similar expressions with a mix of shock, doubt, and intrigue.

I gulp my margarita down—I went with strawberry tonight because I'm feeling sassy. It's been two weeks since I last felt Carter's hands on me.

Since I last stared into his hazel eyes.

Since he made me come undone.

And I've been sulking ever since.

When pictures of him from a charity dinner surfaced in several print and online tabloids, I cried into a bag of Chex Mix.

Okay, two bags.

Three.

I only pull out the salty snack in dire situations, and last week was a low point, for sure. I've never cried like that over a guy. I barely cried like that when I broke my freaking arm as a kid. But to my defense, which I stated to the girls when they expressed concern, Carter was decked out in a tuxedo that was made for him—literally. It was a custom job, and it fit his form perfectly. He even kept the beard.

It was trimmed and groomed, but he'd kept it, nonetheless.

I like to think it's because I told him I liked it, especially when his head was between my—

"Are you going to keep us waiting for long? Maybe I should get a refill?" Bree points to the empty margarita pitcher and the glasses surrounding us.

I nod, slumping in my seat.

"Come on," Erin says, dipping her head to meet me at eye level. "You said you weren't going to pout."

"I also said I'd only drink one skinny margarita, but things change." I wink and sip my *regular* strawberry margarita. Licking my lips and savoring the sweet, fruity taste, I set the glass down and sigh. "Okay. I'm sorry. I know I'm being a drag."

This is my first time out besides going to work. I was tempted to skip this dinner too, but the girls threatened to come to my apartment and kidnap me if they had to.

"It's just not like you." Madison leans forward and squeezes my hand. "You weren't even this upset when you broke up with Wyatt."

"Carter just…" I meet her gaze. "He meant more to me than Wyatt or anyone else. My few days with Carter were real. I just wish he saw it that way."

"Oh, honey." Erin frowns.

"What? What did I miss?" Bree sets a full pitcher in the middle of the table, the liquid sloshing dangerously close to the edges, and plops into the seat across from me. "Did you start without me?"

I shake my head, giggling. These girls know how to put me in a good mood.

"Okay, then what gives? What did Carter say when he called?" Bree waves for me to go on.

I finish off my drink and pour another, feeling a hint of buzz burning through me from the tequila. "He said he just needed me to know. What the hell does that even mean?" I spread my arms. "Why would he care? It's not like I'd call him to explain myself if I went home with the bartender tonight." I mumble the last part about Harvey, hoping it was lost in the chatter of the crowded restaurant, but my friends definitely hear me.

Their eyes and ears have been glued to me since we sat down, given that my call with Carter is the most exciting thing happening right now since Erin dumped the foot-fetish guy and became a vegetarian.

At the mention of another guy, they widen their eyes and purse their lips like they're scandalized, even though they were the ones pushing me to hook up with said bartender a couple weeks ago.

Just like he did then, Harvey looks good tonight too.

I immediately caught his attention when we walked in earlier, and he flirted when he took our order. He even complimented me on my glasses, giving me a once-over that would make any grown woman's toes curl, but I felt nothing.

Anything the bartender said, I compared to Carter.

Because Carter still has a hold on me, no matter what I do to try to get him out of my damn head.

I wave my arms at my friends. "All right! You all begged me to come out tonight so I could get my mind *off* Carter. This inquisition about him isn't helping." I tsk at them and practically slurp my fresh margarita.

"You're right." Madison leans back in her chair, seemingly letting this go, and turns her focus on Erin. "Why don't you tell us about the new guy you met? What's his name—Paul?"

Bree snickers. "God, could his name be any more boring?"

Madison covers her mouth as she laughs, and I swat at Bree. "He doesn't have control over his name, you know."

"Exactly." Erin glares. "People with boring names can still have exciting personalities, an affinity for interesting foods, a love of poetry. Perfect guys could have generic names."

"But…" Madison urges.

"But this Paul is not one of them." Erin cringes. "He actually thought the Empire State Building was secretly Stark Tower. Like, from the Marvel movies. And when I asked if he was kidding, he called me a Chitauri and left, making me pay for the check."

"Oh my God," Madison says, spitting margarita down her shirt.

In a fit of giggles, I hand Madison a wad of napkins, and I'm suddenly really glad I came out tonight.

Erin buries her face in her hands, then quickly drops them back to her lap. "Seriously, what is wrong with me? Why do

I attract weirdos? What about me screams, *Hey, freaks, come hither?*"

I snort and almost choke on my strawberry margarita.

"You do attract some wackos, but I feel you." Madison gives her a sympathetic smile and a pat on the hand. "The most awkward thing a guy did to me was take me to church on Valentine's Day because he was trying to get right with God and didn't want to be tempted to sin with me."

I cover my mouth as a loud burst of laughter escapes. "Oh, yeah! Wasn't that the guy who also wore flip-flops in the dead of winter?"

"He wore them the night we went to church too. That was also the last time I saw him." Madison holds her glass of margarita up. "To sex!"

The rest of us cheer and clink our glasses to one another's.

"This is why I will happily remain single. Seriously, dating is too complicated. The occasional plow from a good-enough-looking guy is plenty." Bree gives us a devious wink.

"Plow?" I raise my eyebrows. "How romantic."

"Who needs romance? I just need someone to scratch the itch and go on their merry way, preferably before I learn his favorite kind of bagel and how much he loves his grandma. Because if I know those two things, I'm a goner." Bree shrugs.

"That's all it takes, huh? Damn, I should tweak my long checklist." Erin giggles into her drink.

"You're welcome." Bree winks.

"Hey, ladies. How are we doing tonight?" a familiar voice sounds from the end of the table.

I give myself a brain freeze from the margarita. "Graham?" I cough, grimacing from the pain in my head. "What're you doing here?"

"I need to, um, talk to you." He stuffs his hands into his pockets.

My friends wave. I think Bree sighs, and Erin definitely melts into her seat a little—they've made plenty of comments about how *hot* they think Graham is. Madison seems to be the only immune one. She gracefully gets up and rounds my chair to give him a hug.

"Madison, hey. How are you?" Graham asks, pulling back. "Haven't seen you since Tessa's grad school graduation."

"Right? It's been too long. I've been crazed at the salon, which is a blessing, but it's also kicking my ass." Madison picks up her full glass. "This, and the fact that Sunday is only a couple days away, definitely help."

"I hear that. Next round is on me." Graham nods toward the bartender who's heading our way. He hands Harvey some cash and talks in a hushed tone while pointing to our pitcher. I can't hear exactly what he says over the clapping and loud *thank-yous* from my friends.

When Graham returns his attention to us, he chuckles at our rowdy cheers, then glances at me, nodding toward the door. "Ladies, enjoy the evening."

I follow him out the front, still unsure why he's here. I'm not ready to speak to him, and I thought he wasn't ready for me, either, given he left the cabin under the pretense that a patient needed him.

I knew he was lying, and Bree confirmed it when she ran into him in Brooklyn soon after he would've arrived in the city, and he didn't seem to be in a hurry to get anywhere.

For an upstanding doctor, he's not always very mature.

"How did you even find me?" I ask, not recalling any texts or calls from him tonight.

"It's Thursday. You've been coming to this same restaurant for girls' night for the last year." Graham drags his hands down his face, drawing my attention to the circles under his eyes. "I know you, Tessa, and I know you don't understand why I reacted to you and Carter like I did."

I cross my arms, trying to ignore the sting in my chest from hearing his name.

"The thing is, I know him too. I know *too* much, which is the problem, and you shouldn't have to deal with pictures of him and models shoved in your face every five seconds."

"Ah." I nod. "So, that's why you're here. You saw the picture and wanted to check on me."

"Of course I want to check on you. You're my sister." There's an underlying *duh* in his tone, and it eases the crease in my brows. Graham's affection for me has always been obvious and welcomed, and this shouldn't be any different, right? He's always wanted what's best for me, and he was clearly right about Carter.

It doesn't change how much I hate that Graham was right, though.

I exhale, dropping my arms and lowering my shoulders, relaxing into my stance. "It's an old picture. It's fine."

"What do you mean?"

I tense—my relaxed posture was short-lived. "Well, the picture of Carter and Ginger is an old one. So, no harm done. Besides, he and I are not together. Even if it was a recent one, he wouldn't have done anything wrong," I ramble.

"Wait, how do you know it's an old one?" Now, Graham crosses his arms, mirroring my previous stance like the times we used to play the copycat game.

Except he never got as angry then as he is now.

I roll my eyes in an attempt to downplay the situation. I don't need another outburst like the one he had at the cabin here on the sidewalk in front of a crowded restaurant. "Carter called, but we only discussed the picture. He explained, and that's it. The call lasted about thirty seconds total."

"That son of a bitch."

"I don't know why I'm even explaining myself to you. It's none of your business, which is the reason I've been pissed at you for the last week and a half. You were four days late to our vacation to celebrate my birthday, and when you did finally show up, you gave me more hell than the time I had one glass of wine while I was on an antibiotic."

He roughly exhales, tightening his arms across his narrow chest.

"You overreacted and treated me like a child. It wasn't Carter's fault. It takes two people to have—" I stop myself, especially when Graham's glare snaps up at me. "It was *my* decision, as well as his, and I'm not going to apologize for it except to say that I'm sorry it makes you uncomfortable."

He breathes in deeply through his nose like he does when he runs, which I've seen only a handful of times in my life. The guy runs faster than if he were being chased by the subway, so we don't make it a habit to run together. "I'm not asking for an apology, and you don't owe me one. I'm not even mad at you, and I shouldn't have taken it out on you. It's Carter I'm mad at. He betrayed my trust—literally, the one fucking thing I asked him to do was stay away from you."

"It's not like he planned it. He didn't come to the cabin with the intention of getting into my pants. Come on, Graham." I laugh, but it's strangled.

"Why are you defending him?"

Holding his stare, I step out of the way for a couple to pass and run my hands up and down my arms as a gentle breeze drifts over us. The sun has long set, bringing with it the fall chill I love so much, even though I'm not off to the best start this season.

I clear my throat and answer Graham with painful honesty. "Because Carter didn't do anything wrong. As much as it sucks now, I knew what I was getting myself into and that it wouldn't go anywhere. I mean, it's not like I expected to be the one to change his playboy ways."

His jaw tics, and his lips form a straight line.

I lean into him, nudging his shoulder with mine. "Jeez, Graham. I'm not the naïve ten-year-old you once knew."

His gaze bores into mine. "But you're hurt."

"Of course, I'm hurt. I really liked him." I shrug. "I'll be okay, though. I just need time."

He pulls me into an embrace, his arms wrapping around my neck, and he kisses my temple. "You're going to give me gray hairs," he murmurs into my hair.

"Isn't Dad supposed to say that?" I tease, my nose pressed into his shoulder.

"Well, I'm saying it too." He backs away. "Blame Mom and Dad. It's their fault I have a sister who's seven years younger than I am. If you were older, maybe I wouldn't be so protective."

"Yeah, sure." I tilt my head in doubt.

"You're right." He winks, scratching the back of his head. "I am sorry I blew up at you. It wasn't fair."

"And Carter?"

"Now him…" His lips form something between a frown and an evil Joker smile. "As for Carter, I'll continue being mad at him for the next fifty years. Long enough to still be able to kick his ass."

I giggle, shaking my head. "If you think you'll still be in good enough shape to lift your leg at that age, you'll have to share your secret with the world. You'll make millions."

"You think?" He wraps his arm around my shoulder, walking me back to the door of the restaurant and out of the cool evening. "Because I believe the way to go is to sue Carter for all he's worth. I mean, why settle for millions when I can have billions?"

I breathe a sigh of relief to be joking with Graham like this again.

I hate being mad at him and vice versa. It doesn't happen often, but when our arguments do blow up, his silence is torture.

The longest we've gone without speaking has been these last couple weeks, and it's taken a toll.

I can finally relax now and even hope that my heart will eventually heal the rest of the way.

TWENTY-FOUR

Carter

"**W**here were you last weekend? Graham had a party at his place for the Nashville Fury game." Miles smacks my shoulder, his enthusiasm on a higher level than mine. It's partly because he always gets excited about anything to do with Nashville since that's where he's originally from, but it's also that I'm in a particularly sour fucking mood and don't give two shits about football right now. "Man, the winning touchdown was killer. I'm not going to lie—I felt it in my pants."

I make an incoherent sound, focusing on each rep harder than usual.

"Were you with Ginger? How long have you two been together now? Because I thought—"

"We're not together," I growl, flinging sweat off my lips in his direction. I drop the weights by my feet with a loud clink and stand. "Your turn."

"Damn, dude. What's up with you?" Miles takes my place on the bench, wiping his brow with the hem of his shirt. "The promotion?"

I sigh. "No."

And it's the truth. Our clients and partners feel confident in me again, given the extra efforts I've made to reassure them of my competence. Last week, the board gave us the details of my promotion, and we'll be announcing my official takeover soon. Not that I had any doubts they would make the right call, but it was a relief to hear it from them directly.

It's finally happening.

No, the promotion isn't at all what has my head spinning these days.

Miles lies back with the dumbbells hovering above his face. I go around to stand behind him as a spotter and instinctively breathe in and out with him, focusing only on counting reps.

Once he's finished fifteen—three more than me, *the showoff*—he stands and takes the weights to the rack. "So? What, then?" he asks, turning toward me with hands on his hips.

"I slept with Graham's sister," I blurt.

His jaw falls open as he drops his arms to his sides. "You did what, now?"

I clasp my fingers behind my neck and stare at the ceiling, then glance around us at the small fitness center in the building of my office. Miles and I are only accompanied by another man who seems to be in his seventies, so I assume it's safe to chat here—this isn't the kind of place that's crawling with paparazzi.

That's just what I fucking need too—headlines from every corner of the internet outing Tessa and me. Although, her beautiful face would light up every page…

"Hello?" Miles waves his hand in front of me. "Are you going to repeat what you just said, or what?"

I wipe the sweat from my forehead and speak up when I say, "I slept with Graham's sister, man. Several times too. Like a fucking marathon with no finish line, and it was incredible. It was—"

"I don't need the details, but shit, Carter. Graham's *sister?*" His eyes bug out of his head like I'm telling him I got her pregnant and ran away. "That's so wrong."

"I know. I screwed up, okay?" I hang my head, then snap it back up. "But it's not like I did it on purpose. She's hot and smart and funny, and she's an adult. Graham's pissy, acting like I preyed on her, but she's capable of making her own decisions. Which she did."

"You are too, and the decision you should've made was to go stay with Daisy as soon as you laid eyes on Tessa. That would've been smart."

I groan, hanging my head again, because he's right. The moment I saw her, I should've run. I should've pretended there really was a bear and run far away from her.

"From your sad-ass mood these days, I can only assume things with her didn't end well?"

I cringe. "No, they didn't. I didn't even want to end things, but the look on Graham's face… The things he said…" I look up at Miles, who's leaning forward, waiting expectantly for me to finish. "They're all true. I'm not good enough for her."

"You really like her. This isn't a game?"

I stare at him pointedly, but I can't get pissed. It's a fair enough question, given my past.

He studies me, and I'm sure he's looking for any sign that I'm lying. That I'm messing around. But when he shrugs like this is all so damn simple, I'm caught off guard. "I think you could be."

"What?"

"You could be good enough for her."

"I'm not, though." I wave my arms around. "Just look at my history. You know only half of what Graham knows, and even you can admit I'm a mess when it comes to women."

"Sure, but it's because you haven't met the *right* woman."

I furrow my brows at him like he's speaking a foreign language.

"Think about all the guys you know. Which of them didn't sleep around before they met *the one*? They all did! Come on, Carter. You're smart. Use your head." He smacks my shoulder, then grabs his bag from the floor. "I'm hitting the showers—need to get to my next session. I suggest you get to work too. Oh, and you should call your girl."

"What about Graham?" I ask before he gets too far away. I didn't realize how badly I needed to talk to someone about this. It's been hell keeping all of it inside, but unleashing all my thoughts onto my friend has been a damn relief.

He toys with the zipper on his bag, again nodding calmly. "Give him a chance to see what I see—this new side of you." He waves up and down at me. "He'll come around."

My head in a shitstorm of a mess, I rinse off and slip my suit and tie back on, studying my reflection in the mirror. I never thought I'd say this, but I miss lounging around the cabin in my sweatpants and eating brownies with Tessa.

I haven't been out to my usual bar or club since I returned to the city, but I have been hiking up north once. Although it was enjoyable, the scenery wasn't as special. Not because it wasn't stunning, but because Tessa wasn't there to share a sandwich with me.

Or to make jokes about my heavy breathing.

Or to share almost-kisses with along the trail.

As I make my way back up to my office, Miles's words are on repeat in my head. For every ding of the elevator up the twenty floors to my office, I hear one more reason in his defense.

He's right. Drake, a friend from college, slept with countless women until he met Kiersten at a restaurant opening in Soho. They were seated next to each other and reached for the same glass of water. He made a joke that he'd really wanted a beer, anyway, so she could have the water, and the rest was history. They've been married for five years and counting.

If he can do it, why can't I?

I could call Tessa. She answered the last time I did and didn't hang up on me. No, I hung up on her like the fucking jackass that I am. What was I thinking? She was vulnerable and honest with me, and I was too chicken to respond.

I'm always too scared to get close to someone, but Tessa's the first and only woman to make me think I could handle it.

There's a first for everything, after all, and I've never been one to shy away from a challenge.

I've just sat in my chair in front of my two computer screens, my hair still damp and my soreness settling in like clouds before a storm, when my office phone rings—my assistant.

"Hey, Yara, what's up?" I answer, my chair squeaking as I lean forward to talk into the speaker.

"I'm sorry to bother you, Mr. Fields, but there's a Mrs. Rollins here to see you? She says you called her."

Tessa's here?

I freeze.

"Mr. Fields?" Yara asks.

"Send her in please." I hang up, run my palm down my dark slacks, and straighten my tie over my racing heart.

She's here.

Frantically, my glance darts around the office, and I rush around the desk to straighten the chairs, then push the bar cart to the side.

Tessa's here, and I wish I would've asked Whitney to straighten up. I also should've had Yara stock the minifridge and get the window cleaners to work around the clock. I stand in front of the nearest floor-to-ceiling window to inspect it for smudges, and there are too many to speak of.

Fuck, why didn't I get the cleaners?

I jump when there's a knock on the door and turn toward it. Sliding over the leather couch, I fumble toward the door as if I'm a baby gazelle just learning how to walk.

Out of breath, I open the door, ready to look into Tessa's bright eyes—it's been too fucking long. "Come in—Mrs. Rollins?"

Standing before me is not Tessa, but rather, her mother. "Weren't expecting me, huh?" She lifts a brow, and it's eerily similar to the way Tessa challenges me with a simple look.

"No, I'm not… I wasn't expecting…" I stammer. Shaking the tension out of my shoulders, I offer her a smile and remember my manners. "Please, come in."

I spread my arm to the side and step out of the way. As she comes inside, I nod over her head to Yara and mouth *thank you*, then close the door behind Tessa's mother. "Can I get you anything to drink? A snack, perhaps?" I ask.

"That won't be necessary, but I appreciate it." She drops her purse onto the couch and sits next to it, crossing her feet at the ankles. "I hope it's okay I stopped by like this."

"Of course," I reassure her.

She interlocks her hands in her lap and relaxes into her seat. For someone who's never been here before, she seems oddly at ease and comfortable already, and her words come out evenly when she says, "I know you're a busy man and you have your schedule. If you don't have time now, I can come back—retirement keeps me much freer than I used to be. One of the perks I didn't think I'd enjoy, but truthfully, it's been a blessing."

"I bet."

"No, I mean, truly a blessing. It feels like my husband and I have seen half the world already. We don't need to worry about our work or risk losing patients. We come and go as we please and can see the kids anytime we want. Well, Tessa, that is. As you know, Graham has a busy schedule of his own. I swear, it's like that son of mine has taken on the country's ailments all on his shoulders."

I do my best to hide my instinctive flinch and force a smile, instead, but I'm sure it appears as more of a grimace. It doesn't even feel natural on my face.

Quietly, I sit across from Mrs. Rollins on the second couch, the skyline expanding behind her and making her appear more intimidating than the previous times I've met her.

She eyes me, her expression unreadable.

I squirm in my seat, suddenly nervous as though this isn't my own office.

After a pause that feels like it stretches for hours, she leans forward, clasping her hands between her knees, making her gold bracelets clamor together. "You're wondering why I'm here."

She says it as more of a statement rather than a question, so I don't answer.

"You called me, though." She laughs.

I squint as I mentally sift through the calls I've made the last few days—and there have been a lot—until I land on the one she's referring to. "Right." I jump up. "You're here about the fundraiser I want to host. Perfect. I'd love your help, but"—I glance down at her, tilting my head—"we could've done this over the phone. I'm sorry. I should've specified in my voice mail so you wouldn't have had to come all the way down here."

"Nonsense. I told you I'm retired, remember? I have literally nowhere to be." She smiles, and it's genuine. It's not the forced one my mother usually gives when she greets my father's guests, nor is it like the one she gives my father. My mother barely smiles at him at all.

I clear my throat, gathering my scattered thoughts—I'm never this fucking flustered, but I chalk it to be my nerves from the brief moment when I thought Tessa was here. "I'm glad you dropped by, then."

"So, let's discuss the charity. It's to benefit Darby's Dreamers, yes?"

Nodding, I turn my phone on to check my notes and add to them. "When I was in Connecticut, I met Kyle and Eugene's parents, Trina and the sheriff."

"Lovely family, aren't they?" She beams, clasping her hands in her lap again.

"They really are, and I'd like to help raise funds and awareness for the cause and other families like them. It's a bit last minute, but I think it would be optimal to have it during the holiday season. Donors tend to be more generous around that time." I wink, halfway sitting against the front of my desk, facing her. "My plan is to host a fundraiser dinner the first weekend of December. I've already contacted Mr. and Mrs. Loffley, but they have a prior engagement that weekend. I'm hoping you can ask the Thompsons if they can attend. I'd love it if they might even consider speaking at the event, but I figure such a favor might be better received if it comes from someone they know and trust." I extend my hand toward her.

"This is a splendid idea, Carter, and I'd be delighted to help. Trina will be tickled, I'm sure. I'll call her when I get home."

"That would be great." I clap my hands in front of me and freeze in a prayer-like manner. "I can email you more details on the date, time, and location of the event to pass along, and then, I'll have my assistant send a formal invitation as well."

"Perfect." Mrs. Rollins stands and moves toward me, quirking her eyebrow again. "Can I ask you a question, though?"

"Anything," I blurt. She has this way about her that makes me feel like I'm under interrogation, yet I'm comfortable in her presence too. What is it about these Rollins women?

"You called me for help. Why not Graham or Tessa? I'm sure they'd love to assist you." She squints at me like she's ready to catch me in a lie—is this a test?

Surely, she knows Graham's not speaking to me, and asking Tessa for a favor right now is like playing with fire. So, this must be a test of some sort, right?

I cross my arms and give her a tight-lipped smile. "I did call Graham, and as for Tessa, well, I didn't figure she'd appreciate me asking her for anything. Honestly, I'm surprised you're here and that Graham didn't forbid you from contacting me."

"I see." She purses her lips.

I avert my gaze, and my arms strain against my suit jacket

as I tighten them across my chest. The next words tumble out of my mouth like they did with Miles earlier—I'm on a damn roll today. "It's not that I don't want them to help. I'd like for both of them to attend, but I know it's a lot to ask. Especially for Graham. You saw him the last time we spoke. It wasn't exactly a party at the cabin, but a swift and brutal kick to my ego. Left me pretty scarred. And that's saying something because I've had my ass handed to me by my father, among other terrifying—" I clear my throat, suddenly realizing I'm unleashing these things to my best friend's mother. Who even am I right now? "I'm sorry. I don't know why I'm telling you all this."

"I think you do." She steps up to me and places her hand on my shoulder, her expression warm and generous. "Besides, this is what I've done all my life. People find it easy to talk to me, so I'll take it as a compliment that you do as well, even if I am off the clock." She winks.

"Right." I loosen up a fraction.

"My daughter is an adult, even though Graham has trouble accepting it. In general, he has trouble accepting that he can't control everything—he gets it from his father, mind you." She laughs, and the sound soothes me further. She squeezes my shoulder before dropping her hand to clasp the other in front of her. "Tell me, what is this thing with you and Tessa?"

My jaw comes unhinged. "I'm not… She and I are…" I stammer, surprised she's asking me about this. What the fuck do I say about our fling to Tessa's mother?

My God, what fresh hell is this?

She tsks. "I'm not asking for the dirty details, Carter, so relax. I'm only interested in your feelings for my daughter. Are they serious?"

I'm speechless. I haven't confessed my true feelings to Tessa. How can I do so to her mother? This is going to bite me in the ass either way, and I can't help but curse Graham for all this—it's his fault, anyway. If he would've introduced me to Tessa years ago—when I first met his parents, even—maybe things wouldn't have turned out this way.

Although I'm not sure I'm upset with the way it happened, except for the ending, that is.

As if reading my mind, Mrs. Rollins says, "As I'd previously tell my clients, wishing things would've happened differently isn't going to help. All you can do is sort through the present and figure out what you're going to do about it to ensure you have the future you can be happy with."

"The future is out of our control, though."

She shrugs. "Maybe parts of it, sure. But some things, such as love, we can act on. We can ensure the ones we're meant to be with are next to us in five, ten, fifteen years and beyond. If Tessa's that person for you, are you willing to fight for her?"

"Yes," I say without hesitation, and a sense of calm washes over me.

My office phone rings, making us both jump.

She brings her hand to her chest and laughs. "Well, I'll let you get back to it."

All I can do is nod because I'm at a loss for words.

Once she reaches the door, I push off my desk and round it to grab the ringing phone—Yara.

"You don't have to be your father, you know." Mrs. Rollins voice sounds again, drawing my attention to where she stands by the door. "You can be your own man and make your own decisions."

Giving me one more smile, she pulls the handle open and disappears.

I'm stunned, to say the least. How did she…

She's good.

I shake my head, chuckling. What an unexpected afternoon.

Still smiling, I accept the call, putting it on speaker. "Yes, Yara?"

"Your two o'clock is here and waiting in the conference room."

"I'll be right there." I stand, buttoning the front of my jacket, and make my way to the door, an extra bounce in my Italian loafers.

And the lightness in my chest doesn't leave me for the rest of the day as I formulate a plan.

TWENTY-FIVE

Carter

As the sun drops low in the sky, the dim glow casting over the tall buildings outside my window, I'm reminded of the sunrise through the trees at the cabin. As if I wasn't already thinking of Tessa nonstop since I left, her mother's visit the other day brought an onslaught of regret that I've been carrying with me like an anchor.

I've been slammed with work, so I haven't been able to call her yet.

I also haven't figured out what to say. At this point, words don't feel like enough. I need something bigger. Something to *show* Tessa I'm serious about her.

There's a knock on the door, cutting through my thoughts. I rub my eyes, not having realized how long I've been sitting in front of my computer, and stand.

I'm just past the couches when my father enters.

"Dad?" I stop in my tracks, standing taller out of instinct. He taught me that posture is everything. It exudes confidence and power, which is what our clientele is most attracted to.

Every deal starts with the tone that first impression sets, beginning with posture.

"Hey, son." He scratches his jaw and remains by the door. "Got a minute?"

I stare at him, noting the wrinkles around his eyes and the dull gleam there that matches the setting sun. The gray in his hair. The tired lines around his mouth.

I haven't seen him up close in a while, even though we work down the hall from each other.

We haven't grown this billion-dollar company by sitting around chatting.

Once the shock of him standing here to do just that wears off, I spread my arm toward the couch for him to take a seat. "Please."

He nods and makes himself comfortable while I move toward the bar cart by the window.

"Whiskey?" I ask over my shoulder, already opening a bottle of his favorite.

"That's fine."

I hand him a glass and clink my own against it, then open my jacket to sit across from him, my mind racing through the reasons to explain his unusual request to talk in person.

His retirement?

A new deal to hand off to me?

To celebrate that he was right about Shanty? He proved to be useful with the Heiderman acquisition after all.

Once my father swallows, the sound echoing in the

silence of my office, he says, "I heard about your impromptu fundraiser in a few weeks."

I give him a smile that reaches my eyes. "Ava's not entirely happy, but the large bonus I'm giving her for Christmas makes up for the double-time she's working to make it happen."

"I'd be more worried about guests not having enough time to commit to it."

"Come on." I wave him off. "I'm giving the socialites of the Upper East Side an excuse to be social. They'll show," I say with absolute confidence. I've already had several acquaintances confirm they'll be in attendance.

"Good thing you're doing." He raises his glass.

I nod, swirling the liquid in my own.

"About our conversation a few weeks ago…" For the first time in my life, I bear witness to my father—Victor Fields, prominent billionaire of New York—squirm.

Exhaling, I lean forward to set my glass on the coffee table between us with a clink. When I look at him again, the sun is low in the sky outside, casting a shadow over his expression.

I know the conversation he's referring to.

The one where I questioned his and Mom's marriage.

We haven't mentioned it since then, and it's been well over a month. I didn't think we'd ever revisit it, not with him dodging me any chance he gets. After each meeting, he rushes off with the phone to his ear, or he claims he's leaving the office early in order to prepare for his impending retirement.

With him, it's always something.

I sink into the couch cushions and brace myself for a lecture full of sighs and grunts.

Here we go.

"I'm sorry I was short with you," he says.

My jaw drops.

Okay, I didn't expect that…

"The truth is… you were right." He sets his glass next to mine and locks eyes with me. All I see is remorse in his. His tone is apologetic and maybe even a little sad when he says, "You have to understand—your mother and I married out of love and devotion, but…" He swipes at the corners of his mouth, and it's obvious this is difficult for him. I've never heard him have this much trouble with words before.

The man in front of me is very unlike my dad.

When was the last time we had a conversation that didn't involve the board, business, and media attention? Have we ever?

Even when I was twenty-five and went to the hospital with a ruptured appendix, he sent flowers with Whitney and called to let me know he rescheduled my meetings. I think somewhere in between he might've asked how I was feeling, but it's hard to say.

I still when he continues. "Conceiving you took a toll on us and our marriage. Having a baby became our priority, and after you were born, we completely forgot how to be a couple. A *real* couple. And our shortcomings just became our norm." He shrugs, his frown deep.

I clear my throat. "You can be a real couple, though, if you want. If you can't live without each other, you should fight for your marriage, Dad. It's not too late." I find myself smiling as I realize I'm repeating some of the words Tessa said to me.

I didn't believe them then, not like I do now.

"We're going to work on it." My dad shifts in his seat.

"*Really* work on it? Or pretend to go to counseling to keep up appearances?" I lift an eyebrow, still in disbelief that we're having this conversation, let alone that he's owning up to his and Mom's problems.

He throws his hands up. "No, no. I mean it. Your mother and I have been talking, and last night, we made headway. It was perhaps the first genuine conversation we've had in years. We even switched therapists since Dr. Hubbert didn't prove to be useful over the last decade."

My shoulders ease, releasing the tension as his confession settles in.

We sit in comfortable silence as we sip our whiskey, and after a beat, he chuckles. "You met a girl, didn't you?"

I freeze with the rim of the glass against my lips, then lower it. "What?"

He chuckles harder. "I'll be damned. I never thought I'd see the day when you, my son, would settle down."

I wave my hand from side to side. "I'm not. I haven't even…" My voice trails off. He can't hear me over his chuckling that's turned into howling laughter, anyway. "Fuck it. Yeah. I met a girl." I laugh along with him, equally surprised.

It's surreal, to say the least, to be talking with my father for longer than thirty seconds about anything outside this office building.

All it took to open my eyes were a few days with Tessa Rollins.

I tell Dad about her. About her sweet smile, genuine heart, and smart mouth—both intelligent and quick with a witty comeback.

"She's a damn good poker player too."

"No kidding?" he says over his shoulder as he pours us another round.

"I swear. She kicked my ass." I accept the full glass and nod.

Dad throws his head back and laughs, the sound deep and unusually carefree. Maybe all he needed was to have his eyes opened too. From the sounds of it, the last month has been the nudge he's needed to be proactive.

We continue talking this way, easy and open, as the sun completely sets. I have no clue what time it is when my dad looks at his phone. He turns the screen toward me and points to the long line of missed calls, texts, and emails waiting for him. "See? This is what happens when I turn my phone on silent for a couple hours."

"It's been on silent this whole time?" I pat my coat pocket but come up empty. "Come to think of it, I don't even know where mine is."

He tucks his phone into the inside pocket of his jacket and stands. "It was your mother's idea for me to look at my phone less. Says I'm retiring soon and need to learn to slow down. I agree."

I stand too and clap his shoulder. "I'm glad we talked."

"Me too." He nods, and the sincerity in his voice is almost palpable. "Say, this impromptu charity dinner wouldn't have anything to do with your woman, would it?"

I inhale deeply and let it out, feeling a weight lifted after this day. "Actually, yes. I believe in the cause, but I also plan to win her back that night."

"Oh, you're not together right now?"

I work my jaw back and forth. "I left that part out, didn't I?"

"No, you didn't tell me you were up shit creek without a paddle." He furrows his thick brows, a lightness in his tone.

I meet his gaze and match his amusement with a chuckle. "Hopefully, it won't be for long."

"You've always been a master of persuasion." Dad offers me a kind and proud smile, one I've rarely—if ever—seen.

What even fucking happened tonight?

"This may be my most difficult deal yet." My lips form a thin line, my nerves suddenly rattled.

"And the woman outside a couple weeks back? Does she have anything to do with this?"

"Who?"

"Tall blonde woman? She stopped me out in the hall."

I mentally run through the events of the last couple weeks and the faces I saw, until understanding dawns, and I stop on the one he's referring to.

Tessa's mother.

"That would be Tessa's mom, yes."

"Ah, I see." He shrugs. "Nice lady. Very insightful."

"Comfortably intimidating too." I chuckle, nodding. "She definitely knows what she's talking about."

"Had me figured out before I even said a word. I thought I was more complicated than that." He coughs into his hand, which turns into a laugh, and I join him.

He pulls his phone out again and checks the screen. It's still on silent, and I assume it's out of habit that he grabs it now—can't fault him for that. The man's been glued to his phone or computer screen for the last fifty years.

I applaud him for enduring this long with only checking it twice this whole time.

"Shit. Your mother's called three times. I better see what's going on. It could be a fire, or she chipped a nail. I never know with her. She's very—" He clamps his mouth shut and snaps his gaze toward me, holding his hands up and sighing. "That's the kind of shit I need to watch. I'm working on it."

My eyebrows rise so high, they touch my hairline. "Well, I'm…" I'm at a loss for words is what I am. Surprised. Proud. Happy for him and Mom.

I never thought I'd see the day my dad would admit he needed to change some of his ways. He's stubborn like that.

"I'm a new man, I know." Dad spreads his arms. "I think it's impending retirement. In a week, I'll have nowhere to be at all hours of the day and night. I'll be alone with your mother or planning and attending your aunt's annual wedding." He rolls his eyes, his tone good-natured and fun.

"I'm happy for you, Dad. And I hear retirement's not so bad." I wink, recalling Mrs. Rollins's take on the notion. I've only met her a few times in the past, but even so, she seemed so much happier and more rejuvenated when I last saw her.

It gives me hope for my father.

"We'll see how long I last in linen clothes and flip-flops. Richard retired last year, and all he does is go out on his yacht in linens and a hat that makes him look like an ass." He pulls his jacket tight around him like he's hugging it. Like he'll miss wearing suits come next week. "God, I'm in for a real kick to the ball sac, aren't I?"

My laughter bubbles up my throat of its own accord, and he waves me off, joking with me.

I've laughed more with my dad tonight than I have in many years combined.

And once he leaves, a sense of peace settles over me.

If I wasn't already determined to win Tessa back, I'd be ready now after talking with my dad. Because if he can change after all these years—after all the mistakes he and Mom have made—I can change my ways too, right?

I can be the man Tessa deserves.

More importantly, for the first time in my life, I want to be committed to a woman.

I want to be the one for *her*.

But before I can do that, I have one more loose end to tie up. I pull my phone out and scroll through my contacts until I find and click on the one I need, then hold my breath.

"What do you want?" Graham's voice booms through my speaker. "I haven't been answering your calls for a reason. Take a hint, asshole."

"So glad you're talking to me again," I say sarcastically, suppressing the tickle in the back of my throat. This is not the time to laugh.

His frustrated exhale travels through the line loud and clear.

I pull back the phone to ensure he's still with me. "Since you haven't ended the call yet, hear me out."

He answers me with another heavy grunt, but I take it as a win.

"I need your help," I plead.

TWENTY-SIX

Tessa

"I saw the press release," I say, clutching the phone to my ear. "Congratulations are in order, so that's why I'm calling." I shift, switching the phone to my other ear and rolling my eyes because I sound so formal and impersonal. Running a hand through my hair, I continue. "So, um, congratulations on the promotion. I know you'll be great. Hopefully better than your poker game, because if you let a sweet girl trick you with her bluff, then I don't know what to say about your business tactics." I giggle into the phone, then catch myself, my face heating.

Good thing he can't see me.

"Okay, bye." I end the voice mail and hang up, sighing.

I swore I wouldn't call Carter. It's been three weeks since I last talked to him.

Three weeks.

That's how long I've lasted without speaking to him. In that short time, though, I've Googled him more times than the bags of Chex Mix I've had—which were shockingly a lot—and picked up the phone to call or text him even more.

But I'm getting better. I didn't do any of those things yesterday or the day before. I'm carrying on with my life, even if some days feel like I'm on autopilot. But today, I couldn't stop myself from seeing all the excitement of the new Fields Company CEO.

He looked good in every picture and video I found. It's not surprising, but would it kill him to dampen his appearance a little? Maybe roll around in mud before a photo shoot?

"Who am I kidding?" I mutter to myself as I sit on the couch, my book open next to me as I settle in for a quiet evening.

Carter would still look good even covered in brown stains.

I sigh, tucking my feet underneath me. "Ow." I wince, using my hand to hold my ankle up.

A stinging pain shoots from my calf muscle and shin up to my aching quads, taking me by surprise. I didn't realize how sore I was from jogging this week, and I've started asking myself if it'll ever go away or if I'm doomed to never be able to walk comfortably again.

I set my leg back down and pick my wine up for a sip.

Even with my constantly aching muscles, it's a good thing I'm exercising again. I got winded from hiking with Carter, and the elevator went out at work last week, forcing us to go up four flights of stairs to reach our offices.

I'm at a good place in my life—not including my sex life— with a respectable and fulfilling job, my own apartment, and loving friends and family. But my fitness has been lacking. I've re-upped my membership at the yoga studio and have been going with Erin again just like old times.

I'll even attempt to complete one of the many 5k runs for various causes around here.

But one step at a time. I'm still in the beginning stages, where it's difficult to even sit on my couch.

I pick up my book and read the same line five times, finding it hard to focus, when my phone screen lights up from the coffee table in front of me. I drop the book to my side and check my new text.

Madison: Oh my God, the SON OF A BITCH.

"What the hell?" I mutter, instantly tensing as I click on the screenshot of a social media post below her message.

I don't react when I see a smiling Wyatt, my ex, or the gorgeous woman on his arm in the image.

Nor do I flinch when I see the large rock on the woman's engagement finger.

I have no feelings left for the man, but what makes my stomach recoil and blood boil is the caption: *A year and a half with this beauty. Glad to make her mine forever.*

Which would mean he started dating this woman when he was still with… *me.*

I clutch my phone so hard my knuckles turn white.

I drop it by my feet and stand, pacing by the couch as the dishwasher in the kitchen rumbles, swishing water within. After a moment, I stop and throw my head back. What escapes me is a laugh so hysterical it can't be mine. *Is it?*

Biting my lip, I bend down, retrieve my phone, and call Madison as I resume pacing, my bare feet digging into the plush rug.

She answers on the first ring. "I swear, the asshole will pay for going behind your back while you were dating. Karma is a bitch, and it has a large red target on his stupid, motherfucking face."

"I appreciate the sentiment, and I'm sure he'll get what's coming to him, but I won't be sticking around to find out." I laugh, but this time it sounds more like my own.

"How can you be laughing about this? You should be wanting to crucify the sleazeball." If she were in my apartment, I'm certain her eyes would be as wide open as her mouth. Madison doesn't get riled up often, but when she does, she looks crazed, as I imagine she is right now. On top of that, the southern twang in her accent—thanks to several years of living in Texas as a teenager—thickens the angrier she is.

"You know? I'd wish him harm if I still had any feelings for him, but I'm really over him. I'm over the whole thing." I shrug, staring at the floral painting on the wall above my couch.

Silence answers me.

"I mean, I knew the moron was cheating on me, but I didn't want to accept it at the time. It's why we broke up, remember? I finally realized how unhealthy we were."

"And good thing you did. I wanted to punch him in the jaw so many times," Madison says, audibly irritated.

I squeeze my eyes closed, giggling with my friend. She's usually level-headed and calm, but she'll kick some ass when her friends are threatened.

"You sure you're okay?" Madison asks, her voice laced with more concern than is necessary. *Her and her big heart.*

"I'm fine. Thanks, Mads."

"Anytime." There's a squeaking sound on her end—a

sound I know well from the source of it. I've sat in that chair many times over the years. No one cuts and colors my hair like Madison.

"Are you still at the salon?" I check the time and see it's way past her closing time.

She sighs. "Yes. I had a few stragglers I couldn't turn away, but I'm all cleaned up now and about to go home." There's more shuffling on her end and then some jingling, which is probably from her keys. "Hey, did you catch the press release today?"

I take a deep breath in. "How could I not? It's everywhere. They act like they didn't know Carter was going to take over."

She snorts. "I can come over if you need."

"It's not necessary. I'm just going to read my book and pass out before my neighbors start trying to tear our shared wall down. It's getting late, which means they'll start fucking like rabbits soon."

"Remember when you were excited to finally get new neighbors?" Madison muses.

"Oh, how naïve I was," I joke.

Once our giggles subside, she says, "Call if you need anything, no matter what time."

I thank her again, and we end the call as I sink onto the couch, pulling my green throw blanket over my lap, my chest sinking. If I were still hung up on Wyatt, I'd be more pissed right now, but the truth is, his deception isn't news. I've known he's an asshole for a while.

My connection with him wasn't real, and if I didn't have enough proof of that already, this is just more evidence.

"I'm not Wyatt."

Carter's declaration rings in my head right as his name pops up on my phone screen with an incoming call.

My breath catches as I swipe to answer. "Carter?"

"Hey," he says, his greeting more like a question as if he's surprised. "I didn't expect you to answer."

"Why? I'm the one who called you," I tease.

"Right, but I figured you'd be asleep by now in order to get up early. You do tend to get up before the sun even on your days off, so…" His chuckle shoots through my ear and straight to my heart.

As if on cue, I yawn, unable to stop the loud sound from escaping me.

"I'd say *I told you so*, but you're doing it for me." Another chuckle rumbles out of him, and I'm almost a goner.

His laugh is the sound version of a drug.

I clear my throat, resisting the urge to sink into this friendly banter. It's too hard to do that with him. And too soon. "What's up?" I ask, trying to force the pep in my voice.

"I got your voice mail and wanted to thank you." He grows serious, and I envision the dimples slowly disappearing from his cheeks.

"Oh, well, you're welcome." I nod, my body as stiff as my tone.

There's a pause.

I can't take this torture anymore, and at the same time as I say, "I need to go," he says, "Will you do something for me?"

"Um…" I bite my lip.

"I'm hosting a charity dinner a week after Thanksgiving. Your invitation was already sent, but I'd like to personally invite you to attend."

I freeze. Is he asking me out on a date? It sounds like a date.

"I don't know," I whisper.

"It's for an amazing cause, and it will give us a chance to… talk."

"Talk? What is there left to say, Carter?" My heart races, hope suddenly smashing the carefully constructed wall I've been rebuilding around my heart the last few weeks. "I can't be your date."

"I'd still like for you to come." After a brief pause, he says weakly, "You can even bring a date of your choosing. If you want…" He lets the offer hang between us, and his sharp intake of breath is deafening.

My chest swirls with overwhelming confusion and uncertainty. Treading lightly, I say, "Not that it's any of your business, but I wouldn't have anyone to ask."

He finally exhales, his relief more obvious than the skyscrapers are tall in Manhattan. "No, you're right. It's not my business, but I can't say I'm not happy to hear it."

Gripping my phone, I steel myself. I will not let his amused tone affect my resolve.

I will not allow myself to be giddy that he's happy I'm not seeing anyone.

I will not—

"What is that?" he asks, making me pause.

"Um…" I blink toward the wall behind my couch. The banging against it, along with the sensual moans, are louder than the dishwasher. There might as well be a live porno in my living room, especially since it's noisy enough for Carter to hear it through the speaker. "That would be my neighbors. They're very… sexual."

I head toward the safety of my room, where their escapades aren't heard, as Carter laughs. "That's putting it lightly. It sounds like two animals in heat on the last day on Earth."

I sit on the edge of my bed and giggle.

After a pause, he sounds genuine, his voice as smooth as honey when he pleads, "Just think about the dinner, okay? Please."

I run my fingers through my hair, my glance darting toward the kitchen through the small opening of the doorway like the running dishwasher will give me answers. One pause in rinsing means yes, and two means no.

I chew on the inside of my cheek and stand from the bed, my bare feet padding across the rug and out toward the kitchen toward the refrigerator for more white wine. "What charity is it benefiting?"

"You'll have to come find out for yourself." I imagine he's winking.

Which makes my heart flutter.

"Is that so?" I quirk an eyebrow and head back to the confines of my room, bottle of wine in hand. "I don't have enough diamonds in the vault to attend such a decadent occasion, though."

His chuckle is deep and throaty. "It's not a ball at the queen's estate. Just a dinner."

"A black-tie event isn't *just a dinner* to regular people like myself." I roll my eyes, giving in. His good mood is infectious.

"You're anything but regular." His inhale is quick and overwhelming, like he didn't mean to say that out loud.

My heart automatically soars at his words.

He sounds lighter during this call than he did when he called to explain about Ginger. There's an air of amusement and mischief in his tone that matches his personality. It's the same tone he used at the cabin when I first met him.

Fun Carter.

The one I'm falling for, but even the other side of him is endearing as well. He's the whole package.

"Please," he says, his voice gruff, yet melodic somehow. "Think about it."

"I will," I promise.

Once we end the call, I hold the phone to my chest, warring with myself.

What happens if I go and we *talk*?

More importantly, can I be okay if I don't go?

TWENTY-SEVEN

Carter

Graham steps inside the event hall, tugging at his bow tie. He's either angry at it or me for making him come—or both.

I've called and texted Graham repeatedly since I called to ask him for a favor. He needed some convincing to attend this evening, but I think I got through to him.

And not just to be here tonight.

I've been trying to convince him that my intentions with his sister are not fleeting. I don't know what we have exactly, but Tessa and I are too fucking real to pretend it meant nothing.

To pretend it was just sex.

The sex was great because we have something more than lust between us, and I'm determined to convince them both that I'm not going anywhere.

I straighten my own bow tie and smooth the lapels of my tuxedo, my fingers trembling and nerves firing like they're canons and I've lit the fuse.

The moment of truth comes tonight, in more ways than one.

"Great turnout tonight, son." My dad sneaks beside me, clapping my shoulder and making me jump. "Don't be so nervous. The media's forgotten all about your run-in with the mailbox and moved on to discuss an actress's new nose or whatever. They're not even talking about you taking over the company anymore. Seems they only like scandals." He shrugs, but then he smirks, obviously sarcastic.

Of course, the media loves a chance to gossip about the latest celebrity intoxication mishap, wardrobe malfunction, and nasty divorce. I'm not surprised they turned a cold shoulder at my promotion—it's too boring.

I sip my champagne, stuffing my free hand into my pocket as I scan the room. Where is she?

She's going to come… right?

"I'm proud of you, Carter." My father squeezes my shoulder, drawing my attention to him.

He's said that a couple times in the last few weeks, and it's strange not having him give me so many lectures as he would have just two months ago. Instead, he's actually been trying to be more encouraging. This new therapist he and Mom have been going to really seems to be helping, and I'm already seeing the benefits.

I shake his hand and nod. "Thanks, Dad."

We both turn to watch the crowd. The women in sparkling dresses and high heels and the men in sharp tuxes. All for a good cause.

He's about to turn away but stops himself, holding a finger up at me. "I forgot to ask—how was your stay with your cousin Daisy? And Gary?"

"It was pretty brutal. Listening to him discuss the four types of estuaries without a drink in my hand was quite possibly the worst conversation I've ever had." I sigh, my chest immediately flooding with guilt. "It was nice of them to let me crash there, though."

"That's the spirit." He sips out of his flute and nods when my mother waves him over to her huddle of Manhattan's wealthiest couples. "Loosen up and enjoy yourself. Everything will work out tonight."

As he retreats with a wink, I drain the rest of my champagne and place it on an empty tray as a server passes.

"You didn't save me any?" a familiar voice sounds from behind me. "And here I thought you didn't even like champagne. According to my friend Bree and her gossip magazines, anyway."

Exhaling, I turn to find Tessa standing behind me. "I love champagne, and there's plenty more—" I freeze as if I swallowed my tongue.

Her red lips are bold, like her, and a drastic contrast to her black dress. The floor-length gown accentuates her feminine shape. Her short hair is wavy and barely brushing the tops of her bare shoulders, off which the straps of her dress hang.

The neckline dips low, pushing her breasts up in a classy, yet sexy way.

And her eyes shine, glistening under the bright chandeliers hanging from the ceiling.

I haven't seen her in person in two months, not since the

cabin. Her voice through a phone hasn't been enough to curb my need for her, and I've fucking missed her.

My body jolts toward her of its own volition.

"You're absolutely stunning," I say, drinking her in, my breathing suddenly labored. I bring the back of her hand to my lips and brush soft kisses across her knuckles, relishing in her soft skin. "I'm so glad you came."

"You mentioned free food and a good cause. I had to make an appearance." Her glowing expression is brighter than her gold necklace.

I smirk, but it quickly falls into a frown. "Were those the only reasons?"

"I also wanted to see you in a tux," she says in a hushed tone, her pursed lips breaking into a striking grin as she fingers my bow tie, then runs her palm flat against my chest down the valley of my pecs.

I'd give my left arm for her to pull me in so I can kiss her. *She's so damn close.*

I lick my lips, the ghost of her taste on them, and I groan as her hand falls back to her side.

She clears her throat, gazing up at me, all humor gone.

I gently grasp her arm, stopping her from leaving, and blurt the first thing that enters my brain. "What've you been up to?"

Shit. I didn't have anything better? I haven't seen her in weeks, and all I can manage is a lame, generic question.

Fantastic.

She shifts, clutching her wristlet to her stomach. "I've taken up jogging."

"Oh?" I ask.

"Yeah." She relaxes her stance, and I reluctantly remove my hand from her, but not before I give her arm one last squeeze. "I realized I need to be more proactive with my health like I used to be, and it's fun."

Beaming, I nod along and tamp down the urge to tell her I'd be happy to show her a thing or two in the gym if she needs help, but it's too soon. Keeping it casual and slow like this is good... for now.

I also want to pump my fist in the air. I can't believe my dumbass question is working to keep her here with me.

"How've you been? The new promotion going well?"

I stare at her lips like we're having a sensual conversation instead of a friendly one, catching up with the happenings of our lives since we parted. "The first day of my full reign was pretty tense, so I decided to lighten the atmosphere with a little comedic routine at our morning meeting. I made jokes about Derek's tuna sandwiches he brings in for lunch every day and Marta's use of *urgent* subject lines in every email. All in good fun."

"Sounds like it." She sways to the side.

"It didn't hit the mark quite as I expected or intended, so I was kindly told to officially retire from comedy. Which means I'm left to work my jokes on my friends and family. So, it's their loss, really." I scratch my chin, feeling lighter than I have in a while. Talking to Tessa feels natural and comfortable, and I've missed this feeling I have from being around her.

She places a hand over her chest as she laughs, her eyes squeezed closed.

"See? It's working already," I say, my focus stuck on her every move.

"Okay, you can take a bow now and pull the curtain."

Grinning, I nod. "If we're being serious and honest, there have been challenges. But slowly, I think people are warming up to me being their boss. My dad's been in that position for most of them for the last thirty years or more, so I don't blame people for being wary. We're establishing a respectable dynamic, though."

"Keep being you, and it'll be more than enough for them to trust you."

I rub my jaw just to keep my hand busy as an overwhelming need to hold her consumes me.

She shifts. "I—" She cuts herself off when she zeroes in on something over my shoulder. "What is Graham doing here? And is that my mother?"

I smile, turning to stand next to her.

As I place my hand on her lower back, she takes in the space for the first time, her gaze traveling over the Christmas trees in the corners and the linen-covered tables, on top of which are brochures of the organization of honor. The yellow and red colors of the centerpieces match them, and the backdrop behind the stage is full of pictures of families the organization has helped.

Smiling faces are everywhere.

That's what this organization does—it completes families in so many ways. I knew it was special the moment Tessa told me about it, but after talking with Trina and the founders, it's come to hold a special place in my own heart.

Tessa covers her mouth with one hand, her dainty fingers trembling against her flushed cheeks. "Darby's Dreamers? You did all this for them?"

"Thanks to you for introducing me to them through the Thompsons."

Dropping her hand to her side, she turns her teary gaze up to meet mine.

I bring her fingers up to my chest, unable to keep my hands to myself any longer. "Tessa, you opened a whole new world for me. Less than a week in a cabin with you, and I'm a changed man."

She gulps, heavy tears building in her eyes.

"I'm sorry for not saying so sooner. I'm sorry I left the cabin without telling you how I really feel. I didn't know how." I lean my forehead against hers, happily drowning in her sweet floral scent. It washes over me, soothing me better than a Swedish massage, as my confession rushes out of me in a single breath. "I was too scared and doubted my capability to make the commitment to you that you deserve, but I'm not anymore. I want to be with you."

She lets out a shaky breath, then inhales deeply as she steps back to peer at me.

I continue holding her, though. I can't let her walk away. I have to convince her. Letting her leave is not an option until I put everything on the table. Clearing my throat, I step up to her. "I'm serious. I mean, it's crazy to think, but I want the marriage, kids, and family vacations to create our own traditions. I want it all if it's with you."

"Carter Fields, a family man," she whispers, gripping my hands.

"I never thought I'd say it, let alone *want* it, but I fucking love the sound of it." I chuckle, my heart pounding in my ears over the music.

"Me too." She beams up at me, her lips parted. I've obviously taken her by surprise, so I give her a minute, standing back to give her an inch of space—that's all I can manage. And I hold my breath, especially when her frown slowly seeps in. "But first…"

My heart falls into my stomach like the other shoe is dropping. I thought her coming here meant she wants to be with me too, but maybe she only came to tell me she doesn't.

Fuck.

Tessa bites her lip, her white teeth a stark contrast to her red lipstick. The small gesture makes my whole body harden, even though I'm a sudden cluster of rattled nerves.

The effect she has on me has only strengthened in the time we've spent apart, and I know in this moment, no matter what she says next, I'll do everything I can to convince her to be mine.

To be worthy of her.

We fucking belong together.

"I owe you an apology too," she says.

"What?" I shake my head, taken aback. "You have nothing to apologize for."

"But I do." She gives me a crooked, shy smile. "I was scared too. I kept myself guarded because I didn't want a repeat of my last relationship, but you're nothing like Wyatt. I know you'd never hurt me like he did. What you and I have is very different. It's special and a once-in-a-lifetime kind of thing."

"What… I mean, how…" I search her expression, dumbfounded.

"When I left Wyatt, all I felt was relief, and it only got easier to be without him until I felt nothing at all. But after you left, I was heartbroken, and it only got worse." She places both hands on my chest, and the rest of the party seems to fade as I cling to each of her words. "Even though I think I knew it all along, I was scared to let myself get carried away again. But you're it for me, Carter, and I'm not going to let either of our pasts get in the way of this."

Elated, I close the gap between us, pressing our bodies together. "What now?"

"Now… you kiss me." She tilts her face up and touches her nose to mine, giving me access to those teasing lips.

I cup the back of her head and kiss her, loving the way she fits so perfectly in my arms. I have the urge to deepen the kiss, but the soft music reminds me we're in public. Pulling back, I lean my forehead against hers. "Fuck, I need you."

She grips my shoulders, panting. "God, yes."

"I see you two made up."

We jump apart and turn toward the voice—Graham.

Busted.

"Listen, I'm not going to try to keep you two apart, but you have to watch the PDA." He squeezes his palms together in front of him, then weaves them between us, his knuckles against our chests, separating us. "Much better."

Tessa bites her curling bottom lip, and her eyes sparkle brighter than all the sequins in this place.

"Fuck it." I push Graham out of the way and cup her cheek, molding my lips to hers. I snake my hand to the back of her neck, wrapping her hair between my fingers and tugging until she melts against me.

Graham groans beside us, and Tessa's giggles vibrate down my body. "Okay, okay," she says against my lips, holding my arm as she presses her cheek against mine and whispers in my ear, "Maybe later we can…"

"Find a dark closet where I can feel you up?" I growl.

"The slit in this dress was not an accident," she whispers.

Immediately, I bend at the knees and curse under my breath.

"Tessa, sweetheart!" Her mother gracefully steps up to us,

a full flute of champagne in one hand, and I find Graham still beside us too.

When Tessa and her mother pull back from a hug, Mrs. Rollins looks at me over her shoulder, seemingly unsurprised Tessa and I made up.

When a server comes by with a tray of champagne, I grab two and give one to Tessa. I resume holding her hand, threading my fingers through hers as my body hums.

As we chat, my gaze involuntarily falls to the aforementioned slit in her dress, which reveals most of one leg. The fabric starts at the open *V* midthigh, her legs tan and smooth.

I don't know how long I'll last without getting her alone.

At one point, Tessa scans the room. "Where's Dad?"

"You will never believe this." Mrs. Rollins places a hand on her hip. "Your father thought it was a good idea to learn Tai Chi. I agreed because I thought it would help center him, but what does he do? He trips over his own feet while walking into the yard to practice and sprains his hip. He's at home resting and icing it."

"Oh, no." Tessa holds her mother's arm.

"I have no idea when and how your father became so clumsy."

Graham finishes his champagne and chimes in, "He's pretty much always had two left feet. He was usually at the clinic, though, and got immediate and efficient care."

"Oh, the things I'm learning about him," their mother jokes.

I lean down to Tessa's ear and say in a hushed tone, "Sounds familiar."

"How so?" Tessa inches into me, her eyebrows high.

"I seem to remember someone hurting themselves on the

way to whitewater rafting," I say. "Now we know you get the clumsiness from your father's side."

"How's your father liking retirement, Carter?" Mrs. Rollins pulls my attention toward her.

I glance over at my own parents. My dad has his hand on Mom's lower back, and every now and then, as they converse with guests, they gaze at each other. It's the smallest gesture, but I can tell their commitment to making things work is already benefitting them.

I focus again on Tessa's mother, grinning. "It's only been a couple weeks, and he's been at the office every day. Says he's only there as a visitor, but I think it's going to take time for him to get used to a slower pace of life."

"Ah, yes. I remember the first few weeks of my own retirement. I went to my office every day simply to smell the leather couch." She inhales like she can still smell it.

"Really?" Tessa asks. "I didn't know that."

"Well, it's hard to give up your business when it's been your whole life, but once you get some distance, it becomes easier to see how much more is out there."

"Sounds brutal." Graham grimaces.

"Oh, you'll learn." She pats him on the back and nods. "Trust me, your father is learning, and you will too."

Graham grumbles incoherently, obviously bracing himself to fight retirement, even though it's light-years away. But I know him. When the time comes, he won't go easily.

"Carter, if your father needs tips, have him call me." She smiles, then waves to someone and brushes past us. "Excuse me, kids."

"So…" Graham rocks on his heels, his eyelids appearing heavy.

"Dude, how much have you had to drink already?" I study him.

"Not enough." He glances around, and I assume it's for more champagne. When he turns back to us, he stares at me, his expression softening. "But in all seriousness, if you two are happy or whatever, I'm… well, I'm happy for you too, then."

Tessa places her hand over her chest, and I step back, squinting at him. "I don't know if it's the bubbly talking, but I appreciate that."

He nods, then bumps my shoulder as he leaves.

All our close friends and family seem occupied, so I slide my arm around Tessa's waist and dip my head until my nose is buried in her hair and ask, "So… closet?"

Instead of answering, she grabs my hand and tugs me toward the door.

"Wait! It's this way." I pull her in the opposite direction, where I think I spotted a storage room during a tour with Ava a few weeks ago.

Tessa raises the long side of her dress in one hand and hurries to follow me, her heels clicking across the floor. The music is too loud for others to hear her, and everyone's preoccupied with champagne and conversation to notice us, anyway.

Even if they did notice, though, nothing could stop me.

As soon as we reach paradise—a dusty storage room with cleaning supplies along the shelves on the walls—I plan to make all the filthy fantasies I've had of Tessa come true.

TWENTY-EIGHT

Tessa

Carter locks the door behind us, then pushes my back against it, pressing his arousal into my lower stomach, which aches for him.

My body is on fire for him.

Clothed in darkness, my senses are heightened, and I feel his kiss deeper than I did out in the open. Here, in the private solitude of the closet, his mouth is eager, much like our kisses at the cabin.

I've missed this. His touch and dominant presence.

His expert tongue is hot and determined.

A hint of champagne lingers on his lips, and I lap it up like it's the first drop of water I've ever had.

He moves his mouth along my jawline, brushing his soft lips down the column of my neck and across my exposed collarbone.

This dress, with its low, sweetheart neckline, was a sound decision if there ever was one.

Carter runs his hand down my side and stops at my hip, his fingers digging into me over the fabric and making me whimper. There's too much separating us, so I claw at his waist, the silk material of his cummerbund smooth under my fingers.

"Jesus, I've missed this mouth," he growls right before he plunges his tongue between my parted lips, cupping my chin with his thumb and forefinger to hold my face in place as he continues his frenzied assault on my mouth.

I'm at his mercy, and it drives me absolutely wild.

He slides his hand from my hip to the opening of my dress, where he dips underneath to find the surprise I have for him.

Grunting, he leans his forehead against mine. "Fuck. No panties?"

I peek up at him and bite my bottom lip, which he wiggles free with one thumb as he trails his other hand across where my panties should be until he settles between my legs.

When he slides a finger into my wet heat, I gasp, and he swallows it, capturing me in a kiss so passionate, my knees weaken.

I rock my hips, riding his hand, as we continue devouring each other.

Moaning, I run my fingers through his hair and tug on it, ruffling it all up and making him look as chaotic as his movements are. "Oh. Oh." My mouth hangs open as he finds the bundle of nerves tightening above my clit. He puts pressure there, moving his thumb in a circular motion and bringing me to the brink of euphoria.

"That's it." He pants, watching me with lust-filled eyes. "That's it, baby."

"Yes," I repeat over and over again, along with his name. When I grow louder, he clamps his hand over my mouth to keep me from blowing our cover—we are still at a big event.

Right when I'm about to fall over the edge, he pulls out and holds my gaze as he licks his fingers, one by one. It sends even more heat down to my core, ready to explode, and my eyelids flutter.

"I need you," I whisper, my need so great I can barely speak.

He moves backward, hitting what sounds like a bucket, and it scrapes across the floor. I grab at his clothing again, but he's already lowered his pants, his hard and thick length standing at attention between us.

Working quickly, he sheaths himself in a condom and kisses me again, pulling my dress to the side. Cold air hits my slick heat, and a whole new wave of arousal washes over me.

Carter doesn't stop our kiss as he adjusts himself at my entrance and slides inside me with ease.

"Oh God, yes." I cling to his shoulders as he wraps one of my legs around his waist, then slides his hand underneath the material of my dress to palm my bare ass.

Each time he thrusts into me, my back hits the door, and the string of it further jolts me alive.

Because I have Carter.

He's here, inside me, loving me.

He didn't say the words out loud before, but he declared his feelings and desire for a commitment. It's more than enough for me to know he's mine and I'm his.

I moan, lost in this moment, when the doorknob jimmies to our side, making us freeze.

My eyes widen, and his snap up to mine. I open my mouth, but he covers it with his hand again as we look down to the moving shadows beneath the door. Muffled voices filter inside, and I glance back up at Carter, panicked.

He doesn't move.

He's completely still and hard deep inside me, and my leg squeezes the side of his waist right above his hip, the heel of my stiletto digging into his firm ass.

The voices fade, along with the shadows. After a moment, Carter nods, a slow and devious grin spreading across his lips, making his dimples appear.

I trace one with my finger and smile back as he resumes, rolling his hips and reaching the spot deep inside me that makes me see stars.

My pants grow louder as he quickens his pace.

The knocks of my back against the door are more frequent, drowning my whimpers.

"God, I've missed you," he growls against my lips, his voice strained.

"Me… too," I stammer, the words high-pitched and difficult to release.

With one more deep thrust, we both collapse onto each other, shuddering as our climaxes overwhelm us.

Our chests heave.

Carter's cheeks are flushed, and the veins in his neck slowly relax, as do his shoulders.

I link my fingers together behind his neck and kiss him, keeping him inside me.

We're one.

Carter and me—we were joined from the moment we first saw each other, and I have no doubt we have a future together, one I'll fight to protect.

Because I can't live without him again.

"Come home with me," he whispers, twirling my hair at the nape of my neck between his fingers, causing shivers down my spine. "Stay with me tonight."

I lick my lips, savoring his request.

"I want you in my bed. Tucked into my side. Waking up next to me, Tessa."

I nod since words are caught in my throat, clogged with all these emotions as my heart continues racing.

"I never want to be without you again." He places a firm kiss on my lips, seemingly for reiteration. "You're mine. Okay? You're mine."

I kiss him back with every ounce of energy I have left, agreeing all the same.

In the restroom, I apply my lipstick and smack my lips together with an extra pop, freshening up. I wiggle my dress into place and run my fingers through my hair, untangling the mess Carter created when he fisted it during our secret rendezvous.

How wild.

How reckless and dangerously sexy it was to be with him like that in a closet, outside of which a hundred people filter.

I thought we were almost caught at one point, and it only added to the thrill of it.

When I decided to take Carter up on his invitation to come out tonight, I didn't know what would happen. Our last phone call gave me hope, but up until I saw him, I thought I might be too naïve.

When our eyes locked, though, and before he said the words, I knew.

I knew why I'd come and why he'd asked me here. Because we can't resist this pull between us, and I trust the words he spoke to me.

I believe him when he says he doesn't want anyone but me.

His intensity when he moved inside me was breathtaking. All-consuming. Natural. Like we're meant for each other.

With rosy cheeks and a playful smile, I leave the restroom and find Carter in the hall, leaning against the wall, his tuxedo in place.

He's no longer disheveled or unraveled like he was in the closet when I undressed him.

On the contrary—he's impeccable.

Strong, square jaw. Mischievous, yet thoughtful eyes. A boyish grin that brings to life the butterflies in my stomach.

I'd sell my soul for him to smile at me like this for the rest of my life, but as he pushes off the wall and grabs my hand, I know I won't need to.

Even though he hasn't said it out loud, I can feel his love for me through each of his fingertips as they thread mine.

As Carter and I rejoin the party, the music filters around us, and we steal coy glances at each other as we squeeze our intertwined hands together.

This is where I belong.

"Mr. Fields, there you are! And Tessa, my gosh, you're a vision." Trina appears at our sides, holding her hand out toward me, her mouth agape as she glances between us.

We both jump, laughing under our breaths as we greet Trina, who's decked in a floor-length gown with shoulder pads. She grips Carter's arm with both hands, pulling us apart. "Thank you so much for handling our travel and accommodating our stay in the city, but more importantly, thank you for all this." She turns her head from side to side. "You have such a big heart, and our Tessa is a lucky woman." She turns and reaches out to me as well, grasping us both.

I smile warmly at her as Carter says, "You're very welcome, Mrs. Thompson. I'm glad you could make it, and thank you for your kind words." He peers down at me, his eyes on fire. "Tessa is one special woman, to say the least."

"Please, call me Trina," she insists, then waves around us, beaming. "This is all so extravagant. I wasn't sure what to wear. I've never been to something like this."

I gush, "You look absolutely perfect. Your dress is stunning."

"I'm not sure about all that, but I appreciate it." Trina tucks her hair behind both ears as Sheriff Thompson joins us.

He kisses the side of her head in a loving gesture, then says, "The boys are here."

"Oh my goodness!" Trina claps, her eyes lighting up, and when she looks at us, she pleads, "You two have to say hello to Eugene and Kyle when you get a chance. They would absolutely love to see you, Tessa, and to meet you, Carter."

"Of course. We'll catch up with you all after dinner and your big speech," Carter reassures her as servers swarm into the event space balancing trays of food on their shoulders.

She throws her arms up. "Oh, I cannot believe I agreed to speak in front of all these people. I wish the Loffleys could've been here to do it, instead."

"You'll be great, Trina." Carter smiles. "Just do what I do when I give an important speech, and imagine the guests are all puppies. It's easy to talk with enthusiasm to puppies, no?"

Trina and the sheriff both chuckle, thanking him again for having them here.

Once I'm alone with Carter again, I tuck myself into his side, and the lapels of his jacket wrinkle when he snakes his arm around my waist. He kisses my forehead, and I sigh, melting against him as we make our way to our table.

A feeling of contentment that I've never known washes over me.

One of peace that I'm in the right place, at the right time, with the right person.

With Carter.

TWENTY-NINE

Carter

Tessa's smile is radiant.

There's a lazy tilt to it, one that has me itching to constantly touch her. To be near her. To revel in the fact that she's mine.

I don't deserve her, but I'll spend the rest of my life cherishing her and striving to be worthy of her.

Using the white linen napkin, I wipe the corners of my mouth, sated from Tessa and the five-course meal we just inhaled like vacuums. I expected nothing less from Chef Ingrid, whose high-end restaurant catered tonight. She's known for her perfect blend of comfort food and upscale cuisine—a combination that always has me salivating.

Judging from the hum of approval from guests, I'm not alone, either.

I place my napkin on top of my empty plate and stand,

but I remain low. "Dance with me," I whisper in Tessa's hair, curling my fingers through hers at her side and squeezing. I twirl her onto the dance floor as a Christmas tune echoes across the hall.

She hums to the classic song as we sway, her hand in mine at our side while the other grips the back of my neck.

We continue this way as though we're in our own world and not among this big crowd.

It's how I know it will be with Tessa in the future—just us.

I dip low to rest my chin on top of her head, content, when I notice Graham at the bar… and a familiar woman checking him out.

I will Graham to stop brooding for a moment, long enough to notice her, and when he finally does, I snicker under my breath.

They exchange coy glances and a few words in between his glares in our direction. They're obviously talking about us, so he should really be thanking me for the conversation starter.

The song fades to an end and transitions into a quick, fun one, which has Tessa bouncing in my arms, her breasts pushing against my chest in agonizing bliss.

"I'm going to get Graham out here to dance!" She hoists her dress up in one hand, and she takes small but quick steps toward her brother, pulling him away from the woman.

Once Graham comes close, I lean over to whisper, "You sly dog."

"Shut your damn mouth," he growls, glancing over his shoulder at the woman, who moves away from the bar to talk to a few other guests I recognize. They aren't her usual crew, but they're friendly, nonetheless.

"I didn't see you jot anything down in your phone or on a napkin. Want her number?" I quirk my eyebrow, offering my assistance since I know her through a mutual friend.

Graham squirms, shifting on his feet. "Mind your own business, okay?" he clips, but I don't miss the playful note in his tone.

Much like the old Graham. The one who didn't want to kick my ass.

I slap him on the back and let up, glad to have any semblance of normalcy between us.

We haven't talked much since the cabin, but his attendance tonight and the hint of teasing have me optimistic that we'll be okay in time.

I open my mouth to say something, but Mrs. Ruth catches my attention from the other side of the room. She waves for me to go over, and I inch toward her.

Not before I kiss Tessa on her temple, though.

Once I'm done doing a little schmoozing and catching up with old friends, I find Tessa, who's still on the dance floor with Graham.

As I approach, she stands back and points between Graham and me. "So, when are you two going to explain what the hell happened?"

Graham tenses beside me. "Like I told him, it's none of your business. If you can do what you want—"

"I think she's referring to you and me, dude," I chime in to keep him from outing himself and whatever he and the woman were discussing. It had to have been enough for her to keep eyeing him over the rim of her glass as she works the room.

Hook, line, and sinker.

Dr. Rollins has fucking game, and he didn't even need

to be wearing his stethoscope to impress her. I'll give him shit for that later, but right now, there are other pressing matters.

"Oh, right." Graham clears his throat, scratching his chin. I've never seen him so fucking squirrely, and it takes everything in me not to let the tickle in the back of my throat become full-on howling laughter.

"Well? How are you here tonight and in the same room? You're really not still mad?" Tessa studies her brother, twisting her lips, then glances at me.

Her doe eyes are too adorable.

Graham places his hands on his hips. "Look, Fields and I talked, and… whatever. I'm here. I'm cool. You two don't have to worry about me standing in your way."

Tessa squints. "Why do I feel like there's more to this story?"

"Because there is, but it's between us." I wink at her, then nod to Graham.

He smacks my shoulder and points. "We're even for the whole Trixie bit, okay? No more favors for you."

I throw my head back and laugh. "We're square. Although you did owe me for the whole Talladega debacle."

"No way. That was payback for Diana."

"The drunk asshole poured his beer on me when I asked him to leave." I lower my voice so I don't draw attention from the respectable donors milling around us.

Graham tosses his head back in a laugh so loud, I almost have to cover my ears.

"What?" Tessa screeches, tugging on my arm. "The guy who pissed himself? You didn't tell me the part about the beer!"

"Now, that"—Graham catches his breath—"I didn't plan

the beer shower or the skunk, but it was all a nice touch. You deserved it."

"You never told me about Diana. How was I supposed to know?"

"I did tell you about her! You just don't listen when you already have your eyes set on something you can't have." He points to his sister. "Exhibit A."

Tessa snorts, and I hang my head, chuckling. "Touché."

"I thought you said you'd be cool." Tessa nudges him.

Graham shrugs as he backs away. "Didn't say anything about keeping my joking jabs to myself, though."

I groan, facing Tessa, who reaches up to wrap her hands behind my neck. "I'm never going to live this down with him, am I?"

"For a respected doctor, Graham's not exactly known to be super mature and forgiving when it comes to his personal life. At the cabin, he actually blew out the candles on my birthday cake like a damn toddler throwing a petty tantrum."

I laugh. "That sounds about right."

"He got over it, though, and even apologized. Maybe there's hope for his maturity yet."

I pull her to me and kiss her smiling lips, so close to eliciting one of her sexy sighs when my father's voice interrupts us.

"So, this is the girl."

We jump apart, and Tessa swipes at the corners of her lips for what I assume is any smudged lipstick.

I hold my arm out to her and say to my father, "This is Tessa Rollins."

"Rollins, huh? You wouldn't have any relationship to—who's that friend of yours from college, son? Grant?"

"Graham," I correct him.

"Right. My mistake." He gives me a sympathetic tilt of his head. Between the two of us, I've always had the better memory when it comes to names. It's one of the things I often did for him—remind him of names before we arrived at a business meeting. So, I'm unsurprised he doesn't remember Graham, even though they've met plenty of times over the years.

I am surprised he remembered a specific friend of mine at all.

"I'm Graham's sister," Tessa explains.

My dad raises his eyebrows. "Ah, intriguing."

"Not really, no." I shrug in an attempt to appear nonchalant, but it's no use.

"It's lovely to meet you, Tessa." My father takes her hand in both of his. "My son's told me a lot about you, and I must say, he couldn't have found a better woman to settle down with."

I hold my hand up. "Whoa, whoa. Don't go scaring her away with talk of marriage. We just got together. One step at a time."

Tessa dips her head, and my father shrugs, dropping her hand. "What? Tessa here is perfect marriage material. She's the kind of woman I've been on your stubborn ass to try to meet all these years. How could you let her go?"

"I'm not letting her go, Dad."

"You are if you're not going to propose soon."

"Dad, stop." I wave my hand, officially humiliated for the first time in my life—and I've done plenty of embarrassing things over the years.

Tessa interrupts. "I'm surprised he even asked me out tonight after I called the sheriff on him the first day we met."

My dad's laughter thunders out of him like an engine on a jet plane. "No kidding!"

"It's true. I thought he was stalking me." Tessa smiles, her eyes dancing as my father continues howling.

He wipes tears from his eyes and claps my shoulder. "Definitely marry this one."

"All right." I shake my head. "Are you finished yet?"

With one more pat to my shoulder and a wink to Tessa, he leaves us alone. I place my hand on her lower back and lead her away, whispering in her ear, "Don't mind him. He tends to ramble in his old age."

"I found him charming."

"In that case, just know I got my charm from him."

Her body trembles under my palm as she giggles.

We don't get very far before we're interrupted again, but this time it's Landon Shanty and his fiancée, Emmy. The same Emmy I slept with a while back. When they approach and greet us, she smiles warmly as her gaze bounces between Tessa and me. Shanty, on the other hand, looks at me smugly, like he's walked away with the prize.

To be fair, he did. Even though we weren't meant to be, Emmy is a fantastic person, and Shanty, the bastard, is lucky.

I won too, though.

Gripping Tessa's hand tightly, I say to Shanty and Emmy, "This is my girlfriend, Tessa."

Shanty does a double-take, then leans in with his hand cupped around his ear. "I'm sorry, what? I don't think I've ever heard the word *girlfriend* come out of your mouth."

Emmy smacks his chest, her expressive features horrified. "You'll have to excuse him. He doesn't normally drink champagne."

Tessa and I look at each other, our grins too much to

contain, then turn back toward the other couple and wave them off.

The truth is, Shanty's right. Before Tessa, I never would've called a woman on my arm my girlfriend, no matter how many times I'd slept with her. Emmy knows it too, although I appreciate her apology on his behalf, which I tell her now.

"You two make a lovely couple, and I wish you the best," she says, squeezing Tessa's hand, her words sincere. I expected nothing less from her.

As we walk away from them to dance some more, I grab two full flutes of champagne from a passing server and hand one to Tessa, leaning down to kiss her cheek as she accepts it. I want to kiss her lips again, but I don't want to ruin her makeup for the hundredth time. I'll have my chance later on to mess it all up again.

When she's in my bed tonight.

I plan to make up for all the nights she was missing.

I inwardly smirk as she sways to the music with every step, the bottom of her dress sweeping across the floor like a paint brush against a clean canvas—our clean slate.

Tessa is feminine elegance and grace wrapped up into one sexy package.

"What're we toasting to?" she asks, her cheeks flushed from what I like to assume is our *sex-cape* in the closet and the fun evening we're having.

"To the future."

Her breath audibly catches.

"I know my father was a little premature in his comments, but someday, Tessa Rollins, I'm going to ask you to marry me. Because I'm falling for you, and I know that every day I spend with you, I'll only fall harder."

She hums against my lips, searching my expression.

"I'm falling in love with you," I say hoarsely as I stare at her lips. "All it took was a few days in a cabin with you, but I want to take things slow. For starters, I want to take you out on a real and proper date, just the two of us."

She sighs dreamily, melting into my side. "I'd like that. All of it."

My chest swells, straining against this restrictive tux, and I clink my champagne flute to hers, confident in our future.

One I've already set in motion.

I won't tell her until the time is right, but the truth is, that's what Graham and I discussed during our phone call.

I asked for his blessing.

When the time is right, I'm going to ask Tessa to marry me and be mine forever.

It had taken Graham by surprise. He asked to meet me in person to look me in the eye too, which he did. He made me repeat my intentions with his sister about ten times, without blinking, until he finally sat back in his chair at the café where we met and nodded.

He said he believed me and that if I want to ask Tessa to marry me someday, I have his blessing.

I walked away from that café a new and lighter man.

I'm a man who knows what he wants, and I want Tessa for the long haul. I plan to make it all happen too, one day at a time.

Because love happens in an instant—from the moment I laid eyes on her—but a life together takes time and effort. A life with Tessa is something I'm more than ready and willing to work toward.

It's us from here on out.

EPILOGUE

Tessa

One year later…

Carter grunts by the door, followed by a thud as he sets my bag down. "What the hell is in here? Books?"

"Yes." I place both hands on my hips, quirking my brow. "Is there a problem?"

"You realize you won't have time to read during this trip, right?" He inches toward me to where I stand in the kitchen.

"Oh? And what else will be occupying my time?" I ask coyly.

"Me." He wraps me in his arms, nuzzling his face in the crook of my neck as he slides his hand down my stomach to the waistband of my leggings. "I have many plans for you," he whispers against my neck, making me squirm.

I hum, about to give myself to him, when a realization slams into me. "My parents will be here any minute, though. We can't."

"They got delayed. Did they not tell you?" He pulls back.

"What? This is dangerously familiar, don't you think? Graham has to work. My parents' flight is delayed. We're here alone…" I leave my naughty reminder hanging in the air as I run my fingertips up his arm the way I know he likes.

"I vaguely recall these events you speak of," he teases, obviously remembering my birthday trip last year.

At this cabin.

We're celebrating my birthday here again this year. Everyone promised they'd be here, but I have to admit, I'm more than happy to get the party started alone with Carter.

We live together in the city now, but I still can't seem to get enough of him—and vice versa. His hands and mouth are like moths to a flame, the flame being my body.

"I think strip poker was a staple game last time too, and I definitely need a repeat." Carter tilts his head toward the living room.

This place is exactly as we left it over the summer during our last visit.

It always looks the same, which is part of the charm—cheesy decorative pillows, quirky patterns on the blankets, and the same tacky dishes for everyday use.

No one touches my grandmother's china.

"After we go to the store. We don't have any coffee, lasagna, toast, or anything, and you know how hungry I get after a sex marathon." I lean into Carter, fingering the hem of his shirt.

"Oh, I love when you talk dirty to me." He kisses my lips, holding me snug against him.

I mold my body to his, losing myself in his muscled frame, feeling his strong pecs beneath my palms.

"Okay, let's hurry and go so we can get the fun started." He stands back and reaches around to swat my ass. "It's my lady's birthday, and she deserves orgasms. A *lot* of orgasms."

I suck in a sharp breath, staring at his lips. "What if we wait for…"

"Nope. My lady also needs food and energy because we have a lot of sex to fit in before everyone gets here, and you'll need all the carbs."

"Now you're talking dirty." I giggle, brushing past him.

We've been here a couple times since my last birthday, splitting our vacations between this place, his family's estate at Martha's Vineyard, and their house in the Poconos. We have to be careful and make sure to call before we show up, though, given how his parents have learned to enjoy his father's retirement.

Walking in on them doing it on the kitchen counter at the house in the Poconos was a picture Carter and I could've both lived without. But once we got past the horrific incident, it was hard not to be happy at how well they're getting along now.

"I'll drive." Carter grabs the keys from the hook by the door, next to which a picture of him and me hangs.

That is the only thing that's changed. We've added his pictures around the cabin because, even though we're not married, Carter is family all the same. He and I have been living together for almost seven months, and every day, we grow closer as a couple, planning our life together.

The luxuries of his penthouse are nice too.

I didn't know if I could get used to his lifestyle—cooks, housekeepers, and private security guards. It's still overwhelming to have everything—literally *everything*—at my fingertips.

Not to mention the media attention. Being recognized as Carter's bimbo fling, then serious girlfriend, and then marriage material by magazines was flat-out insane at first.

Then, it was surreal.

None of it has been easy, but Carter's helping me navigate his world. I'm getting him acclimated to mine too. Introducing him to the girls was an *interesting* event, to say the least. Bree had a million questions—including boxer briefs or boxers. Erin stared the entire time, and I think I even saw her miss her mouth when she tried to eat a chip. And Madison sat back with me to watch it all play out.

The day I moved in with Carter, Whitney hugged me for what felt like an hour. She was so happy I was moving in, repeatedly telling me how good I am for Carter. She was also excited not to have to clean up after his messy overnight *guests* anymore, a comment that earned Carter a glare from both of us.

But that's his past.

We all have them. What matters is the present and the future. And Carter's both of mine.

On top of that, I've even started helping his company's philanthropic efforts. I'm a part-time assistant to Ava, who needs the extra hands now that their efforts and events are increasing. After the dinner for Darby's Dreamers, I took a special interest in that department and enjoy the rewarding work.

It's a way for me to help even more people outside my regular job.

It doesn't hurt to get to work with Carter on occasion too.

This last year has been one whirlwind after another, but

when I fall into bed with Carter every night, our bodies wrapped up in the sheets, I wouldn't trade any of it.

He's home.

"Oh." Carter stops on the porch, snapping his fingers, and I bump into him as I close the door to the cabin behind me. "We need to check the mail. Mrs. Thompson said she dropped us off some goods and a card."

"I already put them inside. They were on the rocking chairs when we arrived," I say as I brush past him.

He doesn't move from the porch. "I think we should still check the mailbox, though. Maybe there's something else? A piece of gold? Now, how would you feel if you just left a piece of gold in your mailbox?"

"What do I need a small piece of gold for when I have *you*?" I bat my lashes sarcastically.

He tsks. "I knew you were only with me for the money."

"Duh. Nothing else is worth the torture of your snores," I tease.

He fakes offense, gasping loudly.

I plant a kiss on his lips and resume my walk toward the mailbox—obviously there's something inside he wants me to check out.

But I don't expect what I find when I open it.

A black velvet box.

A *ring* box.

"Oh my God." I spin around to find Carter on one knee next to the mailbox, my family's cabin standing behind him. It's a picturesque moment.

I blink several times over in order to commit this to memory as my body erupts in goose bumps.

With shaky movements, I remove the box and hold it

between us. He places his hands on mine and smiles. "I came here to stay with you and your family because I drove my car into a mailbox."

A teary laugh escapes me.

"I was a different man, then. I thought I had everything, but this last year with you has shown me how much I was missing. You've made me a better man, and I'll continue to be better for you. To be the man and partner you deserve."

Joyful tears pour down my cheeks.

"We fell in love at this cabin a year ago, and I want this to be the place where we vow forever. Because that's what I want. What do you want?"

"I love you." I nod and try to swallow around the lump of emotions in my throat. "I want it all with you, Carter."

He smiles his dimpled grin at me, one that melts my heart and will continue to make me weak in the knees for the rest of my life. "Tessa Rollins, will you marry me and be stuck with me for life?"

"Yes," I breathe like I've been waiting for this moment all my life.

And in many ways, I have.

He opens the box, revealing the most brilliant halo engagement ring I've ever seen. It fits perfectly on my finger, and I don't immediately pause to inspect it closer.

Right now, I need to kiss my fiancé, and that's exactly what I do.

I wrap my arms around Carter, crushing my mouth to his like he alone has oxygen for me to breathe. I repeatedly murmur *I love you* against his lips as I take him down to the ground, straddling him as I continue kissing him with only the birds around as witnesses.

"What did she say?" a muffled voice sounds from somewhere in the distance.

"Is it a yes? What's going on?" another deep voice follows.

"What is that?" I whisper to Carter.

"Oh, right." He turns toward the cabin and waves, calling out, "You can all come out now. She said yes!"

In a blink, both of our families jump out from behind the cabin and trees, racing toward us with their arms wide open. My mom reaches us first, her cheeks tear-stained as she wraps her arms around both of us.

And we celebrate.

My birthday, our engagement, and love.

In the chaos, I catch Carter's beaming eyes over our excited families' heads. The billionaire I once thought was out of reach—he's here in a group hug after professing his love and commitment to me.

I smile wider than I ever have and count myself lucky to have been stuck with him last year.

And forever.

THE END

ALSO WRITTEN BY GEORGIA COFFMAN

Stuck with You Series
Stuck with the Billionaire
Stuck with the Movie Star
Stuck with the Boss
Stuck with the Single Dad

Stuck with You Spinoffs
Stuck with a Date
Stuck with the Rock Star

Stuck with You Holiday Spinoffs
Stuck at Christmas
Stuck Under the Mistletoe

The Heat Series
Falling for a Stranger
Falling for a Player
Falling for a Bachelor
Falling for My Roommate

Standalone Novels
Official
Heartbeat
Unbreakable

ACKNOWLEDGMENTS

Thank you for reading Carter and Tessa's love story! This book was not a planned release for me. The idea came when I joined several other authors for a collaboration to write the short version. I fell in love with the characters, and when it was time for me to decide what my next release would be, I knew I had to write something funny with little angst. Something light that would make me smile and in turn, would make you smile.

I decided to return to the billionaire short I wrote for the collaboration. As I was expanding it, I found exactly what I'd been looking for. I was excited. Giddy. I fell in love with this story and its characters all over again, and before I knew it, I'd added almost 60k new words!

And I hope Carter and Tessa brought you joy. If they did,

I'd love and appreciate it if you could please leave a review on Amazon, Goodreads, or BookBub.

I couldn't have finished this book without my team. They keep me motivated, focused, and sane. I couldn't do this without you, Amanda! Working with you has changed me and my books for the better.

To my KKSB girls—thank you so much for listening to me talk about this book for months. Your feedback and encouragement during the whole process made it so much more fun. You've changed the authoring game for me, and I'm forever grateful for you ladies.

To my mom—I thank you in every one of my books, and that'll never change. You've been my cheerleader since before I ever wrote a word. Thank you for teaching me to believe in myself. Thank you for everything.

Lastly, my husband. No words can adequately express how thankful I am for you. You're the reason I have any clue what love is. You're my person. My forever. My special HEA that I wouldn't trade for anything. Love you, forever and always.

ABOUT THE AUTHOR

Georgia Coffman is an author of steamy contemporary romances and romantic comedies. She has a Master's in Professional Writing and loves the TV show *Friends*, as well as shopping. She and her husband enjoy working out and playing with their two pups. Georgia loves to connect on social media or through email, so feel free to reach out with any questions, your fave book recommendations, or even a funny joke!

Newsletter
www.georgiacoffman.com/newsletter

Website
www.georgiacoffman.com

Facebook
www.facebook.com/authorgeorgiacoffman

Instagram
www.instagram.com/authorgeorgiacoffman

Pinterest
https://www.pinterest.com/authorgeorgiacoffman

TikTok
www.tiktok.com/@authorgeorgiacoffman

BookBub
www.bookbub.com/authors/georgia-coffman

Amazon
amazon.com/author/georgiacoffman

Goodreads
http://bit.ly/georgiaonGR

Verve Romance
https://ververomance.com/app/authorgeorgiacoffman

Georgia
COFFMAN
ROMANCE AUTHOR